Hugh,

Thank you for
are 8 the windows
Always in Christ

BLACK HEART REVENGE

BLACK HEART REVENGE

Kristy Morgan

iUniverse, Inc.
Bloomington

Black Heart Revenge

Copyright © 2013 by Kristy Morgan.

All rights reserved. No part of this book may be used or reproduced by any means, graphic, electronic, or mechanical, including photocopying, recording, taping or by any information storage retrieval system without the written permission of the publisher except in the case of brief quotations embodied in critical articles and reviews.

This is a work of fiction. All of the characters, names, incidents, organizations, and dialogue in this novel are either the products of the author's imagination or are used fictitiously.

iUniverse books may be ordered through booksellers or by contacting:

iUniverse
1663 Liberty Drive
Bloomington, IN 47403
www.iuniverse.com
1-800-Authors (1-800-288-4677)

Because of the dynamic nature of the Internet, any web addresses or links contained in this book may have changed since publication and may no longer be valid. The views expressed in this work are solely those of the author and do not necessarily reflect the views of the publisher, and the publisher hereby disclaims any responsibility for them.

Any people depicted in stock imagery provided by Thinkstock are models, and such images are being used for illustrative purposes only.
Certain stock imagery © Thinkstock.

ISBN: 978-1-4759-7006-7 (sc)
ISBN: 978-1-4759-7008-1 (hc)
ISBN: 978-1-4759-7007-4 (ebk)

Library of Congress Control Number: 2013900055

Printed in the United States of America

iUniverse rev. date: 01/02/2013

DEDICATION

To my beloved sister, Katherine Renee Threlkeld Cleaveland. You are my hero. You are what it means to be an overcomer. I am thankful for every struggle that I have witnessed you come through. For it is in those struggles that I have been reminded of the kind of strength and fortitude that it takes to make it through life. I will pray God's favor over your life for as long as he grants you life. I am so proud of you and I am happy to know someone as courageous in her ability to fight for life and love as you.

ACKNOWLEDGMENTS

Thank you to my Lord and Savior Jesus Christ for his unending grace and gentle mercy. I could have never accomplished this or any other endeavor without His help . . .

I would like to thank James Morgan and Judy Threlkeld for their efforts in editing Black Heart Revenge . . .

I would like to thank Jessica O'Neal for the vision that she showed in creating the Cover page for Black Heart Revenge . . .

Thank you to Melissa Royster and Ashley Torbert for their efforts in keeping me sain throughout this project . . .

Thank you to all of my family, friends, and co-workers that have been so supportive while I was completing Black Heart Revenge . . . . Also for all of their support during my other two books The Adventures of Rocky and Skeeter, Rocky Goes to Jail, and The Legend of Garrison falls . . . just to name a few . . . (the love of my life, my best friend and husband, James Morgan . . .) (my mother, who is my constant biggest fan and always pushing me to be my very best, Judy Threlkeld . . .) (to my daddy, for his hard work and determination to support his family, and always make me feel safe, Marvin Threlkeld Jr.) (my children, who have listened until I am sure they believed their ears would bleed as I rewrote and rethought passages in my books, Jesse O'Neal, James R. Morgan, Jessica O'Neal, and Rebecca Morgan . . .) (my sister, for allowing me to see myself through her eyes, and for making me feel as though I was already a bestselling author, Katherine Cleaveland . . .) (My best friend since I was in middle school, who has been like a sister to me, and has made me feel as though I belonged in her world if no other place, Melissa Royster . . .) (my co-worker and friend that sacrificed to go to breakfast, lunch, or whatever I needed at the time just to listen to all that I had to say, for making me feel valued, and appreciated, Kisha Leverette . . .) (my co-worker, and friend, who has listened to me and believed in me even when I thought I could not make it another step, Ashley Torbert . . .) (my co-worker and friend that has prayed with me and for me, Angela Simon . . .)

CHAPTER 1

The whole week before coming out to the misty bluff that over looked the large town of Darlington, South Carolina, she could barely keep her thoughts from careening out of control. Jordan had imagined the ride even as the airplane lifted off from the airport in New York near the compound where she worked.

Flying could be both exhilarating and exhausting for Jordan. Exhilarating because she loved the adrenaline rush that poured through her veins . . . soaking her senses, but exhausting because of the fear that encompassed her entire being . . . Heights had never been a source of pleasure for her, but if Jordan was being honest most of the time she welcomed the fear. The adrenaline that etched its way through her, soaking every part of her mind, body and soul . . . was overwhelming. That was another kind of fear. An enjoyable fear that left her drained and satiated all at once. This she felt, this anguish . . . built from the years of guilt and fear that marked her childhood did nothing to set into motion the usual rush that she had become accustom to feeling. No, this was a sensation, which permeated her entire being; chiseling away at the usual fight or flight response that followed after a fear induced thrill. It left her desolate and defenseless in its foreboding aftermath.

Jordan waited expectantly for the usual surge that normally accompanied take off. Frustrated, she closed her eyes as she tried desperately to give her mind over completely to anything but thoughts of the past.

The turbulence began. Normally her ears filled with air and her head spun with the excitement that spawned from the feel of being out of control but not on this trip. Nothing filled her mind more than the thought of riding to her old home place in the back of her brother's eighteen-wheeler.

Jordan's brother, Garret Buckley Jr., drove for one of the small trucking companies that littered the community of Darlington, South Carolina and Jordan could see the inside of his coveted rig even now as she tried to focus on the in-flight instructions being issued over the intercom by the pilot. Nothing could order her thoughts. No matter what she tried she was already in the truck and she was already feeling her mind as it was once again being pulled back into the past. She was not looking forward to the ride with her brother but even as she tried desperately not to think about it she could feel the turbulence again as the plane groaned with the effort of landing. With a sigh, she knew with utter helplessness at that moment that she had done the one thing that she had been determined not to; not only had she lent her mind to the dreaded trip, it had been the only thing that had taken center stage in her scattered thoughts.

Now as she checked back into reality once again and tried to allow some semblance of peace to take over even if for only a fraction of a moment, she knew it was pointless. In no time at all she would be in the back of her brother's truck wishing with all her might that she were any place else on earth.

Jordan watched as the light flickered to life indicating that it was safe for the passengers to take off their seat-belts. She blew out a frustrated breath and decided that hiding away in the aircraft would not make for a good impression. Especially if she was to convince her brother and his family that nothing had changed about her . . . she was the same . . . mentally scarred, clumsy gangly mess she had always been. Just like her sister-in-law, and her niece she was chilled to the bone with the fear of her brother and the threat that he imposed. Quite simply it was imperative that she appear just as determined as she had always been not to anger him.

Jordan collected her carry on luggage from the compartment above her seat, and stepped into the flow of people exiting the plane. She looked around at the excited faces and inwardly cringed. She would give anything to be excited about something . . . anything. She had never known such peace, as she was witnessing on the faces of the passengers of flight 230. Most of the passengers were returning home in hopes of a grand family reunion. Some she imagined may even be leaving home in search of a new life beyond what they had always known. She had found that knew life. She had left all of the things of her past just exactly where they belonged in the past, or so she had thought. As she looked around she was fast becoming aware that she could not have been more wrong. Not only had she not left the past in the past, but it was all that she dwelled on. It was defining her life; carving huge sections out of her mind, body, and soul. It was deciding the course of her future, as though she were in the passenger seat while her memories called the shots. This trip was not only crucial and unavoidable; it was long over due. It was time that Jordan Buckley took responsibility of her life; past time.

Jordan stepped from the plane and scanned the crowd for any sign of her brother. In the front of the crowd holding up a piece of tattered cardboard, with several smudge marks around the perimeter, Jr. stood amidst the other onlookers waiting with true love and expectant hope coloring their features. Her brother on the other hand, held the makeshift sign in the air with one hand while his other hand hung lazily at his side; his fingertips ended at his pocket. He adopted a confident stance that was only skin deep, one leg bent at the knee while the other was bone straight. Tobacco stains shadowed deep grooves at the edge of his mouth and his front pocket just under his hand had the faded outline of the can of tobacco that was bulging its protest against the fabric of his tight fitting jeans. Wisps of thread protruded from the hole made by the bulging can.

Jordan allowed her eyes to trail up from the evidence of his addiction to his face. All of her confidence faded in an instant as she came face to face with the reincarnation of her father. Jr. was not just the essence of the man that their father had been, more to the point he was a cookie-cutter-cut-out version of their father; the likeness was uncanny. Jordan knew that people had often claimed that her brother looked a lot like their father, but in the time that she had been gone training for her knew life, her brother had seemed to morph into her father.

"Well are you going to stand there staring?" Her brother grouched. Jordan dropped her head and shook it slightly as she walked in the direction that he was indicating the truck to be in. She decided not to answer. She had worried with all of the confidence that the organization had filled her with that she would not be able to pull off the pretense that she was afraid of her brother. Her eyes filled with tears that burned their protest to be released at the outer edges. Jordan shook her head and batted her eyelashes . . . she needed to appear to be afraid, but she had no intention of giving into this . . . this hold that her brother seemed to have on her. She would not allow her mind to get caught up in the onslaught of emotions and carried away in the current . . . as devastating as it was to see her father standing before her once again, alive, young, thriving, and capable of his worst; She would stay focused. She had a job to do and she was going to see it through if it killed her. This was not her father, it was an illusion. One of life's cruel jokes. Not only had her brother grown up to be just like their father, but as if fate was mocking her with this taunting gesture, her brother looked exactly like the man their father had been when Jordan was still a child, still hiding from him in the bottom of her closet praying for a reprieve.

The truck felt like a tomb, encompassing her fear. Jordan Buckley hated this ride; she knew it would not be an easy trip. As the door slammed behind her she felt her heart skid into an unrecognizable rhythm. Now, Jordan sat in the backseat of the big rig caressing the fleece fabric on the small bunk. A picture of two wolves howling at a big-yellow-full-iridescent-moon lined its feather-soft surface. Just as she had predicted she was already wishing she were any other place on earth. She looked back at the fleece blanket again as she allowed her mind to begin scrutinizing the picture.

The moon seemed to over shadow everything else in the image. As if all that existed in its world was there only to pay homage to it. How ironic she thought . . . that her brother would possess something that so completely depicted his life. Jordan moved her hand higher up the fleece as her hand circled the outline of the moon and then gripped into a fist; struggling to keep at bay the memory that was ripping through her consciousness.

Jordan was three again and her father had staggered into the house after spending the evening at a bar that was at the end of their street. She could smell the bitter stench of alcohol as it permeated the air around her almost becoming tangible like it was a living, breathing entity. Capable of erasing all that she was; all that was left of her purity. She could feel herself slip away with every pungent inhale.

"Jordan! Where the hell are you girl?" Garrett Buckley was the epitome of evil. He stunk of cheap wine and cheaper cigarettes. Using every profane word imaginable bringing to the surface the fear that he had long since embedded in her subconscious . . . Obviously, he hadn't grown weary of the vicious tirade against her mother and sought yet another victim.

Jordan hid in the closet hoping that she could somehow become a part of the wall. If she sank deep enough into the closet . . . that maybe he would peer in and she would be camouflaged . . . part of the scenery, but every time no matter how much she wished, it never made it so.

Jordan's fist tightened around the iridescent-moon, of the fleece as the last of the horrible memory slipped away. Her father was brutal with the beatings, but they were nothing when compared to the guilt that she carried. She could remember as she hid in the closet, many times she would hope shamefully that her father would grow weary of his relentless ambush on her mother and not have the energy to launch an attack against her as well. The guilt of that one wish had plagued Jordan for longer than she could remember. It was the one thing that kept her awake at night. It mattered not that she was a little girl. That made no difference . . . somehow she should have been stronger. Sure she had sustained her fair share of broken bones and bruises but that would never be enough to absolve her of her crimes . . . the crime of leaving her mother to be beaten to a pulp while she sat trembling in the corner of her closet thanking a God that she did not even believe in, for being excused his vicious rampage even if for just this once. That was the one crime she could never be pardoned of. Because no matter what good she may do in life, no matter how much evil she may rid the world of, she, Jordan Buckley was the deepest and most profoundly disgusting kind of evil she could have ever imagined. She was a coward.

Her mother would do anything for her of that she had no doubt. So why had she failed her mother so miserably? How could she be so awful as to wish such a horrible fate on her mother? Why could she not be brave and just run to her mother's aid? She could have ran into the room and jumped on her father's back and pulled the attention from her mother. Couldn't she? It's what she would have done now. If only she was given the chance. A do over . . . if somehow by some miracle she could face her father while he attacked her mother and be the Jordan that she was today things would have ended so differently.

Jordan would have made so many things right. So many things would have been different for her mother. But it was too late. Her mother was gone. She had died five years earlier only three months after Jordan's father had passed away. He deserved to die. Jordan knew that. But why did her mother have to die so suddenly after him? Why was she not given more time to enjoy life? Maybe, it was as her mother had said. That day would never come. Three months after Jordan's father died her mother had passed as well. Judy Buckley never left her husband's side. Jordan was horrified by the idea that her mother had wasted away at her father's beck and call . . . her mother never thinking of herself had spent years in the care of others and was certain that God would reward her greatly for her efforts. What a load! Jordan hated that her mother's misguided beliefs had placed her in a sort of prison. Her prison was not steel but it was a worse kind of prison. It was a prison fashioned of misguided loyalty . . . loyalty to her father . . . loyalty to God . . . Jordan would have thrown her father out if she had been given the opportunity, but she could never do anything that would cause her mother even a moment of pain. So in the end she had sat by and helplessly watched as her mother foolishly pledged loyalty to nothing. At least that was the way that Jordan viewed it.

Not long after Jordan's father died her brother moved his wife and child into their old family home. Erica, her sister-in-law, and Penny, her niece, had been very good to Jordan's mother. Both had treated Judy Buckley with the utmost respect. Jordan could still see the haunting look in her mother's eyes as she watched Jr., kick off yet another generation in the Buckley family legacy of abusive drunks. Jordan could only imagine it to be a contributing factor to her mother's early demise. In the end Judy Buckley could not watch as the cruelness of her own life was mirrored in the lives of her daughter-in-law and her precious granddaughter. It was quite simply more than Judy could stand.

Jordan closed her eyes and forced the tears that threatened her back. Not today . . . She was on a mission. Jordan had thought about this everyday for the past two years. She would not allow the past to make her weak. She had studied mixed martial arts, worked out religiously, and even learned how to meditate. Her body and mind were both chiseled to perfection. She could separate the past from the present. She would not allow her brother, Garrett Jr., or his reminder of her father to change what she came here to do . . . Penny, Jordan's niece, needed her, and Jordan intended to be there.

Jordan recoiled at the hiss of the air breaks. Jr. pulled the truck to a stop in front of the old white house. Chills ran down her spine as she allowed her senses to take in the place where she grew up. The four granite pillars that lined the front porch were lined with cracks snaking their length. The shutters that made up the perimeter of each window were a dingy-grey-color, hung slightly to the right, leaving none of them symmetrical with the windows. The roof had piles of pine-straw and leaves matted in clumps lining the edges of the tattered gutter system. Weeds snaked up the porch, that was a mix of red and brown and had holes between some of the boards big enough to put a fist through. Some of the windows had spider-web-crack formations that stretched their length, making Jordan imagine that they were one more storm away form sitting in a pile of rubble. Jordan would relish the thought of the old house falling to the ground, but she would not want anything so horrible to happen while her niece and sister-in-law occupied its dreadful domain. Her brother was another story, the world would be so much better off if only he would follow their father's example and just die. Jordan shook her head only slightly as she tried to imagine how sorry a man would have to be to allow his wife and child to live in such an unquestionably condemned structure.

It still amazed Jordan her brother's ability to bring his family to live in the very house which they had all been tortured. Jordan could not ask her brother about his choice in places to raise a family. Garret Jr. had fast become an exact replica of their father and just like their father he was both swift and harsh with his punishments. Not that she was afraid of her brother she would have long since angered Garret Jr. if it would have been her that he would come after . . . but it would not be her that he would attack . . . it would be his wife and child . . . that was too unbearable a thought. She would not allow her emotions to override the plans she had worked so hard to set into motion. Every aspect of her being here had not gone without careful scrutiny on her part. She was even careful to make it seem as though she needed her brother's help, because she had no where to go. She had to give him the false sense that he was always in control. It would be that one misconception that would allow her to end all of their suffering, and to end the evil that spawned with each new member of the Buckley bloodline.

Jordan clenched her fist as she looked at the small girl on the front porch and forced a weak smile. Soon . . . she thought. Soon Penny's nightmare would be over. All she had to do was stick to her plan, and then Penny could come live with her. Jordan was Penny's next of kin, second only to Erica, Penny's mother. Jordan was certain that Erica would embrace the way of life that Jordan would gift her and her daughter with. The ability to defend themselves . . . the idea would be intoxicating; to never have to live at the mercy of Garret Jr. or any other hell-bent-individual that was self ordained to be the head of their lives. No one had the right to stand in righteous indignation demanding undeserved loyalty . . . loyalty that had not been earned, from any other member of the human race. The idea of taking away another human's freedoms by force sickened Jordan and it demanded swift punishment; a punishment that she was well equipped to issue.

All that stood between Jordan, and claiming Penny, as her own, was a simple process of elimination . . . a process, in which she was certain, her brother would be the eliminated . . . and she was even more certain, that he would not be missed.

* * *

Jordan never had any children of her own. She never married, for that matter she had never been touched, intimately by a male. She did not trust them. If her father's cruel punishments had taught her anything it was you never let anyone that close to you. The only person responsible for Jordan . . . was herself. Looking at Erica and watching her poor excuse of an existence was proof that Jordan was right in her decision to stay alone.

Jordan kept tight emotional inventory; if she ever had feelings for a man that transcended a warm regard; a kind of friendship, he was quickly eliminated from her life. Jordan would never allow herself to fall prey to a man's intentions; foolishly, letting her guard down and trusting him. No, that would not happen. Jordan would never relinquish that amount of control to anyone. She was certain that it would take losing control of her life, her mind, all that she had become, in order to find any semblance of a relationship, and she knew better than anyone what that meant for women. Jordan's mother had been living proof.

* * *

Penny sat poised, on the top step, hugging one of the round marble pillars, which were stationed every few feet apart, an anchor for the dilapidated roof. In her eyes, a fear flashed just beneath the surface. It was in that moment, that Jordan felt her resolve grow. She would be cold, calculating, and precise. There was no room to let her petty fears cloud her thoughts. No time to slip back into a past that's presence was so tangible it threatened to drain the very life from Jordan. For what she was about to do she had to remain focused and clear. There would be no room for error.

Jordan looked from her brother to her sister-in-law as she cleared her throat. Then inwardly, collected her thoughts, as she chided herself; for yet again allowing her fears to get the best of her. Pull it together and ask the question . . . she thought. Good grief, at this pace she would become like one of those wolves baying at the moon on the fleece blanket . . . only instead of the moon it would be her brother. She cleared her throat again as the thought scorched her senses. It wasn't her brother that ignited such fear within her, but the memories here in this house. The very idea that she would lose her focus, her resolve, within its walls, control was an illusion . . . Jordan knew that all to well, but she also knew that it could be a comforting illusion. One that she needed in order to survive what lay just inside the walls of her family home.

"Where do I sleep?" The question seemed to be simple enough. It was just being in this place, the way her brother was the mirror image of her father . . . with his cool dead gray eyes, flushed red cheeks from too much alcohol, the same smell that emitted from his pores and permeated her senses, threatening to make her vomit. How would she do this, when her skin seemed to slip from her body and lay in a puddle at her feet; as even it refused to be in his awful presence.

Jordan could feel the inward volcano of fear . . . which erupted through her veins, and left her the scared little girl in her closet hoping to become a part of the scenery . . . rising up within her. Though, in some ways the fear was good, because she was certain it would allow her brother to relax and become over confident; she could not allow it to consume her, in essence causing her to lose her edge.

"Erica, can you hear?" Garrett snapped at his wife. Erica barely one hundred fifteen pounds with stringy black hair and blue eyes that brimmed always with unshed tears; jerked to attention. Fear resonated from her the same way alcohol did Garret Jr. Its sickening stench accosted Jordan's senses antagonizing the burgeoning anger that Jordan was desperately trying to hold at bay.

There before Jordan, in the same house of torment she grew up in was another woman and child that their only hope was not of a tomorrow without violence, but of making it through today . . . minute by excruciating minute, hoping that every syllable that slipped through their lips met with his approval.

"Yes of course, I am sorry. Right . . . right this way Jordan. How was your trip?" Erica babbled incoherently, through trembling lips. "Are you hungry? I prepared a meal for all of us to eat. After you are settled in maybe . . ." The words were never completed; Jordan winced as she watched Garrett level Erica with the back of his hand.

"Shut all that jabbering up! Stupid woman, can't you see that she just got here? Just show her to her room and spare all of us your mindless chattering." Garret's body was vibrating with need as he stood hovering over Erica. His six foot two stature dwarfed that of her four foot eleven one. Jordan glowered as Erica's hand, flew protectively to her cheek, and then she lowered her gaze. Like a subdued animal, careful not to anger its owner any further she uttered sheepishly. "Follow me."

The fury of the moment nearly blindsided Jordan. She knew that she would have a hard time with his abuse of Erica and Penny but this was beyond anything she could have imagined. She could feel her body tingling with pent up furry. Adrenaline flushed through her veins, like a geyser. Everything in her being, begged for his blood to spill on the spot . . . more than that she wanted to examine it. Watch it as it drained, purposelessly from his worthless body. Jordan stifled the anger within her as she reached down deep; finding that little girl that hovered in the corner of her mind and allowed her to come to the surface for the moment. She had to appear beaten and afraid. She would have to watch Erica and Penny and carefully imitate their actions. It had been a very long time since Jordan had felt fear's sharp talons grip her heart and quicken her breath. But being at the old house was pulling her fast into its unrelenting grip.

Jordan was careful not to provoke her brother then. She had the plan and she would stick to it. He would absolutely have to be killing one of them for her to intervene and in essence deviate from the original strategy. She knew all too well how protective the abused could be of the abuser. She would be careful that her strike did not engage her sister-in-law or her niece in an attempt to protect her brother through misguided loyalty. He, like her father, did not deserve their loyalty but she had seen it be given in similar circumstances. Women beaten to a pulp would call the police for protection, have the man locked up, and then bail him out, only to start the whole viscous cycle over again.

She definitely, could not trust that Erica and Penny would not come to Garret Junior's rescue. Sometimes women or children would help their abuser because they were afraid of the repercussions if they did otherwise . . . maybe, their attacker would be the victor in the struggle, and turn on them for their disloyalty . . . sure it would only indemnify that the victim live in their present torment for longer, but logic did not always have the last word . . . Stockholm syndrome was real; and it could cripple a victim, making them a prisoner forever due to the sympathy that the victim would sometimes feel for their captor; make no mistake about it, anyone in an abusive situation was living in captivity, whether by choice or by force, it made no difference. Prison was prison and Jordan was determined to put an end to the captivity that had been allowed to continue for generations . . . the generations that poisoned her own bloodline indiscriminately, just as the plague had taken the lives of many; so had this been a plague that had claimed not only the wellbeing but the very freedom of every woman and child that lay in its path.

Jordan would free them of the hell they were living in, and once it was all over this porthole to the abyss known as her family home, would be forever closed. Jordan would stand by and bask in the ambiance of the fire; as its flames licked feverishly at the corners of the wasted structure, until at last there was nothing left of its offensive memoirs.

CHAPTER 2

The scene on the porch had ended abruptly as Jordan was able to talk her anger back into the iron box deep in her mind, the place that she would only allow come to the surface in those moments that she needed to step beyond what was acceptable in normal circumstances; societies idea of rational had no dwelling there. It was trapped and there it would stay until Jordan gave it the free rain that it cried out for now. Jr. moved into the house, leaving the two women and child to struggle with Jordan's bags . . . Jordan stepped in front of Erica as she stayed by the ripped-screen-door keeping it at bay so that Penny and Jordan could carry Jordan's things into the house without interference. A small brown spider with spindly legs dangled from an intricately splayed web that hung from the porch light trying to ready for its next meal. Jordan turned her attention from the spider's tireless efforts back to Erica as she allowed a small understanding smile to color her forlorn features. Stepping through the front door, Jordan's breath caught. Time seemed to stand still as she stepped back into the past. The yellowing-tobacco-stained-walls still held the same cracks and crevices from Jordan's childhood, but with the years of disrepair added from her brother's lack of care, the living room seemed to somehow be different yet the same. An old living room suit lined the walls with its blue floral print. The same as when Jordan had lived there as a child; Jordan had not really expected her brother to spring for new furniture, but walking into the house, seeing the same furniture had just impacted her senses in such a way that she had not been prepared for. Jordan could see that the house was managed by her sister-in-law, but the old-brown-shag-carpet gave little hope of ever allowing her efforts to shine through, as it was matted with cigarette burns and beer spills. The floral print couch, love seat, and chair was the same as when Jordan had lived there as a child, but with years of disrepair and a lot more punishment, it no longer held the same luster as before. The set had been a present from her grandparents. Jordan could remember the set, its otherworldly beauty as the delivery men brought it in to the ugliness that was her family home; even the its campaign for luster could not transcend the ambiguous evil that darkened the Buckley home. Jordan's father had been on his best behavior the day that it was brought. He was careful to never make a seen with other men around. Garret Senior cared nothing for Jordan's grandparents but he always welcomed the gifts to their daughter . . . or more to the point to him . . . as Jordan knew her mother would never be allowed to enjoy anything sent to her home as long as her father was there. Jordan looked back at the couch as she followed its length to the floor where the surrounding area was filled with an orange-yellow-tinted cushion. Bits and pieces of the cushion now dry rotting after years of abuse were spilling from a huge hole in the side of the fabric. Jordan could imagine that Jr. was the only one that was allowed to enjoy the couch enough to lay on it, and judging by the burn holes in the carpet in front of the couch she could see that her guess had been right.

A look of ashamed resignation flashed in Erica's eyes and then she moved further down the hall, quietly directing Jordan to her old bedroom. The hall dimly lit with only the suns raise straining to light the way, snaked its way to Jordan's old room, seeming to taunt Jordan. She could see the past unfold as it whispered its threat of taking what was left of her sanity. Jordan moved with measured steps as she brushed past her parent's old room and moved thoughtlessly to the adjacent wall. She half expected her father's ghost to jump out of the old room and grab her. She picked up the pace slightly as she pushed down the hall to her old room.

Once she stepped into the old bedroom she grew up in, Jordan secured the door behind her. She hastened to the bed, carefully taking inventory she pulled out all the contents of her suitcase. After putting her clothes away, she stepped over to the closet. She would not open the bag that contained her weapons until she allowed her mind this time. So without wasting another minute, she crawled to the corner. It was then that she allowed the memories, of the past to claim her. She had to get it out of her system. One by one, she looked at the memoirs, of the past; holding them up and examining them, allowing all the facets of each horrible moment access to her innermost being . . . so that her mind's eye could see them at last for what they were. She would look, no matter how ugly or hard the recollection. She would allow the fear to turn into something beyond rage, something beyond anything she could imagine. Because when she stood at the threshold of life and death, when she held her brother's life by the thread of wasted existence that it truly had become, she would be able to take the proverbial scissors and snip, without hesitation. She would thrust her brother into the hell that her mother had talked about. Forcing him into one of the darkened chambers, of the abyss, that would house pain and aguish, that had been designed specifically for him alone. Specifically for his cruelty . . . and once she had assured that he was no longer on this plain, she would throw away the key, and never think of him or their father's ruthless tyranny again. For from that moment on she would be the builder of a new future; a future in which she would never again have to see another woman cower at the hands of a Buckley offspring. Because she would be the one to finally stand and do what she should have done from the beginning; she would end it.

Jordan showered and dressed quickly; she donned a pair of old blue-jeans and a white-loose-fitted t-shirt that had a bouquet of pink, purple, and white flowers. Jordan had stopped at a local emporium to grab a few things to make up a wardrobe that would lend to the look she was trying to pull off; innocence, purity, and timid-uncertainty. It was assumed that if she looked the part it would better encapsulate the illusion that she was trying to sell to her brother. It was his belief that she was the same as when she had left ten years earlier that Jordan was hoping for. It was exactly what would keep Penny and Erica out of harms way; making her brother feel comfortable around her as well. That way he would not think twice about attacking Jordan when the time came, and Jordan was sure that if her niece and sister-in-law believed that Junior was not in danger . . . they would simply slip away to sulk in whatever part of the house gave the most sense of false security. Jordan reached down to her tennis shoe and hid the first of several weapons. She was careful to keep the weapons out of site so that her family would not be able to detect their presence. She was sure on some level at least that she would be able to overcome her brother without the use of weaponry, but the bureau had taught her never to underestimate her enemy. So operating under that guideline, Jordan attached the sheath for her trusty six-inch-blade around her leg just under the bulky material of her too big blue jeans and slid the blade home. Jordan scanned her image in the mirror and after being satisfied with what she saw stepped from the room. She would have to endure dinner with her brother and his worshipers. Jordan hoped with all her might that she was up to the task. Image would only get her so far, while the clothes she had picked were an excellent touch, they would not be all that she needed to convince her brother that attacking her would leave him the victor to the spoils of battle.

* * *

The meal passed with all the gloominess she could stand. Jordan scanned the old dining room; so many mixed feelings shrouded the moment. Many of the fixtures that marked the room's history were splintered with memories of her mother . . . her mother's taste was simple yet elegant, but watered down by her poorly managed budget. Thanks to Garret Sr.'s lust for the night life so many dreams had been left unfulfilled in her mother's life. There was nothing of Judy's taste represented in the room; not in a real way. Not in the pictures that Jordan's grandmother had shared with her as a young child. The pictures depicted her mother in a way that Jordan had never imagined. Beautiful frilly dresses embellished with lace and beads. Fact was Jordan's mother had traded a life of privilege for a shabby existence with Garret Sr. Jordan had taken the old photo from her grandmother. The picture testified of a different life. One that had held promise. Judy Buckley's room was bedazzled in a beautiful princess bed with lace and jewels. Huge two feet tall stuffed animals in every shape and size lined the perimeter of the room. Pale pink walls were divided by embellished cherry-wood molding. Bay windows adorned in silk-maroon curtains that were tied back with golden braid-work tassels, protruded from the room and surrounded a makeshift lounge area. Jordan could imagine her mother sitting in its secure comfort with a book, losing herself in its pages.

Her mother's parents had been full of life; they loved to travel and had a love for life that was only over shadowed by their love for each other. They loved their children as well and were not rich but well off. Jordan's grandfather was a Baptist minister and her grandmother worked in the local mill and had worked there for over thirty years when she retired . . . she worked in the office on payroll and made a decent living. The two had insisted that the church not pay for his time as a minister. Her grandfather was more than willing to work in the local mill as a weaver, but the church had other ideas and would not hear of it. The church paid for her grandfather to attend night school to get an associates degree in psychology and was soon taking advantage of his skills through marriage and family counseling. He had gone from preaching on Sunday morning and night as well as Wednesday nights to counseling the parishioners two nights a week. The new hours put in on the church's behalf were taking away from his family; a perfect excuse for the church elders to veto the young couple's vote in not receiving any money for his efforts and family's sacrifice. The extra hours would make it impossible for Jordan's grandfather to work outside of the home. He would be unable to earn a suitable income that would buffer the money needed to placate the family budget. It was decided not only would the church pay him a salary but he would move into the new brick home that was being built next to the church for their benefit . . . rent free.

Jordan listened to the creak of the old wooden chairs as she scrutinized the cobwebs that hung from the four-bulb light fixture that curved in delicate arches, (a wedding gift supplied by Jordan's grandmother) the only claim to true elegance that the old house could boast. The dark wood of the dining room was rich; the knots in the pine bringing the wood together in the perfect ensemble of rugged beauty and delicate grace. Jordan breathed a sigh as she allowed the loss of her mother and her grandparents to cripple her emotions. Death has no sting . . . Jordan allowed the words her mother, quoted from the bible to wash over her. Death does sting mama . . . Jordan thought as she again took one last look at the old room. It was the only place in the house that Jordan did not completely despise; for it was the one place that her whole family had come together twice a year . . . Christmas and Thanksgiving . . . the two days a year that almost seemed normal . . . almost. No one entered the room any other day of the year . . . so her father's destructive behavior had not touched the room's timeless beauty. Like a time capsule, holding evidence of a beauty long since lost, in the mist of ugliness left in the aftermath of a terrible storm . . . the room told a story of better days past.

Jordan stood and dismissed herself as she headed for her room. She knew that her brother would put her in her old room; she was counting on it. After all, his cruelty like their father's knew no end. Both her brother and father shared the same jaded sense of humor; she never saw her brother show any sign of true happiness, but she knew what brought him pleasure, he wanted all of the people in his world, like the wolves depicted in the fleece fabric on the bunk of his truck, to pay homage to him. Oh yes, Jr. wanted exactly what their father wanted; to be in control. He wanted to be the overseer of pain and discomfort in other's lives . . . he thrived on the fear that emitted from his victims eyes. To him it said. "You have me right where you want me." That was exactly what he wanted. She counted on this unwitting mistake on his part, to put her in the one room of the old house that she knew more than any of the others. She had spent most of her time hiding in the room, cowering in the closet's corner praying that she would go unnoticed. It was in that room that she knew so well, that she was least likely to be surprised, for she would be on her own turf. Also the memories of the room would lend to the lack of fear that she was starting to sense; the longer that she stayed in the house and witnessed her brother's blatant disregard for his wife and child the angrier she was becoming. Jordan knew that she would need a healthy dose of her past fears to help her tap into the one emotion that no longer held center stage in her mind . . . fear. Her brother would not try to attack her if he felt a lack of trepidation; he was a coward after all, and cowards would never start a confrontation in which they were certain they would not be the victor.

* * *

Jordan was certain that Jr. had not considered that she had lived in the same torturous hell, she knew that same wrath, and it had made her become the hunter of men and women like him. This was her ultimate test. The one thing standing between her and being signed on as the highest level of secrecy that the government held . . . a black Ops organization known as, 'Black Heart Revenge', the government's answer to crimes that had gone unpunished. There was only so much that the legal system could do . . . after that a person was put on trial, in front of twelve jurors . . . sometimes members of the jury would feel sorry for these members of society that were cruel. The men and women of the jury could be coaxed into a not guilty verdict by a talented ruthless lawyer that cared for nothing but his next payday . . . or sometimes it was the prisoner that played on the jury's tender sensibilities; he or she would sit in the courtroom looking like innocence personified, and gain undeserved freedom. The criminal, in essence would be set back out on society; only to begin another bout of rape and murder against innocent members of society. Jordan and other members of the organization like her were the means to an end; a type of vigilante justice.

Black Heart Revenge, had agents all over the world, going about their lives unnoticed by anyone . . . The member could have any cover imaginable . . . from school teacher to garbage worker. The more mundane the job the better the cover; once an agent was set into mission-mode, they were unstoppable. No matter what resources or what casualty even that of the agent the mission was to be complete . . . and there was only two unbreakable rules, no matter the circumstance, an agent was never to break cover, and absolutely for no reason was the agent ever to indicate Black Heart's involvement. It was completely unacceptable and any agent that broke the rules would be punished . . . death would be the only verdict for an agent caught breaking the rule.

Jordan had lived like a shadow standing on the outskirts of her own world, just being a witness to the life that was hers for years; her head down as if counting the floor boards. The nights of hoping her father would pass out. The inner turmoil of guarding what was fast becoming a black heart had long since quenched any desire she may possess to exist, let alone thrive. Then one day, after stepping out of a cab, heading to her less than desirable apartment; a man reached out and grabbed her. Pulling her protesting into the shadows of the alley that lurked between her apartment building and the neighboring multilevel complex.

The man stood before her, heaving with lust, as he eyed her breast his gaze fell lower, a lust-driven-haze contorted his face. The man was wearing standard-prison-issue stripes, his greasy black hair lay in unkempt clumps, his dark eyes held a murderous glare that spoke of untouched mayhem; the desire to tear her apart after slaking his lust on her was evident in those dark pools that were sunken back in his head . . . His glare sent a rush of adrenaline through her causing her limbs to vibrate with uncertainty. Jordan could feel her heart as it leaped into her throat, the rhythm was pulsing with all the terror that was radiating throughout her body.

With one hand over her mouth, and the other around her waist he drug her deeper into the murky shadows of the alley; where he would sate his disgusting lust on her and then discard her like a piece of used toilet paper. Jordan kicked her feet helplessly, her eyes darting from side to side, as futile whimpers erupted from around the man's cigarette soaked fingers. She could feel his protruding belly as it jutted out and forced her spinal-column into an uncomfortable position. She clawed desperately at his hands. The need to be free of his obvious intent pulsated through her veins as viscous as honey. Instinct screamed through her subconscious and she knew with every fiber of her being that if she made it to the destination she was being propelled, only one of them would be coming out and the chances of that being her was not a bet she would be willing to take. Still she was helpless to stop his unwanted advances.

Jordan's eyes took in the soaring lengths of the apartment buildings jutting into the sky and butting up next to each other lending a scant amount of room for passage. Her breathing became more forced; as claustrophobia took center stage threatening to render her unconscious as its foreboding fingers gripped her airway shutting it down. Her eyes burned as she felt the small amounts of air pass them while escaping around his hand from her muffled mouth. She whimpered helplessly as she flailed against him . . . She felt hot tears start to course down her cheeks and then she felt nothing . . . She was no longer in the driver's seat; that would be the only way that she could explain it . . . In the alley something happened. There was no fear . . . there was nothing but rage, white hot intense filled anger. Jordan was seething . . . with the years of abuse to herself and her mother, the guilt that she had always carried because she had not only failed to help her mother but had hoped her father would satisfy his rage on her mother and not come for her next. One by one, the thoughts seared through Jordan's psyche; blazing trails of unmitigated hatred, and there in that alley, Jordan shed what was left her innocence, her humanity, with the drops of her attacker's blood.

One minute the prisoner was holding her mouth, and demanding Jordan to take off her clothes, and the next he lay in a bloody heap on the ground, at her feet. Jordan stared down at his body then looked down at her right hand as she took inventory of the blood and skin under her long fingernails. Her attacker's throat had a jagged tear, with strings of meat and wormlike vessels protruding from it. Blood oozed from his neck as it filled the ground that surrounded him, and etched its way to her feet. Jordan slowly stepped away and then spun around and headed breathlessly for her apartment.

Standing in the shower, two things donned on her, one she had to get away from here and fast, and the other was that felt . . . good. Jordan scrubbed the remains of blood and tissue from under her fingernails. She washed her hair slowly thinking about the alley and what had happened. She blinked and she was back there again. The guy had her by the throat, he was going to kill her after he raped her; of that she was certain. She felt the years of frustration mount and then turn to anger, and then to rage. Finally she saw herself as if she were on the outside looking in . . . she stomped the heal of her shoe down on top of the man's foot hard, he cried out and loosened his grip . . . she wasted no time as she whirled around slapped both hands as hard as possible against the man's ears, and just as he was about to bend forward and cover his aching head . . . Jordan reached forward and dug her long sharp fingernails into the skin surrounding his larynx, and with a force uncommon to her she yanked his larynx free of his neck . . . nothing fancy, she thought just effective. Some of the moves she guessed had burned into her subconscious from action movies she had watched in her spare time. She was after all an action-movie-junkie, it was the only highlight that colored an otherwise mundane existence, but where did the larynx stunt come from? She supposed it was the movie she had watched about the bouncers in the bar. The male-role was a cooler, responsible for the wellbeing of the bouncers. He had ripped the bad guys throat out after kicking a gun out of his hand. Jordan could not imagine that so many skills could be gained from just visual interpretation, but she had no other explanation.

As she allowed the last of the memory to fade and her mind to grasp hold of the reality that stretched out before her; she would be faced with prison, wouldn't she? She had to get out of the shower, and get dressed. She had to get as far away from this scene as she could. She would have to somehow start over. With the last thought; she stepped from the shower after wrapping up in her robe. Quickly, she grabbed all her things, dressed and then started out the door.

Jordan navigated the four foot hall of her tiny apartment, as she rubbed her head vigorously with the black and white towel that depicted Lighthouses; her favorite. She was headed to her bedroom when something in her peripheral vision caught her eye. Jordan stopped abruptly while peering into her scantly furnished living room. Jordan squealed. She felt her body lift off the ground several inches as she started to run to the back of the apartment. Jordan had only made it a few inches, making it feel as though she had been running in place, when she felt the hard contours of a male hand claim her mouth. Her body felt as though it had been nailed to a washboard, as the man's other hand claimed her arms and with little effort they were deathly tangled behind her back in an iron grip, Jordan stilled herself for the moment that had played out in the alley to return. Instead, she heard the man's soothing voice.

"I am going to let you go." The man said in a careful monotone cadence. His way of holding her was all about containment and had nothing to do with lust. Jordan could sense it not only in the finality of his grip, but the statue-like-stance that she felt as her shoulder blades grazed his chest muscles. His left foot snaked around her left leg where it rested behind her right heel . . . Jordan could not imagine how he was keeping his balance. Nothing about either of the men made her feel in danger, but at the same time she knew that both men would kill her as soon as struggle to keep control of her.

"When I let you go . . . no screaming, no running, and no fighting . . ." The man turned Jordan so that she was facing his partner. "This is Garrison. I am Simon. We are not here to hurt you." The Garrison man simply smiled modestly and nodded his agreement with what was being said. Jordan nodded slightly her understanding and closed her eyes in an attempt to show submission. Jordan waited as Simon unwrapped himself one limb at a time from around her. After being satisfied that Jordan would not make an attempt to escape, the two men waited as Jordan crossed into the living room and stood against the far wall.

"I get that you aren't here to hurt me." Jordan confided with a trembling voice. Her nerves were shattered. First the scene in the alley and now this. How much more would she be expected to endure. She felt an inward wince take root as she scolded herself for the query . . . never ask such a question. It was like inviting more. If nothing else she had learned that from the action movies she loved, as well as some obvious basic self defense moves that she was extremely thankful for now. She pointed to the couch as she gulped air. She lingered against the wall even after the two men took their seat and pushed a couple of plain colored pillows out of the way. Jordan looked at the front door of the apartment as she mentally calculated her chances for escape, and then thought better of it. Best not to test her luck. She figured she had met her quota for amazing feats of escape for the day.

That is when she had her first introduction with the government's answer to unpunished crime. Apparently, there was a few members of the CIA that had come together to form an undercover operation, known as Black Heart Revenge. Those few had quickly spread into many more. Finding people that believed in the militia was not hard. It seems that there were quite a few jaded members of society. The two men that sat in her living room now explained how things worked in depth.

The point was she had committed a crime, like it or not . . . even though he was a prisoner with a shady past, and less than admirable intentions toward her in the alley where he now laid a corpse. Society would still demand that she go to jail, get a lawyer, and take her chances with a jury of twelve of her peers.

Jordan's options were made clear; either they could get the legal ball rolling, by taking her to jail now, or option B, there was a clean up crew, in the alley way, right now that was prepared to stick the scum-bag back in his cell and make it look like an accident.

Jordan could imagine an accident would be tough to fake but the way she saw it, that would be their dilemma. Right now, all she needed from the two agents sitting in her living room was the gist and the dotted line. After all what did she have to loose. Her heart was as hollow as a shell on the ocean floor; she had no one, and a crummy apartment. It was time to make it all yesterday's news.

Jordan considered all that the men had said, and then after only a few more seconds of scrutinizing her worthless existence, Jordan looked around the plain beige walls of her small apartment and shivered as she witnessed a roach taking refuge in one of the cracks at the top of the ceiling. The room in some way made her think of a past that she would love to forget, but until this moment had no options, and no understanding of how. She went to the desk that garlanded the corner of the room. One of the men stood as though he was preparing himself for an altercation. Jordan held up a shaky hand, and assured him she would not be a threat. With a sheepish grin she held up the pen and then stepped over to the coffee table. "Where's the dotted line, gentlemen?"

The two men gave each other a knowing look, as finally, a briefcase was produced; Jordan, quickly, filled out the necessary paperwork as she smiled inwardly, she could already feel her new beginning taking root as it weeded out all the uncertainty of her past. Soon, she would be a new person and with that would come new life, and never again, would she have to live in the shadow of an unrelenting past, that had claimed every happiness, she might have had. She was sure that with the knowledge she would gain from the two men in her apartment, she would be able to forge her own happiness out of any situation no matter how bleak.

CHAPTER 3

The weeks ahead were the hardest, and yet the most rewarding Jordan had ever encountered. After she understood that she would become a killing machine, that what she had done to the guy in the alley had been done in rage and fear, with discipline and training she could erase all doubt of her success in every fight . . . Jordan took to the program and all that it had to offer with complete focus. They also explained that she was absolutely no accident. That she would use everything about her that made her Jordan, to her advantage. They broke her down, rebuilt her, and gave her a confidence that she had only seen in movies or read about in the books that littered her old apartment.

Jordan knew that when she walked into a situation that she would come out the victor. She was trained in the art of Karate; Tai-kwon-do, a type of martial art that taught her how to use anything at her disposal as a weapon, and various other combat techniques . . . her body was honed into a mixture of graceful beauty, seductive curves and sleek definition.

The program was specifically selected to bring all the things that made her a woman together as a vantage point. She also studied the art of Tai chi, a Chinese form of physical exercise, which was characterized by a series of very slow and deliberate ballet body movements. She had catlike agility, and uncanny reflexes. Her mind worked all the time scanning her surroundings for threats or possibilities. She was ever ready for trouble of any kind . . . more than that she welcomed it. She was a different person than she had ever been or even known.

Jordan was also instructed to choose a form of spirituality. She hadn't really understood the importance then, and could not succumb to any spiritual belief that put a male figure at the head of her life. So that had ruled out most of them. Their beliefs in no way affected or persuaded her. She was in all ways her own person . . . . the epitome of woman . . . in her truest form. What a woman was meant to be. Not some punching bag that masquerade as a woman. Jordan would keep to her own beliefs that there was no God . . . no higher power that created it all or over seen all of the little people of earth . . . no galaxy beyond this plain that waited for human discovery. No . . . all that existed was man and that was messed up enough without trying to bring supreme beings into the mix. Here in this place they may hone certain aspects of Jordan Buckley, but if they allowed themselves to believe it spanned beyond those proportions they were sadly mistaken.

Everyday that she worked toward this new, better being she was evolving into she could feel the rage within her turning into something she seemed to be able to control. No more was she the little girl at the bottom of her closet hoping to magically become a part of the scenery, she was now a strong, confident woman that wanted to be noticed in the room so that her demons would come for her, inadvertently allowing for the revenge bubbling beneath the surface, that only she knew about to be satiated. Each time she was able to unload the rage that permeated her being: she could feel that she was becoming a little closer to the person she truly wanted to be. It was invigorating.

Jordan stayed in a compound that was housed beneath the earth, where its identity was kept secret. The dorm-rooms were small with parse decorations and housed two recruits. Every room an exact replicate of the one before was painted white, and was boldly lit with tract-lighting nestled in silver grooves in the ceiling. The silver backdrop of the grooves only magnified the lights potential. On the wall of every dorm was a small turn dial that could tone down the lighting if desired. Jordan kept the lights at their highest setting. The bright glow, a stark difference from that of the dim light of her family home; a welcome distraction. Jordan's roommate, Misty was a very agreeable young woman that like Jordan only cared about the moments that she could legally peel back the restraint on her anger.

Jordan readied herself everyday as she moved as quickly as possible to the spacious room that made up the center of the compound. The outer edge of the room was lined with exercise equipment of various types . . . while the innermost circle of the room housed a mat. The mat was Jordan's favorite place.

Combat training was Jordan's most coveted time of day, the rage that drummed within her like a pulse could be sated; if only for a short time. She had to be careful not to show the true wealth of anger that surged through her veins. The team leaders had been introduced to that part of her many times in the beginning. Lucky for Jordan there was a grading curve, but after the weeks became months, the trainers would watch for those types of behaviors to decrease in a recruit. The members that showed no signs of curving their anger were placed in the garden for six months where they received intense counseling sessions. Jordan had seen the place only once as she helped her partner bring one of the recruits in.

Tommy was introduced to the program around the same time as Garrison and Jordan, though Garrison had been with the program a few months longer than that of Jordan or Tommy. Jordan had been Garrison's first recruit. Tommy was more than angry. The boy had demons that even Jordan could not understand. There was emptiness in his eyes that seemed to burn through his sockets and black out his entire countenance. Jordan entered the garden, and a memory flashed in her mind . . . something about a man and woman being in a garden and not doing what God had told them . . . Jordan was fuzzy on the details of the story. But she could remember that the man and woman had been disobedient. God had soon kicked the two out of the garden for their transgressions.

The Garden was beautiful but held a peace that Jordan found unsettling. Something inside of her was not yet ready for that kind of peace. She had demons of her own though clearly not as intense as Tommy's, they were still demanding. There were desires that needed to be answered. Jordan had to help her sister-in-law and niece, she also needed to destroy her family home and make certain that the family name of Buckley died with her brother, as she had no intentions of caring on the blasphemes putrid taint that was her family's legacy. She could not allow her brother to continue to beat them. He must be dealt with, swiftly; and she could not allow another generation of

Buckley men to pass on their tainted blood. No she could not allow herself to get caught up in the bliss that seemed to encompass such a place. Maybe when it was all over maybe then she could allow the warmth that emitted from the place, the same warmth that Jordan could remember feeling in her mother's presence to have the last word in her haunted soul. But that time would have to wait, too much was at stake.

* * *

Jordan was allowed to choose weapons during training. Her weapons had been simple nothing elaborate. It was with her hands that she found most of her revenge could be satisfied. There was something about the blood of her unsuspecting victims caressing across her flesh in combat that seemed to cool the black desires that scorched through the membranes of her being. Even from her first kill, as pitifully orchestrated as it had been, she could remember the wonderful surge of ecstasy that had forged its way through her being carving a lasting impression on her future. That one moment had told it all. Jordan was a hands on girl.

The weapons that she did choose were a six inch black and purple handled blade that could filet a man with little effort, a colt forty five with a silver and chrome barrel, and a pair of nun chucks with a dragon etched on the handles. Each weapon was carefully chosen for a person that she found to be powerful in her childhood . . . someone that she had admired. Unfortunately, when it came to combat training at that point in her life, Jordan had not been exposed to many women. Growing up the television was flooded with images of men at arms. There simply were not many women joining the military. Most women were being oppressed by public officials.

Every woman in history that had ever made her mark on society had seemed to be erased with one election gone wrong. Where were the Christians then? Jordan would ask herself bitterly. Those people that served their God so blindly. They were supposed to be so loyal to the cause. It was actually humorous to Jordan. They allowed the Ten Commandments to be stripped from the courthouse . . . then prayer to be taken from the schools, and so on and so forth. It just snow balled out of control. Everyday she woke up there were more media images, of people inflicting hate crimes on the Christians? Still these people that were supposed to be power houses of faith would allow it all to continue . . . each time, the followers diminishing in number.

Most of the people that were left to serve God were in hiding. They dare not show their face and claim Jesus Christ as their savior. Jordan had thought that it all had started simple enough; one state in the union had demanded that no one be allowed to have bible study in their homes . . . it was not taken seriously. The idea seemed asinine, and no one paid heed to the undercurrent of Christian hate crimes that were already spawning from the demands in areas surrounding the state. Soon enough, though, the crimes that had only been whispers of things done in the dark had soon come to the surface, as more and more Christian figures were being thrown in jail for preaching in public. Soon homes of suspected Christians were being raided as if there were drug paraphernalia on the property. Jordan shook her head as the memories of slight-grey-haired preachers were being thrown into jail first, and then in no time whole committees of women and children were being disbanded by using almost lethal force. Jordan could not help but think of her mother.

* * *

When Jordan completed her combat training, anger management classes, and classes suggesting that she should choose a spiritual outlet, finally she was set loose on society. Each situation or job was different. She would get a text message that would simply be a number. Each digit in the number stood for specifics in a location where a message would be housed. The number was generally ten digits . . . each digit having a specific meaning. For instance . . . 1234567890—may mean locker 1, on the 2nd floor of the airport. The other numbers would usually be digits in an address . . . for example . . . 34—would be the number of the specific airport and the 5—would be the street number that the airport was located. 67—Would be the designated code for how the person should be eliminated. Black Heart housed an instruction manual in which all of the agents had to know completely . . . In the manual was 99 ways that an agent was allowed to dispose of a mark. The agent had to stick to the agency's command without deviation, because each number selected had at least three different evacuation plans that the agency used to cover up the crime scene. The last of the number-890 was simply the amount to be paid for the job ... for example 890 = 890,000.

Everything was set up very simply in the agency, so that there was no room for error. There was no need to make the numbers hard to remember or to make the process complicated, because no agent had ever revealed their source and even if they had each agent's phone was fitted with its very own tracking device ... so no matter where a agent was they could be tracked. Also every agent had a microchip implant, in the back of their neck, just above their shoulder blade, to the right of their spine.

The microchip could be activated at any moment. This would only take place in the unlikely event of a rogue agent ... the microchip allowed the organization complete access to anything that the agent was hearing. This would allow the organization to set off a detonator that was in the agent's phone and destroy the agent and anyone within a fifty foot radius. Also there was a code-word set into place incase an agent were being tortured and wanted the agency to detonate, to end their suffering.

After retrieving the number of the locker at the airport ... the agent would go to the specific locker and obtain details on the mark. Such items would include pictures of the mark and other general miscellaneous information that would be useful to the agent in ascertaining the whereabouts of the mark ... such as where the mark may work, or members of the mark's inner circle, meaning the people that were most intertwined in the mark's life. Jordan never thought of a mark as he or she ... the mark was quite simply a loose end and she was charged with tying up. She never asked questions; quite simply she did not want to know. Her life had become a far cry better since Black Heart's impromptu appearance in it, and that was all she would ever need to know.

If an agent was caught the process was quite simple; they would take the fall like any other citizen. Then to satisfy the public eye, the agent would be thrown on the mercy of the court and after the sentence was passed, which most of the time would be the death penalty, because the judge was paid off by the agency. The agent would be found "dead" in their cell. In the event, that an agent was not found guilty, and was released back out into general population; the agent was the victim of a hate crime by an angry unidentified member of society, which was apparently dissatisfied with the court's ruling. The agent was then put through the usual process that occurred once they were "killed" in the cell. If the agent was given the death penalty . . . the fear of the death penalty was too much for them and they would kill themselves either by hanging, or any other form of suicide that the organization had deemed acceptable. In reality the recruit would only take a pill that was designed by the organization; and then carefully through an old method taught to the recruits dangle from a rope with enough force to cause attention from the other inmate that was sleeping at the time. They would kick away whatever they had used to step on and hold to the rope cinched tight around their neck with their hands until the other inmate took notice. Normally the other inmate not wanting to be indicated in the death of a cell-mate would scramble from bed and immediately prop the device used to step on back under the recruits feet or in some cases would at least hold the weight of the recruit up and start screaming for help.

Finally after the body was reported found and sent to the necessary media outlets the CIA members that headed up 'Black Heart Revenge' would flash their badges at the mortician; and usually without issue collect the body. In the off chance that a mortician did become problematic the CIA member would simply obtain a warrant from the same judge that had been paid off to deliver the death sentence. Then the "body" would be hauled back to a remote facility. There the agent would undergo plastic surgery and be put back out in the field again with another fake identity . . . of course after the agent had been properly debriefed and put through six months of the garden, to ensure that the agent not make the same mistakes. Most agents did not get caught, so this was not a common occurrence. The few agents that seemed to get caught due to burnout were supposedly given a nice healthy vacation, and then brought back into the agency . . . and were recycled as a trainer. Those who can't do . . . teach, that sort of thing.

Jordan made sure her every move was calculated she weighed everything carefully before setting a plan into motion. She had never had to have plastic surgery and she would not start now. She could not imagine that life as a trainer could satisfy the insatiable thirst for revenge that burned within her.

* * *

Standing in her old room she looked around and made sure each weapon was in place. When she made her attack she would get her brother to follow her into her room. This would assure two things, one it would keep Penny and Erica out of harms way and two it would put the battle on her turf.

Once Jordan had Garret in the room she would lock the door and then her brother's last memories would be shelled out one terrifying blow at a time. The thought was so palpable that she could almost feel his flesh succumbing to her will as the blade sank home and his blood burst forth as evidence that her own revenge was finally satisfied.

CHAPTER 4

The first few days with exception to the slap were just as Jordan had predicted. Garret Jr. had behaved himself. Of course, that was partly due to the fact that Erica had played the part of a good little wife. The picture of submission, she walked around her husband as if egg shells littered the floor around him. His beck and call girl, his wish was her command. The very thought of it sickened Jordan. That combined with certain old demons, which would show their ugly heads, sometimes made it hard for Jordan to stick to the plan. Oh, she could see it all as clear as if she were watching it on a television program; her, walking over to her brother and sinking her blade into that black smug heart of his. It was almost orgasmic the feeling that she knew would accompany the flesh parting way, and watching as his eyes filled with shock. That usual look of how could this of happened to me: that all of them had as the end came. It was a smugness that made her want to puke.

Control was an illusion. No one held all the cards, but these vile excuses for human beings that prayed on the fear of others believed they were in control, of it all. Like the moon that seemed to take over the fleece blanket in the truck; obviously a compensation for the little man he truly was inside. He over shadowed everything that was in his world, sucked the life out of all that came into his grasp; not just expected, but demanded they worship him and only him . . . Just like the wolves worshiped that moon.

In Jordan's heart she knew she brought with her a new world order; for the two shells of human existence that robotically moved around the old house like the pit of despair it truly was. Today would be a day of reckoning; the first day of the rest of their lives, and today would start Jordan on the road to recovery.

After she had her revenge Jordan knew she could return to the agency and prove that she could be a new person. That it could be about business. Despite all the things that the chief of recruits had said to her at the last meeting, Jordan knew that she could control her anger. She knew what the price for her freedom was and she was looking at the toll bridge to that freedom in the form of her brother. It was his part in her ugly past that kept things from moving forward in her life. Wasn't that what she felt? That she had to rid the world of her brother, to know that the woman and child he abused without prejudice were at last free of his tyranny.

Jordan could not know what it truly meant to be at peace until every piece of the puzzle was in place. She had to rid the world of her brother's kind of evil. The kind of evil that forced life and happiness from a little girl sitting at the back of her closet . . . the kind of evil that drained every link to innocence from that same little girl . . . the kind of evil that sat across the table from her now and hoped that his wife or child would do anything that would give him just cause to retaliate against them . . . his belief that it was that transgression on their parts that literally separated him from the cold-hearted-monster that he truly was. His mind was filled with the absurd notion that proclaimed him innocent if he were somehow provoked; they had asked for it. That was the perception that became his all consuming reality, and that was the evil that Jordan had vowed to destroy. She would rip it up by its roots and free everything and everyone in its path. Maybe then she would be whole.

*   *   *

Inside of her, the demon that demanded more blood more heinous acts every time was taking on a life of its own. Just like the smell of alcohol had seemed to infuse the air around her with an almost electrical fear, the rage within her seemed to do the same. The more she exacted her revenge the thirstier she became. It was then that she started to understand the need for spirituality. Yet ironically it was the same hate for the opposite sex that seemed to free her and hold her captive at the same time.

Jordan couldn't seek refuge from any god that shared the same gender as the man that had come home drunk and tortured both her and her mother for so many years. Jordan's mother had died a broken shell of a woman. Lying in her casket was the first smile that looked as though it came from true peace, which Jordan had ever seen on her mother's face. Why had this woman been put through so much in her short life? Jordan's father died king of his castle. Long after he mellowed after he quit drinking, he still demanded her mother's allegiance and it was fearfully given. He never hit her mother again after putting down the bottle, but her mother would tell Jordan during her visits that she had to keep him happy so he would not return to the bottle.

Jordan crossed the kitchen and laid a wary hand on the sink; she eyed the old rust stain, which drifted lazily from the middle of its metal surface to the drain. She shivered and recoiled, reflexively from a roach as it darted frantically away from her hand into the protective darkness beneath the cabinet. The moment took her back to a time when she stood face to face with her mother begging for her to claim what was left of her time on earth and walk in true freedom. Even Jordan was not sure what that was . . . having never felt freedom in her own life, but she was sure that it had nothing to do with wasting away in a house with a selfish-coldhearted excuse of a human being that masquerade around in a man's body. Jordan could almost feel her mother standing there with her. As the memory flooded her senses and she was again standing in this very spot.

Pursing her lips she allowed some of the tension of the moment to be released from her mind before she addressed her mother.

"Why do you stay?" Jordan asked as she closed the distance between her and her mother. Judy Buckley, her mother looked sheepishly around the kitchen for Garrett.

"SHHH!" Judy hissed with urgency while pulling on her daughter's arm. In her eyes were the usual brimming tears that Jordan had become accustom to. It was the "norm". She could not imagine there being anything else in life beyond the family she had grown up in. She could only imagine in all of the homes in the world the same sickening images played out. It was not until she had entered Black

Heart Revenge that she had discovered the truth. Her situation was not the "norm" at all . . . in fact it was the extreme opposite.

"Good lord girl are you mad? Now be off with you before you get him angry." The hiss of whispers pierced the air. Fear flashed in her mother's eyes again, and Jordan could see that even though the man in the other room was only a shell of the beast he had once been . . . her mother had been at the opposing end of his cruel tirades for so long . . . that she now believed him to be just as capable of the same horrible punishments that he had issued for all those years.

"I'm going mama. I just don't understand why you do. Jr. and I are grown now. You could come live with me." Jordan said while trying to make all of the sincerity of the moment register in her eyes. She took her mother's hand in her own before turning to the door as she continued. "Not Jr. though, he is just as bad." Jordan sighed at the last word. It hurt so deeply that her older brother had fallen in their father's foot steps. He had become the same; an alcoholic that would give everything for just one more drink. The same mindless tyrant that took and never gave; the same . . . Jordan dropped her head and then looked back up at her mother. She wanted so desperately to save her mother now. She wanted to take her away from this place and burn its rottenness evil to the ground.

"I said hush girl! I have to stay, the Lord says so." Judy said as she swatted Jordan on the rear, kissed her cheek and gave her a gentle shove toward the back door. She half smiled then blew Jordan a kiss.

Jordan left her mother's kitchen that day feeling as deflated as she had every time she had come to the house and begged her mother to leave. Every time her mother had said no. Every time her mother had stayed. Every time Jordan knew without a doubt that her mother would die; never having lived . . . yet she could not stop the usual thoughts that infected every part of her consciousness . . . Why would anyone have a religion that instructed them to remain loyal to a tyrant as terrible as her father? How long would her mother put up with the degrading way her father treated her? And she couldn't wait to never have to return to that horrible house again.

Long after her father stopped beating her mother, the lasting effects that burned in her heart were still visible; still registering on her mother's face. Jordan could not stand to be around that fear, it changed her. It made her question her ability to stand on her own two feet. How could she feel anything but lost if her own mother the very portal of her existence was so weak?

The things that Jordan experienced in that old house had left a nasty gaping scar in her heart and mind. The innate fear that her mother would not know peace until she was dead was always just beneath the surface; like an old enemy waiting to rear its head and claim all of Jordan's happiness . . . it was never very far away. Would her mother ever know peace? Was there a magical place with streets of gold, where some all knowing supreme being would wipe away her mother's tears? Jordan hoped with all of her being that it could be true; that it was not just some fairy-tale that people held tightly to in order to make it through one horrible day at a time.

* * *

Jordan walked around the house pretending to be treading on the same egg shells as her niece and sister-in-law. Keeping the evil that plagued her heart from being evident on her face was her biggest challenge.

The phone call to Jr. had been the hardest one she had ever had to make. The moment that he picked up the phone she could hear the laughter in his voice. The evil that stormed his soul chortling at the failure that her life had become . . . . Jordan could hear her brother's thoughts as if he were speaking them aloud . . . So you had to come home, huh? You couldn't make it out in the great big cruel world on your own. No doubt you're just a woman. Women are not capable of doing the same things that men are. You need a man to take care of you. . . .

The thought sickened Jordan. The idea that she would lower herself . . . she would never need any man. Oh, no! The day that she ever needed a man she would lie down and die.

Jordan allowed her brother to berate her about the inconvenience of having to pick her up. She just sat and took it all in . . . locking every syllable up, running it concurrent, with all of the other atrocities that he and their father had managed to encroach upon every female that had the misfortune of crossing their worthless paths.

In the end Jr. had done the predictable thing; she knew he would do all along . . . he picked her up. Jordan never doubted it. Of course he would come and pick her up. He would never miss the opportunity to make any female feel less than . . . inferior . . . it was what he lived and breathed for.

Jordan wanted so badly to taste the sweet nectar of revenge, and to feel her mother's spirit cry out from beyond the grave in retribution. The record had to be set straight, and it would be in time. She would make good on her promise. She would see his eyes become still with death. She would finally send the spirit that possessed her brother and father back to whatever hell or abyss it had come from.

CHAPTER 5

Jordan woke up early the next morning. She could smell it in the air, and she knew the time had come for her revenge. She could feel Jr.'s anger building, having not been sated in a week; time was definitely not on her side. His anger was taking on a life of its own refusing to be denied.... Time was growing short and she had to make her move. She knew the cycle. They could only go so long without abusing their victim. This fact had been pounded into her while in training. Just wait; your chance will always come. Don't get sloppy; pick the wrong time and you will be caught . . . it has to be perfect. Play the part of your character well. If you are believable they will let their guard down and become easy prey. Jordan felt the stealthy cat inside of her licking its proverbial claws, as it sat poised on its haunches waiting for the right opportunity.

"Aunt Jordan?" Penny's timid voice broke through the barricade of thoughts. "You are going to do something aren't you?" Jordan turned to Penny and looked at her as if she had been caught.

"What . . . what do you mean; I'm . . . going to do something . . . Penny?" The feigned innocence in her voice was so believable that Jordan patted herself on the back.

"I mean you came to help us. I can see it in your face. I can feel mama's fear. I can feel . . . my fear." Penny said as she smiled weakly, and then pointed a shaky hand in Jordan's direction. "I don't feel fear coming from you, Aunt Jordan." Penny shifted her weight as her eyes darted around the room on the look out for her father. Jordan's mouth fell open as the realization came. There it was; the first rule that you learn in combat. Beware; it takes one to know one. There will always be one person on the battle field that may surprise you; their loyalty not where you think it should normally be. Just as Jordan had been, as a small child, so was Penny . . . desperate for a way out, hungry for help from anywhere that it may come. Jordan had always been ready and willing to leave the bad canvass that was her life, which her father and brother had so easily painted.

Penny hated him; just as Jordan had hated her brother and father . . . so had her niece hated her father. Would she get in the way though? Would she become an obstacle at that crucial moment, or would she prove to be a useful ally? The scene that would ensue after Jordan staged the attack could go either way; the fear that permeated the air around her had a way of turning to hate sometimes. Oh, they were still afraid make no mistake about it, but sometimes there was those that became the beaten animal looking for the chance to lash out. And here she was. Standing in front of Jordan, Penny was a picture of the past. She could see the fears and hopes of the little girl she had once been so long ago standing before her alive in her niece. Or was that a foolish wish, budding inside her, in the face of adversity; laughing at her . . . mocking the dream that always took center stage in her mind, to end generations of suffering. Stopping the pestilence in its track . . . eradicating the awful, fear inducing name. Could she allow her mind the errant hope that her niece, all that remained of her family, its only lingering chance at redemption, could be ready to embrace the future; a future that Jordan had already mapped out for the two of them?

"You stay out of the way and keep your nose clean. You read me? You do as you are told and let me handle what I came here to do." Jordan said as she patted Penny on the shoulder. Then she pulled Penny's chin up so that she was facing her and there would be no doubt that she had penny's full attention. "Are you listening to me?" Jordan searched Penny's eyes for any clue that her niece understood completely that she should remain a safe distance from the battlefield.

"I have no intention of interfering unless I can help." Penny finally admitted, and then turned to walk away. She dropped her gaze to the floor . . . the defiant twelve year old gone, as now standing in her place was the usual vision of uncertainty.

"What are you two wind bags hissing about?" Jr. growled as his hand shot out seeking to connect with Penny's face. Jordan thrust her hand forward warding off the attack then side stepped pushing Penny out of the line of fire tucking the child safely behind her in one fluid motion.

"Go to your room, and lock the door!" Jordan commanded then afforded herself one backward glance at Erica. "This is between me and my brother, stay out of it Erica. Don't make me hurt you. Go to your room and lock the door!" Jordan said as she gave Erica a pointed look that she hoped would instill just enough fear in her sister-in-law to ensure she keep her distance. Erica dropped her eyes to the floor, and slouched forward as she obeyed mindlessly moving in the direction of her room.

"Whoa here! Just who the hell do you think you are coming in here giving my family orders?" Jr.'s voice was full of fire and ice as he looked from his timid wife to his sister and then continued. "I order them about . . . not you or anyone else. It's time you learned a lesson huh?" As the last words left his beer soaked lips Jr. staggered in Jordan's direction.

Jordan side stepped again, clearly playing with her attacker. Her eyes were heated daggers of hate shot from them, as she melted him with an icy glare.

"Maybe you are right Jr., why don't you just come on and teach it to me?" Jordan said as she glanced down the hall and saw the bedroom door close behind Erica.

"What you looking at sis? They ain't gonna help you. They know better than to mess with old Papa Bear. It's time you learned that as well." Jr. looked like a lion that was ready to pounce as the words spilled from his lips. His eyes were dancing with the anticipation of the hunt.

Jordan grinned inwardly as she sensed Jr. stepping willingly into the trap that she had set for him. All that was left was to seal his fate. Jordan feigned fear. Turning for the hall she allowed a fake squeal and then ran to her bedroom and pushed the door behind her. She knew that her brother was on her heels. It was a matter of seconds before he would burst into the room threatening bodily harm and hissing out profanities like the stagnate airbag he had always been.

Jordan closed her eyes and stood facing the window; she forced all the sounds and smells of the house to fade away and focused on only her brother and the sounds of his footfalls. As sure as she was that he was a big yellow coward so was she absolutely certain that he would only go after what he perceived to be a helpless woman. Jordan had to look as vulnerable as she could, otherwise Jr. would not attack. He preyed on the fear of his victims. It's what pushed him, drove him . . . it was the fear that permeated from his victims that fed the beast. In the end she would have to make the scene look as though he had been killed in self defense. After he was dead; she planned to talk to her sister-in-law, to convince her to take the fall. To explain . . . that Garret Jr. had come after her in a drunken rage and had all but killed her . . . she had been left with no choice . . . she had to defend her own life as well as the life of her daughter. And based on the conversation Jordan had had with penny earlier she could not imagine it would be hard to convince her niece to validate her mother's story. That combined with the numerous medical records that Jordan had been privy to through her government clearance, not to mention all the bruises in different stages of healing on Penny and Erica gave further evidence to the story.

Jordan was so absolutely certain that he would come into the room behind her that she stood at the window of her old room smiling inwardly. One by one the sounds of the house, faded away and his steps became synchronized with her very heartbeat . . . . But it was as the sounds faded into nothingness, though he was seconds away that Jordan realized to her horror . . . It was not her room that he was entering but his own . . . Erica! The thought was a soundless whisper that reverberated against the walls of Jordan's anguished mind.

CHAPTER 6

Jordan checked to make sure her knife was loose in the sheath on her leg. She quickly stripped away the bulky clothing that had made up her disguise revealing the sleek-leather of her Black Heart uniform. She had donned the suit that morning. She could feel the change in the atmosphere and new that the time was fast approaching that she would be facing her brother. She had believed that today would be the day, but could not be certain. It was not until her brother had disappeared into his own room that she truly realized the need to be in her own element. Going into the room with her brother she could not be certain if she would be facing one or two adversaries. She thrust the nun chucks into the back of her leather pants, where they was held snug by her belt, and then slowly like the predator she had become started out the door. With her heightened senses she listened for the enemy. With every step she took through the old house, she fought back its vile memories.

Remaining focused on the task at hand even with years of training would not be easy. One excruciating step after the next the memories rained down threatening to take Jordan to her knees. Jordan was four years old again walking through the hall of her childhood home. Head down as usual, hoping to remain unnoticed, not only by her drunken abusive father but also the depraved mind of a brother that was fast becoming his father's exact replica.

Jordan's dad believed that a man's home was quite literally his castle, and in it he would act as he pleased while the women in his home obeyed his every command. He treated her mother as if she lived in a harem . . . as he paraded one woman from the local beer joint after the other through their family home. Her father would join her brother in depraved sexual games with one of Jr.'s girlfriends, while forcing Jordan to stay outside until they had finished. That combined with his collection of nude magazines, depicting women in compromising positions degrading all womankind, kept all over the house, had come together to successfully dement her brother's perspective.

Just as their father would not hide his lust for the opposite sex, Jordan's brother soon learned from that example. "One woman could never truly satisfy the desires that a man possessed". Jordan could not stand the words of her father. Because in her mind she knew it was that dark logic that caused the worst of her pain as a child; having to keep the depraved acts that went on in the old house from her mother, her only friend, was a torture all its on.

Jordan loved her mother with a fervor that was unmatched. She would do anything for her. Jordan knew that her mother could only take so much; the depraved acts of her sibling and father would cost her mother too much anguish. Her mother would be forced to react to the news and in the end Jordan knew that she would loose, because not only was she living in a home with a tyrant that did not care about her feelings . . . but she was living in a world that had quite frankly thrown women away. In the end her mother would not win she would fall prey to the worst beating Jordan's father had ever administered, and that could not happen.

The pictures that flashed through her mind almost brought Jordan to her knees. Once she had told one of her neighborhood friends . . . the girl had lived in a more normal environment and had done what she had thought best . . . she confided in her mother . . . armed with the information the woman approached Jordan's parents. Jordan's father had immediately thrown the woman out of his house, and then slapped Jordan. The beating that came after that taught Jordan a very hard lesson. She had no one. She had only to rely on herself. And again she was visited with the always lingering question that begged for an answer especially in times like these . . . if there was a God . . . as her mother and the people at the church believed . . . then why was he allowing a little girl to be torn apart? Why would cruel people like her father and brother be allowed to govern over Jordan and her mother? The questions kept coming, and more of them mounted everyday. Without the benefit of satisfactory answers for each of the questions, Jordan had but to rely on her own imagination and opinions of the subject. There quite simply was no God and if there were . . . he had better things to do.

Jordan shook her head, as she inwardly chided herself for falling victim to the memories. There was no time for this sort of revere. Had her training not taught her anything? No there were bigger things going on here than the pain that her past caused. She would complete her mission. She would have her revenge in the form of her brother's blood as it left his body and his evil eyes closed in death once and for all, but for now she had to focus, Penny and Erica needed her. Their very lives may depend on her ability to concentrate . . . to stay in the moment.

Unhurriedly she walked into her parents old bedroom that her brother now occupied and standing in front of her was Jr. holding Erica with a knife to her throat.

"What, you think I can't see it all over you sis?" Jr. stammered the words out as his hand shook and sweat dripped from his eyes. "You aren't afraid of me. There is something different about you, a confidence. Sure you walk around here like my wife and daughter pretending you're afraid . . ." Jr. said the words while waving the knife around the room as if he were pointing out the obvious in the air around him. Then he continued. ". . . But it's just an act, ain't it? Where have you been all this time? Why is it so important for you to visit now? You are different. You aren't the same girl that I knew. Something is wrong with you." As Jr. said the last words he regained control of his flailing wife. Erica gasped her disapproval as her eyes went wide with fear. A trickle of blood made a lazy line to her blouse. Jordan imagined with inner delight that it was his.

Jordan could feel her brother's fear, it was palpable and it was hard not to be intoxicated by it. She wanted to bathe in it, to relish it; the knowledge of it poured its sweet nectar through her senses as she stood in the doorway poised for the right moment to strike.

"What's wrong Jr.? It's just me. You beat on your wife and daughter like daddy did us all the time." Jordan crooned as she allowed a simple shrug of her shoulders. "I'm no different than them, a scared little woman for you to beat on." Jordan moved stealthily from one foot to the other in an effort to taunt her brother. "Think about it Jr.

don't you want some competition, someone that you have to work to whip? Look at Erica; I wouldn't waste my time on a beat down shell of a person like that. There is no fight left in her." Jordan said as she pointed her hand palm up at her sister-in-law. "You have beaten it all out of her. Now I'm sure in the beginning she fought back, but now . . . she just walks around here like mama did." Jordan tossed a disgusted look in Erica's direction, trying to appeal to her brother's competitive side. She raised her shoulders and then let them fall in a defeated manner. "No, you need a challenge someone that can give you a run for your money." Jordan pointed her hand at her chest and then let it fall to her side as she began again. "So bro' what do you say? Or are you a chicken? What's it gonna be? Are you going to stand there and let your wife see you for the coward that you are? Or are you going to come after a real woman?"

As the last word left Jordan's lips, Jr. threw Erica on to the bed then thundered toward Jordan. This time Jordan did not run. Sometimes you have no choice but to bring the fight to the enemy. Jordan grabbed Jr.'s arm using the force of his own weight in full throttle to lunge him forward. In moments he was through the door and into her bedroom where she pounced on him like a cat playing with its prey. Jr. turned around just in time to catch Jordan in mid air, but the women he was used to beating on was not the woman that Jordan had become . . . With a blood thirsty scream she grinned as her blade sliced at his face. Jordan pushed her weight off of her brother and with a slight thud almost undetectable to the human ear she landed on the floor just in front of him and then she tossed the knife into the air and whirled around. Pulling her fist to the sides of her body, she curled her right leg up so that her knee was almost touching her abdomen and then with all her might forced her foot out sending Jr. into the nearest wall just as the blade landed pointedly in the hand behind her. A whoosh sound escaped Junior's lips as his back thrust with ample force into the wall behind him. His arms and hands floated upward in an off balance manner that made him look like a person trying to adjust their stance on a tightrope. Closing the distance she sank the cold steel into his chest. As it hit its mark Jr. coughed once and blood exploded from his mouth. His right hand clutched at the huge knife protruding from his chest with a weakened clumsiness, and then he crumbled to the floor in a lifeless heap.

Jordan could feel the beast within her becoming harder and harder to control. Her eyes flashed as she stared down at Junior's lifeless form. She had been so sure this would calm the beast inside of her once and for all. Instead the opposite had been true. The more bloodshed the stronger the urge for the shed of more became.

"Aunt Jordan?" Penny peered around her aunt to her father, and gasped with fear.

Jordan turned to Penny, and thrust the knife against her throat as a single trickle of blood glided to her collar and soaked into the fabric of her pink sweatshirt.

"No!" Erica screamed as she lunged forward. Jordan shoved Penny to the side, and thrusting her nun chucks into the window with lightening speed, jumped through the window; glass shattered to the ground as her feet met with earth. The light of the moon glittered off of what seemed to be a thousand shards of glass; each one testifying to the atrocity that she had almost committed. That she knew with certainty she would have committed if not for Erica's desperate protest.

Jordan's thoughts came in matted heaps. She could not focus on one for another berating her. What had happened? Was she going to hurt Penny? She loved her niece, she had come here to help, but wasn't it she that had shoved the cold steel of the knife's blade against Penny's throat. What was she becoming? Desperation mounted within her as Jordan raced away from the house. She had to put distance between her and the people that she loved, because one thing was absolutely certain . . . Jordan could not be trusted. Not around anyone . . . not even those that she held dear. Not around her sister-in-law and most certainly not around her precious niece.

CHAPTER 7

Jordan screamed out into the night sky as she hit her knees tears fell like drops of rain down her cheeks.

'There is a time and place for everything. Exodus 3:3'. She heard the words breathe across her soul. Jordan could almost hear them as though someone was standing right there in front of her whispering them to her. She jumped to her feet and held the blade up, poised with her feet square up under her ready to do battle.

"Who is there?" She screamed into the surrounding darkness as the tears came harder causing her body to convulse, she fell to her knees again and began vomiting uncontrollably.

"God help me!" She said in strangled gulps between heaves. "What am I becoming? Please help me." She cried as another sequence of cough, heave, and vomit tore through her. Finally, when she had nothing else to give, Jordan collapsed to the ground. Gradually, she could feel her mind slipping into an unconscious state as she surrendered to the darkness.

Jordan's eyes fluttered open. She tried desperately to take in her surroundings. The walls were simple oak wood. Knots littered the length of each wall. She seemed to be in an old cottage or cabin of some kind. The seems where each wooden plank joined were filled with a viscous substance. Jordan could only imagine it to be sap; probably from the tree that had been cut down in order to produce the small shack. A window was cut into adjacent sides of the small home both were shielded with a thick leathery hide covered in a light-golden-brown fur. The wind that howled just beyond the fabric pushed at its leathery hide bulging its protest causing the hide to take on a rounded arch.

Jordan could only put errant pieces of the puzzle together. Focusing her eyes on her surroundings was almost impossible with the piercing ache that was ripping through her skull. Finally, with some effort she lifted herself to a seated position, and then pushed her waste length dark auburn hair out of her face. Her mouth tasted like stale cotton and blood. Her hands on either side of her, she pushed herself forward only to collapse back on the make-shift-bed she was lying on. Upon further inspection she was able to conclude that she had been placed on a shelf that protruded from the wall a few feet, and was only a few feet off the floor. More of the same leathery garment was matted beneath her and made for a warm and surprisingly cozy bed. Realizing that she would not be able to move from the spot, she continued her scrutiny of the tiny room. A door was no more that ten or twelve feet across the room just on the other side of a small two-chair table; forged out of the same oak wood that had been used to construct the small cabin. An X made of two wooden planks that were nailed to several oak-boards nestled between two larger boards at the top and bottom of the bulky structure gave the small cabin its sturdy and ominous security.

Jordan had always been very tall in stature, with a curvy body, one hundred thirty five pounds, dark Auburn hair that seemed to take on a life of its own cascaded down her back in wavy curls that was usually tucked into a neat bun at the nape of her neck.

Jordan was about five foot ten inches tall, and with the muscular bulk she had gained in training she was absolutely stunning. Her eyes were a smoldering shade of green, but most of the time changed with her moods . . . which had seemed to be a constant process lately. The false sense of security and control she gained from killing what she believed to be deserving victims had allowed her to hold her head high. The new found confidence was probably why she wore her hair down these days. She wore a government issued disguise that moved with her body, and had no loose fabric to be snagged on fences or whatever object that she would come in contact with while scaling structures such as tall buildings. Though there was no flesh visual to the human eye, the outfit left absolutely nothing to the imagination. Every curve of her body was made obvious under the tight fitting fabric. Her job was athletically demanding, which only lent to the superb angles of her body . . . her cat-like agility and reflexes allowed her to encounter the most inopportune circumstances with ease. Some things she had learned could be controlled through foresight and preparation.

The confidence that her job afforded had always been intoxicating. In the beginning she had tried desperately to stay focused; to always be mindful that control was an arrogant illusion that she could not afford to embrace . . . but time had claimed her ability to not be seduced by its allure. She for so long, had walked through life like a shadow on the very thread of her own existence . . . so when she had learned all of the things that allowed her to take the upper-hand in most situations, she had embraced the invigorating allure of control. Basking in all of its lies, she was now becoming a victim caught in its trap.

Jordan hadn't felt fears icy talons around her throat for as long as she could remember, that is until she stood ready to kill the one person that meant the most to her, Penny. The realization of what she could have done to Penny was confusing. Why would Jordan have reacted that way? She harbored no aggression toward her niece. She loved her niece. So why had her impulse been to attack? Part of her was boggled down in the guilt of the moment . . . while still another deeper, darker part craved the threat of the unknown. Uncertainty had a way of lighting fires in Jordan . . . it was the moments of ad living taking one moment at a time, making it up as she went, that seemed to push her abilities to the limit . . . It was those times that she could sense the demon inside of her licking its proverbial paws. The demon crouched in the middle of her soul like a rotting toad smiling its approval, waiting and hoping that she would allow it to have control just once more. It was that very feeling that was threatening to take over while she was standing in her old bedroom with the blade shoved close to her niece's throat.

It was the fear of how that moment had made her feel, that was choking off Jordan's air supply. Why had she turned on Penny? Was it because she had approached in the heat of battle? Or was it just who Jordan was? Down deep was Jordan just a cold heartless killer just penning all of her unseemly desires on the "demon" . . . it was times like this that made Jordan wonder was there a demon at all? Or was she the demon? Was Jordan so out of control . . . had she become like the people that she was killing?

Jordan caressed her temples then looked up again as a sharp pain tore through her head. She blew out a jagged breath then decided she had better try to get up again.

"You may as well sit there. You are safe child." A soothing voice came from a dark corner of the room.

"Who's there?" Jordan demanded as she instinctively made a blind sweep for a weapon.

"No need. I removed your weapons. You would not be able to rest with their bulk pressing against your side. Now lie still child, and rest. I am preparing a meal to help you regain your strength." Again the subtle and soothing nature of the voice came in calm assurance.

Shadows lent their cloak of security, making it impossible for Jordan to see the face behind the voice. She strained against the darkness to try and see, but the pain in her temples only doubled. She winced against the pain and then decided to issue a threat instead.

"I don't need weapons to do away with anyone that tries to hurt me. I can kill a man with my bear hands. I will take great pleasure in illustrating for you." Jordan threw the empty threat at her opponent hoping that the searing tone that it had been bathed in would be enough to gain her some respect from the stranger; then she continued. "I don't have a guinea pig so you will have to serve as both audience and example. Will that be a problem for you?" Jordan's eyes flashed into the darkness as she began preparing her senses to be at a heightened awareness.

"There will be no need for examples. For I am well aware of what you are capable of Jordan, now you must rest child. I say to you I am preparing nourishment. You are very weak." The voice was so calming, so soothing that Jordan could imagine how easy it would be to fall asleep while listening to every syllable. It had been like the times as a child when her father and brother had gone on fishing trips, leaving Jordan and her mother alone in the house . . . the days that followed their absence were so calm. Jordan's mother would make the best of each day. She would lay in the bed with Jordan and caress her hair and tell her stories of heaven and God. Jordan had wanted to believe the stories but in the end there had been too much evil in her life. How could any all knowing God, allow all of the things that happened to Jordan and her mother just happen, and then claim to love them? It was those moments that the voice reminded her of now. The safe feeling that it seemed to inspire . . . It was all a vicious lie though . . . and Jordan knew it. There was no all knowing God that loved her or anyone else for that matter. How could there be? All of the doubts and the unwanted trips down memory lane had taken a backseat as something became apparent to her, which she had not considered before . . .

"How do you know my name?" Jordan asked as she tried without success to come to her feet. "I have to get my weapons." Jordan informed the stranger with the annoyingly calm voice. How could the man be so calm. Her nerves for the first time in years were splintering into heaps along with the unanswered questions. "How have I harmed you? Why have you brought me here? Where am I? Who are you?" Jordan grimaced as she acknowledged how foreign her own voice sounded. Each word seemed more and more distant. As if she were falling further into a canyon and her words were scaling the distance while leaving her to the mercies that lie beneath. As the last word left her lips, Jordan fell back on her make-shift-bed and her eyes fluttered closed.

"In time child you will have all these answers and more. For now sleep." The man said as he crossed the room and pulled the covers up on Jordan's sleeping form.

"Father, give me the strength to do what you ask. Never have I seen so much beauty and danger in the same host." As he spoke, Lane looked down into Jordan's face. Slowly, he pulled himself away from her sleeping form amazed at the effort it took. This may be the hardest thing you have ever asked me to do . . . Lane thought as he turned and blew out the candle next to Jordan's bed.

CHAPTER 8

Only a few hours had passed between the last time Jordan was conscious and this, but it seemed to have been a lifetime. This time she came to a seated position with little effort, but getting to her feet was more of a challenge, with a still somewhat spinning head, and jelly for legs.

"Okay, tell me where you have put my weapons and I will be on my way." Jordan announced to the dark corner. She was feeling a little more like herself now so her senses were intact.

"I will." The voice came from the shadows again. "First you must eat. Please sit at the table, and let me serve you." The man encouraged as he emerged from the shadows.

At first Jordan was taken back by his appearance. He wasn't at all what she would have thought. He had golden blonde hair that fell just below his shoulders; the front of his hair and the back were exactly the same length . . . yet it did nothing to take away from its flowing texture. Jordan allowed an appreciative look for that fact, as she thought of some of the more unkempt hairdos that crossed the threshold of some of the beer joints, in which she normally picked her prey.

He stood a majestic six foot five inches tall, and had hazy sky blue eyes. His body was ripped with muscles; that stood out even through the bulky layers of clothing he wore. She could not imagine there was an ounce of fat on his body anywhere. Listening to his voice she would have thought him older. Yet the man that stood before her now couldn't have been more than thirty. His face looked as though it had been chiseled from stone. Not a blemish on it. All was as it should be; like a marble god, his beauty sent chills skittering up her spine.

Jordan tried desperately to collect herself. She cleared her throat, and wanted immensely to break eye contact, but she didn't dare. It was there that your opponent's thoughts, his agenda, and his very soul could be determined. Yet if the eyes were where the soul was exhibited, his were not as clear as his soul was pure. The smoldering blue seemed to sear straight through Jordan. It was all she could do not to tear her eyes away. The years of training screamed out to never break eye contact with her opponent and yet there was a place within her that testified there was no need to keep her guard up with this man. He could be trusted. There was just no room inside her heart for trust, with all the hate that resided there.

"As much as having a man be at my beckon call appeals to my sense of hatred for your gender . . ." Jordan hissed as she pulled herself up from the makeshift bed she had been laying and then continued. "I'm afraid my sense of distrust for your kind is much more defined. So that being said I will have to pass . . . my weapons please!" Jordan said with one hand extended out in front of her. "Please." She added with a sarcastic smile.

"I am not holding you prisoner. You may leave at your leisure. However, unless you are willing to take the blessing that I want to bestow upon you in the form of nourishment, I am afraid I will not be able to allow you to take the weapons for your own protection." As the man said the words, in them Jordan could sense no guile . . . there was none of the usual defiance that she normally witnessed when a male asserted his authority over a female. To the contrary, he if anything seemed . . . humble. The thought nearly crumbled walls that it took years to set in place. Jordan shook her head as if the very act could hold the foolish thought at bay.

"Have you lost your mind? Let me get this straight . . . . You intend to take my weapons if I refuse the meal because you feel it is for my own protection . . . Is that just about the long and the short of it?" Jordan spat the words out with as much hostility as her aching body would allow. She had no intention of mincing words with any man . . . not even one that exuded all the syrupy sweetness that she could stand. It did not matter . . . she would not trust him. He had to be up to something. All men had an agenda and this one, no matter the persona he was trying to put off would be no different.

"Yes, very good you are listening. That is correct. I am unable to allow you to wear weapons that you will not be strong enough to use. You see . . ." The last of Lane's words fell short as Jordan let out a blood thirsty war cry and kicked the chair in front of her causing the back to splinter, and the pieces of wood to fall to the ground. In an instant Jordan was kicking one piece of falling lumber into the air like a volley ball. She spun around and caught it midair then in the blink of an eye was standing with the point to Lane's throat.

"I don't need them!" She growled in a low intimidating tone, and then dropped the wooden stake to the floor and started for the door. Lane never took his eyes off of Jordan, and never flinched during the whole episode.

"Impressive . . . you have all that combat training . . . and not a lick of discipline." Lane said as he turned his back on Jordan and started toward the table.

"I do not take orders from men. I am not your submissive little woman that will do as she is told. You can shove the weapons I will get more." She hissed as her hand touched then shoved at the door of the cabin.

"Please, don't go." Lane allowed a sigh. "Your weapons are in the cabinet. I will get them for you. They are yours." He walked over to the corner cabinet and pulled the wooden door open . . . allowing some of the items to be seen. Jordan's weapons sat on the top shelf, but just below them on the second shelf . . . was something that held her attention. She quickly turned her gaze back toward her weapons. She had no time to get caught up in some sort of soul-saving-revival where she would be the main focus. On the second shelf was a mountain of bibles and tracks, the kind of tracks that she saw the religious people passing out at malls and grocery stores, the kind of people that she avoided like the plague and yet somehow she had ended up in one of their cabins. And why not she figured this is just what they lived in . . . she was surprised he was not chanting and walking around in robes . . . commanding a whole harem of women to do his bidding. By now she half expected to have been passed a hardy cup of death, a nice cup of juice with a pinch of rat poison should do the trick. She peeled her eyes away from the cabinet. She could not help but be confused. Who was this guy? He clearly lived like a mountain man. Yet he spoke with such poetic dignity. He seemed wise beyond his years. His handsome features painted a picture of youth; while his eyes testified of untold knowledge.

"You are right to want them; they are not mine to keep from you. Please forgive me for using them as leverage. It was wrong. I simply wanted you to eat. You may eat or not whatever you wish." He handed the weapons to her and then sat at the table. His countenance betrayed an obvious feeling of defeat . . . nothing was going the way that it was suppose to Jordan assumed.

"I will bother you no more. If I may be of service to you please allow it to be so by only asking. My home is certainly not much but it is yours." He was speaking again and Jordan was trying desperately to hold on to his words as she neglected the subject of the bibles. She took her weapons and returning her gaze to his beautiful eyes where she witnessed the mountain of frustration welling; she moved closer to the table.

It was an odd thing to see . . . Jordan thought to herself. This man of a stature such she had never seen before could probably out power her. He just sat in front of her in his home allowing her to be the aggressor. Sure Jordan was a force to be reckoned with, there was none that she feared, and her combat training was unmatched. She had graduated at the top of her class, and had been the only one in the academy that did not have to have plastic surgery in the first few years out in the field. However, Jordan was not ignorant she had gotten where she was because she had been wise, She was always cunning and never underestimated her opponent especially not one of this man's obvious valor. Here though in this moment . . . he seemed less than . . . but somehow more than at the same time . . . she was at a loss to decide what she felt about him. He was not like the others that seemed obvious . . . but he was not himself either. It was like he had some sort of mission that pushed him and in this moment that mission had fallen completely apart.

Could he really believe all that he was saying? That the Master had sent him? Wasn't it ludicrous to think that some Supreme Being had sent him to help her . . . and for what? Why would she even matter to some Supreme Being? Why now? Her life was certainly not a testimony of someone caring about her.

Jordan had so many questions where he was concerned. Where did he come from? How did he get here? The questions started racing through her mind again. Questions that had nothing to do with her niece. Nothing to do with killing her brother. But everything to do with the oldest and most eluding enigma of her very existence . . . was there a Supreme all knowing Being that stood in the gateway deciding everyone's fate? And if so then where had He been all of her life? Why had He made her mother feel that she was obligated to stay with a horrible man like her father, and why did He feel the need to show up now; after all the years of being unaccounted for? It was then that she cautiously took her weapons and decided knowledge was power. That and she could not remember ever being this hungry.

CHAPTER 9

The meal passed quickly, after a few moments of Jordan circling the room like a lion in a cage. She soon learned that the man's name was Lane. But was still uncertain what his agenda concerning her might be. Sure he had taken care of her, but did that really mean in the grand scheme of things? Her father had put a roof over her head. He had even made sure she had food in her belly, and her clothes were not the worst garments that she had ever seen. But his treatment of her was downright appalling. She knew that based on the simple yet very effective lessons taught to her by her own father during her less than desirable childhood that just because someone provided you with the bear necessities of life did not mean that they would not harm you.

Lane simply eyed her then said thoughtfully. "If I had wanted you dead, I could have killed you while you slept. Jordan how is it you think you came to be here? I am not your enemy." Lane asked as he again pointed toward the chair that had survived her earlier assault. He pulled a stool over from the fireplace and sat waiting for Jordan to take his invitation.

"Who are you? Where did you come from?" Every time Jordan addressed him the questions seemed to pour fluidly from her lips unbidden. Jordan stood straighter as she adjusted a rogue curl back in place over her shoulder.

"My name is Lane. As I told you earlier. I am here to help you. That will have to be enough for now. I do not mean to seem so secretive but the one that sent me says that there is much to learn before you will receive what I must tell you. You are free to leave at any time. You have free will. That has not changed. I will not try to stop you." Each word Lane spoke was carefully chosen. Jordan could tell that he had given it great thought, and there was more. He seemed to be from another place as though he were someone learning English for the first time and trying to choose each word properly. Stranger still was the lack of accent that usually accompanied the careful word selection. As she sat she felt a part of her molding to his words. They seemed to breathe comfort and peace across her soul . . . the soothing cadence and careful selection of each word magically meshed together to sooth any concern that she had for her safety where he was concerned.

"I will not stay. I have to go. My niece and sister-in-law . . . ." Jordan started as she nervously shifted her weight in the hardwood chair. She could not help but note its uncomfortable surface. The mat made of animal pelts had afforded her comfort that she could not allow herself to get used to.

"Are fine. Please eat." Lane finished as he gestured toward the table. "He says to tell you that he is truly sorry for all of the pain that you have experienced." The way that Lane insisted on addressing someone that was not in the room set Jordan's nerves on edge. She could feel a calming serenity that oozed from Lane like alcohol oozed from her brother and father's pores, but she did not sense another presence in the room. So how was it, that Lane could have knowledge of someone else's thoughts on not only the conversation that they were presently involved, but also of the deepest parts of her past. The parts that no one with exception to those that were present, her friend, and her friend's mother knew about. There could be only one explanation. This had to be some sort of test orchestrated by the organization to prove her loyalty or lack there of. He had to be wired or something. He obviously had a microphone in his ear. He was probably listening to his commander right now as he barked off orders on how to disarm her, but what about the past stuff. No one knew that stuff, not even Garrison her partner had privy to that information. Some things would forever stay locked away in the deepest chambers of her heart where no one would see. No one would know the ugly that was her childhood. So how did Lane know anything?

"Who says? What does he know of my pain?" Jordan knit her eyebrows and then grabbed for her weapons and started for the door again.

"I apologize, my words have confused you. That was not my intention. I was trying so desperately to choose them wisely. The one that sent me would not have confusion. He is not the author of confusion. I think it is best if I stick to what you know. I have been sent to help you accept the one that sent me, so that you may know the peace that you have sought and have not been able to find. You have done many horrible things in the name of anger, Jordan. I am here to introduce you to the one that will wipe away all of your tears and take away your anger." Lane confided as his eyes two translucent balls of blue seemed to cloud over with concern.

"What are you talking about? Look guy, I have no time to be brain washed. I've been through enough, and now I am the one that is the inflictor. I am the revenge of the black heart. I stand for the under dog. I will help those that can not help themselves. No more will I stand around with my eyes cast down waiting to be clubbed over the head and drug into an alley way. I am the one that does the clubbing and dragging now, this is a dog eat, dog world mister. The sooner you learn that the better off you will be." Jordan spat out the last word then grabbed her weapons and darted from the cabin before another word could be uttered.

"I'm trying." Lane said as he looked up. "She is stronger willed than I had first thought. I had no idea what I would be facing, Father. Please give me your wisdom. I can't do this without you." Lane's words were full of sincerity as he watched the cabin door at last shut. Time did not seem to be on his side. Jordan was a formidable adversary for any enemy, but Lane was here to help and convincing her that he was not the enemy would not be easy. He would have to keep his eyes and ears open at all times; at any moment if he said or did anything that she perceived to be wrong then it could very well end in bloodshed. He did not want that.

Jordan moved through the woods like a stealthy cat, never making a sound. She had to admit she was thankful for the food, but what was that Lane guy's deal? She had moved in closer, and there was no obvious signs of wires. He was clearly not talking to some commanding officer. Was he some kind of religious nut? She had no time for all of that. She had to check on Erica and Penny. There was no time for small talk with religious nuts in cabins, even if he was the most interesting looking nut she had ever seen.

It was time to focus her energy on the task at hand, find Penny and Erica and explain that she had not been herself. She would never hurt either of them. No, never. It's just Penny had grabbed her at a bad time. After all it was she that had protected them, right? They would accept her apology and take her back into the fold with no problem at all. Then they could become a family. Sure it would take some time after all they had all been through, a lot but Jordan could find them a new home and work hard to protect them both. She would train them. Yes they would learn all her ways. They could start a new world order. She would train her family and after she had taught all of the tricks of the trade to them; they would surely be willing to help in the training of other women. It could become a chain soon there would be no women afraid, once they experienced the way knowledge and power gave them control they would not be able to resist the new way that she offered. Who needed a man, a ruler over them that wanted to beat and take from others? It was time for something different. She had to show women that there was another way.

The thoughts came so quickly and soon without warning Jordan was on the ground sobbing, Jordan could feel her body being lifted into the air. Though she could not stop sobbing to protest she knew with what was left of her frayed senses that it was Lane. She could smell his sweet innocence, and feel the tenderness in his touch. That spoke of a love for her she could not understand.

"Please." She whimpered in a way that she had not, since she was a child. "I have to find them they need me." Her hands weakly pushed at his chest as tears poured from her eyes blurring her vision.

"I have told you they are well. He looks after them as we speak. He is in all places His love stretches beyond your understanding and mine. I am here to protect you. He sent me to you." Lane spoke the words with calm gentleness. The love that dripped from each syllable would be apparent to any black heart, even Jordan's.

CHAPTER 10

Lane placed Jordan's shivering body on the shelf, where she had been before. She only protested a moment longer then finally gave into the nerves that ravished her body and fell fast asleep. Lane watched her sleeping form for a long time as he sat with his back to the raging fire. He hadn't been sure exactly what the Master's plan was in this situation, but he knew with every rise and fall of her chest it became harder to remain focused.

    He knelt down facing the fire and prayed for the strength to not be like the ones she had dealt with before. He asked God to change his heart. To allow him to see Jordan as God himself actually saw her. Not to see her through lustful eyes. He asked God to make it so that her beauty was not such a shock to him. After the prayer ended Lane could feel a growing peace within his heart as it moved throughout his body . . . he felt the strength that accompanied the peace and soon he was able to move to his feet again. He pulled a chair from the table and sat to the side so that he could keep vigil without interrupting her peaceful slumber. Every time he looked at her a part of him seemed to melt away. It wasn't lust that he felt for her, but pity, admiration, love, but there was something more that she seemed to ignite within him. He could not understand it. Something that made him, feel more than the usual protectiveness that followed the job. He was no stranger to his duties as a guardian. Of course he knew the rules, so what was the feeling that this woman infused his very being with?

The rage that burned within her could only be satisfied with the blood of men and women that had wronged others. How could he feel anything but pity for her? He had to focus ... he had to somehow help her understand; she had to know the Creator, before it was too late. Lane had to show her the Master's love for her; she had to know that she was not an accident. That yes she had been through some horrible things but the One that created her had made no mistake in doing so. That she was right it was a demon that had contributed to her father and brother doing so many atrocious things to her and her mother, but when they were created they were given the same free will that all were. Following after what the demon wanted was a choice. It was a terrible choice that could have been avoided if they had only accepted the love that was offered by the Creator.

Lane prayed constantly for the next few hours. He could feel the hunger and exhaustion gripping his body, but he could not stop. The affect Jordan had on him could not have been in the Master's plan ... Could it? He was in the middle of meditating on getting his focus back and did not hear Jordan stir.

"Father please, allow me to be a holy vessel for you. Please help me keep my focus. Lord I have stayed the path all my days on this earth. I have been weak at times but for the most part I have tried to heed your voice. There is something about her. Lord have you misjudged me in this? I do not mean to let you down Father, but how can I help her? All I see is her beauty? Please allow me to see her as you do."

"You already are." The words breathed across Lane's soul, and filled his senses with peace. "You have seen her beauty. She holds such beauty inside all my children possess that same beauty, but are not aware of it. You must teach her of the beauty that she possesses inside. You must teach her to love. You must show her my way. Take the hate out of her fighting teach her to be just. Teach her to love my children, to only fight when there is no other way. Teach her the way of her earthly father is not the way of her heavenly Father. Make her understand that all will not hurt her. There are those that genuinely love, that genuinely want to be loved." The message came loud and clear in his soul. Lane wiped his eyes and tried to get up. He staggered and almost fell over. Without thinking Jordan grabbed for his arm and helped to steady him. She moved quickly with her usual cat like reflexes as she pulled the chair back under him.

"You have to rest." Her voice was but a whisper as she looked away. She hadn't heard, but one side of the conversation, but she had heard enough to know that what she felt for him was reciprocated. The same attraction that stirred inside of her was obviously an issue for him as well.

"Jordan I was sent to take care of you. I am so sorry . . ." His words died as Jordan leaned instinctively forward and grazed his lips with hers. Lane found himself lost in the warm caress of her lips against his at first. Her soft touch, the warmth of her mouth, it all tantalized his senses. Then he pulled back, pushing her forward.

"No." The word was but a gentle protest. "That is not why I am here. You have seen enough lust. I am here to show you love. You will learn the love of your Father." His eyes were a warm shade of blue as he tried desperately to convey the love in his heart that he spoke of to her. To show her the place it came from had nothing to do with the ugliness that had ripped her apart for years. It had nothing to do with the physical. It came from a well-spring that sprung up from within him. A place that only the Master could live. That was the love he had come to reveal to her. He was sent to erase the pain, to hold her in a Godly way, and let her move forward one unsure step at a time. Yet he was here entering turmoil over the most electrifying feeling he had ever known.

CHAPTER 11

Jordan had spent years avoiding contact with the opposite sex. Had she lost her mind? She was trying to kiss Lane like some school girl. What if he had followed through then where would she be? What would she have done? Would she have thrown all that she had learned, all of her principles, her values, her hopes, her dreams, all of it out the window; just to fall into this stranger's arms?

Jordan could feel an electric current so faint that it enticed her in a way that she had never felt before . . . In the past every time a man tried to have anything to do with her it seemed to burn a hole into her soul, blazing another trail of hate and disgust that only served as kindling for the flame of her anger. There was something very different about Lane's touch. He genuinely seemed to care for her, and she could hear it in his words, sense it in his innocence, and feel it in his touch.

Lane tried desperately to stay the course. To only show Jordan the inner love he was feeling for her, the love that flowed naturally from the Creator, he would have to somehow show her all the things that gave him peace, while keeping his distance . . . Because showing her the hunger that she brought to life inside of him would only push her further into the darkness. In all of his time as a guardian, never had he seen such a woman. Jordan was everything all at once . . . strength, beauty, fierce determination, cunning wit, elegant grace, and lethal intent all of which culminated into Jordan being the most desirable woman he had ever encountered, and yet the most formable enemy. Lane was after all a man. Lane was only human, but he prayed constantly for God's guidance in all of his undertakings. But never had he been faced with a temptation as great as the one that stood before him now. He would trade the long days of hunger while fasting. He would gladly take another spirit walk to clear out the frustrations and temptations that life could impose, all of it . . . the days of heat, the nights of cold, imposing hunger; none of it held a candle to not giving in to the enticing beauty of this one woman.

Jordan walked slowly around the cabin caressing the wood panels as she went. Her heart a tangle of confusion and frustration concerning the man that shared the space inside the cabin walls with her. The academy had taught her to use all of the weapons at her disposal, even psychological ones. How would that help her here? In a cabin in the middle of no where with the first man that had ever not been the predictable body of lust that most men were . . . maybe he was. Maybe she had not been direct enough in her approach. Her initial assumption was that Lane would be the type of man that would want a graceful woman, one that would fall back and allow him to take center stage; after all it was obvious that he had spent countless hours honing his body to perfection. She knew the type. Men that spent that much time in the gym lifting weight, running, and meditating had no intention of putting anyone in the driver's seat. But maybe her approach had been all wrong. Maybe he wasn't the kind of man that would want to be in charge at all. Maybe he wanted to be dominated. She had seen the type, of course they were few and far between, but that did not make them extent did it? She sheepishly looked in his direction. She found herself mesmerized by him. What was he thinking? Was this man in front of her for real? He had to be biding his time. This was all an illusion. He had to be playing some sort of game. It just did not add up. She had never seen anyone that looked like this man, and did not assume command in all of the situations they were involved in. Even she had seen a change in her own actions, the way that she perceived her environment, the way that she addressed people in any situation . . . all of it had changed dramatically the moment that her body and mind had been unified in strength. That type of change did something to people, and she knew that better than anyone. Something was definitely askew. There was no way he could be this humble . . . Time would tell it all.

She could wait as long as it took. After all she had no where to be. She had stalked her victims for long periods of time. The second law was to know your enemy. In order to do that you had to mingle with them, get to know them, and soon with enough rope they would be certain to hang themselves. The problem is figuring out what type of rope to use . . .

Jordan made her way to the fire place where Lane sat. With a slow smile meant to give a false sense of security she sat down, and looked at the fire.

"So, Lane . . . It is Lane right?"

"Yes."

"Good. I thought we could get to know each other." Jordan crooned as she crossed one leg over the other and circled a log that claimed the space between them with a long polished nail. "Who are you? Where did you come from?" Jordan continued as she moved closer still. Closing the distance she placed a hand on Lane's chest and allowed a shy look from under her long lashes. "I find you very intriguing." She purred as she dropped her head back while rubbing her hand down the front of her chest.

"Don't bother, Jordan!" He growled. "I'm not your enemy. I've already told you that. If you want to know . . . yes I find you very beautiful most men do. I will go as far as to say, I find you extremely sexy." Lane spat out angrily as he pushed at Jordan trying to put distance between the two of them.

"Mmm . . ." Jordan purred as she repositioned herself closer for the kill.

"Yes but . . . That is not what I was sent for. That is an unfortunate job hazard. I will make it past the stumbling block that it presents. Now would you like some breakfast?" He asked as he pushed himself up from the floor of the cabin.

"What's your hurry?" Jordan asked as she feigned innocence. "Sit down, we won't starve. We will be here for a while let's get to know each other." Jordan caressed her hair as she twirled it around her index finger and tilted her head back to expose her long neck.

Lane had had all he could stand. If she insisted on trying to sleek up to him like some alley cat, so that she could have him shed his senses and most likely slit his throat, he would teach her a lesson she would never forget. Lane wrapped his arm around Jordan's waste then pulled her to her feet by grasping her other hand. Once she was to her feet he twisted her arm around behind her back then pulled her body against his in one fluid motion. Jordan gasped out her disapproval.

"What's wrong Jordan? Based on your actions I would think this was exactly what you want. Or did I misread your purring voice, arching back, and let's not forget your blatant attempt at exposing that luscious neck. Well . . . Let's hear it!" He spat out angrily.

"Let me guess now you are the picture of innocence. Do us both a favor Jordan. Keep your yes . . . yes and your no . . . no. Stop pretending you want to sleep with me so you can prove I'm the epitome of . . ." Lane waved his hands in the air as he searched for the words. " . . . of every other misguided man you have come in contact with. We both know that your desire has nothing to do with sharing my bed. Isn't that right Jordan? You're just itching to sink that cold steel into my skin and watch the floor fill up with crimson. Does that about cover it?" As the last words left his lips Lane's chest was heaving with the effort of keeping his anger in check.

"Yes!" Jordan hissed as she snatched free of his grasp. "I want your blood to flow, just like every one of the other men that . . ." Her last words fell short as her eyes misted and she jerked around to gather her weapons. In an instant she was slammed hard against the wall of Lane's chest.

"Don't touch me!" She spit the words out, but what aggravated her was not his touch, but the way that her body betrayed her . . . she could feel herself being lost there in his grasp. The desperation of the moment dissolving into puddles on the floor of the cabin . . . puddles that lay in heaps . . . of not his blood but Jordan's resolve.

"You were going to say . . . Hurt you . . . Weren't you?" Lane asked as his eyes darted from one of her eyes to the other. Slowly he moved one hand from her wrist, while keeping the other firmly in place, and began brushing his fingers through her hair just above her ear.

"Talk to me Jordan, let me share your burden."

"Please . . . Don't." She weakly protested. "I can't . . . Leave it alone, Lane." Jordan pushed him away. Then grabbed her things and tore out of the cabin.

Lane had to admit that he was certainly getting his exercise. He did not mind the chase that was okay he'd follow her anywhere; it was the fact that she would not or could not face her demons. The demons of her past were haunting her and leading her mind, body and soul to the enemy . . . already he could sense the hate inside her. It was blazing-hot taking with it all of her innocence. He knew that he didn't have much time before the enemy won and claimed what was left of Jordan. Control was an illusion; one that he guessed Jordan was presently being fully intoxicated by. She certainly had the misguided belief that she could toy with the rotting vile that wrapped her soul in its hate-filled grasp and walk away unscathed. It was only a matter of time that Jordan would find out the truth . . . she was in a prison of her on making. Sure at first it may have been her father and brother's fault, and on some level he would suppose that some of the blame would have to rest with Jordan's mother whether she wanted to admit it or not, the woman had some responsibility in what Jordan had endured . . . after all the woman had loving parents that would have certainly taken in Judy and her daughter at any moment. Another fact that was undeniable was the money that Jordan's grandparents had, certainly they could have bank-rolled an escape were one requested. Instead the couple had had their hands tied by the enemy's lies; that God would have one of his children stay in such an awful situation was not only ludicrous it was down-right insulting to any father worth his salt, but especially the Father. The Creator. No one loved his children more! Lane hated this part of his job. The process of removing all of the enemy's taint . . . un-washing the brainwashed as he called it.

If only the world would truly get to know the Creator and not just watch the misguided representations of wayward individuals that claim to know Jesus, but in truth had never spent any real time with the Creator and would not have a clue whom he was, if he stood right in front of them. Lane was saddened by all of it. How many people sat back allowing others to ration information down to them, never taking responsibility for their own spiritual enlightenment. How could they blindly allow anyone that kind of access to their souls? Couldn't they just check behind teachers? Pick a bible up invest valuable worth while time into God's Holy word and see if what the preacher or teacher was saying on Sunday mornings or any other day of the week for that matter was true. Sometimes people were adamant that they were right based on generations of misinformation. Forefathers blindly passed assumed truths that had been passed along to them by trusted, beloved family members to their own family, each generation poisoning the next with lies. Lies, directly responsible for whole lives being destroyed; just like Jordan's had . . . Lane could just imagine that Jordan's mother probably attended a church where the spiritual leaders admonished her for harboring any thoughts that would excuse her from the marriage. Prayer was powerful and was always the way to go, but along with free will God had given his people common sense. Common sense and freewill both were meant to heighten the instinctive desire for survival of His people, instead generation after generation His people refused to use the tools and educate themselves as to what God would truly expect from His children.

Lane allowed the revere of the moment to fall away as he too darted out the door again in pursuit of Jordan. He had to figure out a way to get through to her before it was too late. The ticking time bomb that was crouching inside of her was just itching to sink its anger-filled claws into someone and at times he feared even he would fill that order. He would not be able to let his guard down with Jordan. He loved her and that was apparent. He would even go as far as to say that he believed that she too loved him; but until God could heal her; until she would willingly allow the Father to open her up and scrape all of the hate away from the frayed edges of her tormented soul; like a festering wound, that needed to be rid of the rotting flesh before it could truly heal . . . he would have to be careful. Jordan was not truly herself at this point and could give into the monster that craved revenge and bloodshed at any moment. Lane would willingly lay down his life for her, but he would not foolishly shed his senses to become prey to the beast that fought for the eradication of everyone in her world, even Jordan; a fact that Jordan would have to come to terms with before it was too late.

CHAPTER 12

Jordan etched her way through the woods that surrounded the cabin. She listened as the cacophony of sounds melted in around her raising her suspicions. She was used to the sounds of the night; never before had such crackles and hoots of the night life caused her to be uncomfortable. As a child it was through a trail leading into the woods near her family home that she had first fallen in love with nature. She had made a fort in a fallen oak that had the trunk hewn out by beavers living near the creek that used the collected lumber to make dams.

Lately it seemed with the entrance of Lane into her life that her nerves were tight and on edge. She had to get away from him. She could not allow this man to make her weak. She had a mission. She had to stay focused on the task at hand. There were so many hurting women in the world. That had gone through exactly what she was going through. She had no time to waste. Lane stirred up unwanted feelings inside of her. What good could they be to her? The feelings that had always been like old friends were hate, and anguish; both kept her on her toes. Jordan could count on hate and anguish. She knew what to expect with those feelings . . . not love . . . certainly not this kind of love, and certainly not the love for a man. She had never loved any man, and she would not start now. Men only had one purpose in life as far as she was concerned; to make the women of the world as miserable as possible. Something had died with her grandfather's generation. Chivalry, concern for others, what it meant to be a man . . . Jordan did not know what was lost, but what she did know was she had fond memories of her grandfather, her mother's father, and she somehow knew that with him what it meant to be a man had died with him. He was the last of his kind.

Who did Lane think she was some housewife doormat that would swoon over his touch? Was she supposed to throw her head back and lift her foot like the women did in the movies she had seen from the past? She knew how it worked. Throw your head back and lift your foot for them now and they knock you around later. The thought of allowing any man that kind of power over her caused a sick feeling to grow within her. How women succumb to their charms and found themselves on the receiving end of their mercy or lack there of was beyond Jordan.

"Never . . . !" She hissed into the night air as she ran with the fervor of someone that was being chased . . . and she was . . . she was being chased by an unwanted desire inside of her heart . . . a desire to fall into the arms of the most beautiful being she had ever known . . . Lane. A fear bigger than anything she had ever known gripped her. How could she outrun what was inside of her? This battle was one she could not lose. Yet there seemed no way to win.

After endless moments of trudging forward the sounds of a highway in the short distance became apparent. She could sense Lane's presence even now, she was aware of him every moment. Even that seemed to irritate her. The comfort that knowing he was there, seemed to rub her sensibility the wrong way. He was the enemy and yet she was ready to curl up next to him like a fat cat. She was inches from becoming just like the other pathetic women she knew. Just like her mother standing in the kitchen of that home of disappointment and broken dreams. She could not allow it to be. She had to keep her distance. So much was at stake and Lane was only a distraction.

Jordan watched what that life had to offer. She'd been to the functions held by the local women in the community; an effort to stay in touch and have some semblance of life . . . that is when her father would allow her to go with her mother or even allow her mother to go for that matter. She knew what was expected of a woman.

Some of the women would show up at the functions merely in an effort to keep up appearances; most of the time wearing gallons of makeup to cover the bruises left by their husbands, same as her mother . . . some of the wives were pushed to the side and never thought of. Sitting around reading some romance novel that was just stocked full of fantasies to fill their lonely minds . . . fantasies . . . things that those women would only read about, because no way would they ever know the love of a man that would come close to engendering such attributes as the characters that graced the pages of the books they were reading. Jordan imagined it was that very lonely existence that had pushed the women to hold the parties in the first place. Pretending to have it all; every dream they had ever read about. Setting up their huge lavish homes for the other women of the surrounding neighborhoods to come and gape at, while their husbands were no doubt in some hotel halfway across the planet in the arms of another woman, "The business trip". Jordan never understood the point in the cover up . . . why lie . . . if the men were in control, holding all of the cards, beating the women into submission, what would be the point in lying to them? Why not just say the truth? Tell their wives that they did not love them, and that they would be in a sleazy hotel cuddling with another woman. Jordan could only imagine that the women would welcome the idea of the men leaving them be, if only for a while. She could only imagine that it would take her every effort not to pack the man's bags for him . . . to keep them packed. She would probably constantly remind the sorry piece of work of the other woman hoping that he would go to her and never come back. She would appear all too gracious given the same circumstance, all too ready to have the scum-bag out of her life, and in the life of whatever trashy female he had convinced to share his bed. But it never seemed the case. The men would hide the details from their wives. Could it be that that could be the one thing that would break an already overloaded back, and push the women over the edge? Could that be the missing link that could cause an otherwise beaten and broken shell of existence to rise to the challenge? Jordan could not understand the point? She did not understand why any woman would care where a man spent his free time, and for that matter why would it be that "betrayal" that would send them over the edge. She would have imagined that at some point the millions of beatings should have done the job . . . the treatment of their precious children by the overbearing father, the man that was responsible for their very existence, and yet cared nothing for them . . . that seemed the only ingredients needed to end it all.

All along it had culminated from the foolish dreams of some novelists. Love like that did not exist. That in itself as far as Jordan was concerned was another form of cruelty, and she was certain that it had been orchestrated by a man to torture the poor women of the world that had foolishly allowed themselves to fall prey to the smoke screen . . . the empty promises that always led to the same dead end road . . . living in a house with a man that sat around watching football while the woman took care of the house and the kids. What man would not sign up for that?

Men had it made and there was nothing that women could do about it. Not yet at least. That's where Jordan would come in. She would change all of that as soon as she could put feet to her new world order. An order that would turn things around in women's minds . . . it would show women the world over that all the things that they had been taught up until that point was false . . . it was time that they learned the truth about their self worth. Women would no longer define themselves by their ability to catch the eye of a man, but they would learn of choices that had nothing to do with men. And as for the women that chose to live with their lives beside the opposite sex; so be it, Jordan was fine with that too . . . but no longer would it be a decision made out of necessity; survival for women hinged on them being able to find a man that would support them, work for them and supply their every need.

The man did not have to move a muscle and if the woman thought to request his help she would be slapped around or ignored. What choice did she really have? The man was usually much stronger than her, and she could not make him do anything that he did not want to do. No in the end it was just a hopeless, vicious cycle that never ended. It was all a lie everything that screamed love and romance, a hoax. None of it was real. Rather it was an elaborate ruse, allowing men to live the life of kings while women led the life of paupers.

She would put men and women on an even playing field. Men would no longer be able to shape the futures of women simply by manipulation, due to the woman being the weaker sex. For now on women would be taught the art of self defense, but more than that they would be given the most devastating tool any man would ever find in a woman's arsenal . . . self esteem, Jordan would arm them with the knowledge of self defense and armed with that knowledge they would no longer feel vulnerable. To the contrary . . . a freedom unlike they had ever known would rise up in every woman and allow them once and for all to crawl out into the light of that knowledge and bask in its ambitious glow.

"Disgusting . . . !" She growled into the air. How could they get caught up in the rat race of it all? Couldn't they see that men use the romantic side of women to control them?

"Weaker sex . . . My eye! Come tangle with a real woman! Stop fooling around with little girls in women's clothing. I give knew meaning to Amazon." Jordan said again to the nothingness around her then stopped to look at the highway as a mischievous grin played across her lips. "So much scum . . . So little time." Again she offered the words to no one; the night air.

Lane ran behind Jordan never making a sound. He knew she was aware of his presence. He could read her every thought. Sometimes that was hard to take with all the hate corrupting every contemplation of her subconscious. He had to keep himself from debating her on some of the issues. All men were not like the ones that Jordan was used to seeing . . . either beating the life out of their wives, or ignoring them while they carried on with some girl half their age. The morals of man had certainly plummeted from what the master had initially designed it to be, but man as a whole was not a complete loss. There were still men in the world that cared a great deal for their wives.

The whole idea that women were nothing to the Master was preposterous. On the contrary God loved women tremendously. Why could man not see through the lies of Satan? How had they fallen so far? Why was a lie so much easier to believe? Women were revered. How many countless women had the bible sang their praises and each story had just been swept under the proverbial rug . . . while a lie had taken center stage. Women were towers of faith that in most churches had lead men to the truth . . . but with the lies that Satan had set forth taking root in the minds and hearts of man . . . there was just nothing left of that truth. In the end it was the lie that men were dominant and all that God truly cared about that had been easier to believe. Lane could not understand how women could believe something so ugly. How could they not feel the love of the Father? A feeling so powerful it was tangible.

How was he to make a woman, that hated all men, with good reason, understand that all men were not what she thought. Lane pondered the thought now as he watched Jordan stand by the highway.

"You can go back now." Jordan announced into the air around her. "I'm not going back without a fight!" Jordan hissed as she checked first one side of the highway and then the other for oncoming traffic.

"You can feel my thoughts as strongly as I feel yours. We are joined by our souls . . . by the Father. It is his will for us to be together." Lane said as he took one more step in her direction but then stopped as he thought better of it.

"Have you lost what's left of your medieval mind? Joined by the Father? I have no idea, whom your father is, but I can assure you my father never joined me with anything except his fist." Jordan growled, as she faced the direction she knew Lane to be in.

"Not your earthly father . . . Our heavenly Father. He has joined our souls. We have been put together for a reason." Lane said as he lifted his hands into the air and then let them fall as exasperation flooded his senses. He could not imagine how he would get to the top of the insurmountable grudge she was holding to show her the truth.

"Joined by our souls? Well I can fix that." As the last of the words left her mouth, Jordan flipped into the air with ease as her legs wrapped around the branch, of a tree just above his head. With one fluid motion she was upside down with one hand around his mouth and the other was holding her trusty six inch blade against his throat.

"Why do you hesitate?" Lane questioned as he lifted her from the tree, allowing her legs to uncoil, and her body to align itself with that of his. He closed the remaining distance between their bodies and claimed her lips with his.

Jordan could feel all of her defenses melting away as she crushed her body into his. The warmness of his mouth on hers, and the sweet taste of him seemed to captivate her mind. She couldn't think; everything that had raced through her thoughts only moments earlier, were miles from her now. The questions, the doubts, the rage, all of it replaced with desire, an insatiable hunger that burned through every notion like a wildfire.

Lane was equally lost in the kiss. The sweet warmness of Jordan's mouth combined with the feel of her perfectly sculpted body against his had him held captive. There beside the highway whatever piece of them that hadn't already been glued permanently together by the master was fast being welded by the searing blaze of desire the kiss was forging through their senses.

Jordan was the first to break the embrace. Moving away she held one hand to her throbbing lips while the other pawed against his chest for freedom. She had to put distance between them. He was poisoning her thoughts. That was the last thing she needed. She would not become one of those women.

"Jordan, please. I didn't mean for that to happen. I apologize I should be stronger." Lane said as failure cast its unrelenting shadow over his achingly, beautiful, blue eyes.

"You are only a man. Lust is in your veins. Don't worry . . . ." Jordan hissed as her eyes blazed with furry, she continued. "You are lowered by nature. You can't help it. You have to conquer as many women as possible before you die." Jordan cocked her head to the side as her eyes charred through Lane with the next words. "I hope that you have met your quota, because if you do not stop following me around, you are about to meet this Maker of yours." Jordan hissed sarcastically as she waved her hands through the air.

"You have to stop threatening me. I am not your enemy. Name one thing that I have done to wrong you, that would give you reason to hate me personally, and please do not list my gender. I am not responsible for being born a man. I am also not responsible for the other men in your life." Lane countered as he tried desperately to find the perfect words that would somehow break through the mountain of hate that held Jordan hostage. "I can only be responsible for my own actions Jordan." He held her head with one tender hand as he tried to look deeper into her eyes; to see past all of it . . . all of the aguish, the frustration, the loss. "I will tell you that their actions will not go unpunished. He will avenge you. He said revenge is His. He also said what was done to the least of these was done to him. The least of these, Jordan . . . Do you understand that you are His child? He isn't just my maker, like it or not He is your Maker, too. Can't you see?" Lane's eyes pleaded with her, for her understanding. He could feel defeat grabbing, clawing, at his resolve. It was threatening to break him down. His obvious attraction to Jordan was getting in the way, of his mission.

"Leave me alone! Keep that get a spiritual Being to worship, garbage to yourself. I'm not buying. You . . . or Him . . . !" Jordan screeched as she continued. "Let me get this straight . . . I am supposed to get on my knees and pay homage to the 'Creator' . . ." Jordan held her hands up and pretended to put quotations around the word as it left her mouth. ". . . I refuse to kneel down to a God that encompasses the very gender that has caused me so much grief." Jordan's face lit up with recognition. "You know come to think about it . . . . That makes perfect sense. Think about it . . . . It's just another way for men to get women on their knees. Of course!" Jordan threw her hands into the air and then let them fall again . . . as her eyes seemed to light up as if she had had an epiphany. "All this time and now it is crystal clear. That is why you want me to buy into this ruler of yours . . . You are trying to master the one that fights for women everywhere. If I teach them what I have learned you will loose your foothold. Who sent you?" Jordan was inches from his face poised to do battle as the last word left her lips.

"We have been over this Jordan. I have been sent by the Master. If He wanted to dominate you, He would have made you a mindless robot. He created men and women for His glory. He loves us, He says in his word that He assures us happiness that He will give us life more abundant . . . not that He will turn all of us into mindless robots that run around without a will of our on." Lane was waving his hands in the air. He could feel the frustration mounting. He was getting no where fast. He dropped his hands to his side and sighed. "At times I wish that were true. Then I would not be here trying to convince a wildcat she was going to a place that was beyond any torment she has ever been through. And I would not be fighting every immoral thought in order to do so."

Lane and Jordan had both been trained to keep their emotions at bay, to not allow their anger to compromise a mission. Jordan knew that she was not doing a good job of controlling her anger. She would imagine that Lane was struggling with the effort of restraining his temper as well. She had seen on many occasions that the affect that he was having on her was just as strong as the affect she had on him. Both were trained agents, both had been through countless scenarios and tests to prove that they were ready to handle any field situation. Black Heart and The Truth spared no expense in the efforts that were made to ensure that agents were ready. Now as she stood by the highway inches from this tall-godlike man, she was finding it harder and harder to articulate. Her head spun with the effort of keeping the reins on control, and the more she grasped for the edges of her resolve, the more she could feel the endless gaping chasm grow . . . she was being pulled in, not only to his charms, but to his runaway imagination. What had he said; a place of torment? She tried to double her efforts at maintaining control, but in the end she could sense that it was a lost cause. She felt puny under the weight of curiosity that burned within her.

"What do you mean place of torment? Where do you think you are taking me? And what is this immorality you fight?" Jordan's face contorted into an angry mask as she allowed the questions to come.

"The effect you have on me Jordan. I love you. I knew that from the first moment I saw you, on the ground crying out to the Father, like a lost lamb. I saw you in that moment through His eyes I felt I could do this, but I did not realize there is another love that moves within my soul for you. It is not meant to be. I want to hold you in my arms as a husband would a wife. Jordan, don't you see . . . I can't feel this way. Somewhere along the way I have given into that love and lost my focus. I can not. Your life depends on me keeping that focus. I know the Father chose well in His decision to have a man to prove he was different, I am sorry to Him that I have let his sheep slip through the cracks into the hands of the wolves, and I am sorry to you that you will experience this place of torment because of my failure. Forgive me." Lane dropped his head as the tears that had only threatened to fall cascaded down his cheeks and then he turned and left Jordan standing by the highway.

CHAPTER 13

Jordan stood there watching as Lane walked away, never once taking her eyes away until the shadows claimed his form. What was this place? If he wasn't taking her there then who was? Torment...? A chill whispered through her body and she absently caressed her arms, to stave it off, as she stepped onto the highway and looked first to the left and then to the right. Which way would she go? Whatever direction would lead her as far away from the mesmerizing affect Lane had on her. She was all but certain that she would lose her very existence if she did not run as far and as fast as she could, because she could feel everything that he had said, all of it, every last emotion, was playing around the edges of her dark heart, caressing her soul, and threatening to change her forever. She could not allow that to happen.

The rage that seemed to rise up in her was culminating into something that at times brought with it a terror, of its own right, but it had been her only friend for so long. Sure she had Garrison, but he was a man, same as the rest, though he had proven to be trustworthy on more than one occasion, during their stay at the bureau. But Jordan could not allow one man to cloud her judgment... she could see what the world was becoming, the way women were being discriminated against was not just a symptom that plagued the inner-workings of her own family... no, it was fast becoming the norm. And she would not fall prey to its evil. She would not allow her feelings for Lane to take her eyes off of the truth. She couldn't. Someone had to change things, and if she allowed herself to get lost in the illusion, then who would be left?

* * *

Lane didn't look back. He couldn't. If he had he had stayed there by that highway lost in her gaze, no matter how childlike and terrible it could be, he would not have left her. What good would he be to her with his flesh in the way? He had to get away, to pray, to meditate, and maybe even to ask God to redirect his path . . . So that he could send someone that could help Jordan before it was too late. He could not let the fleshly side of his love for her overshadow what God's plan was for her life.

Lane had been able to follow after God's will for his life, without a problem. Sure there had been times that the road seemed too long, but never had he remembered a road this long. Even the times as a child when his parents were in the mission field providing for the tribe in order to show the people that they cared for them. Lane's father's favorite saying had always been, 'No one will care about what you have to say, until they know how much you care' Lane could still remember the words as if his dad were standing before him saying them now. He tried to take comfort in the memories of his time with his parents as they walked amongst the Cadotion tribe telling them about God . . .

Lane had joined his parents on their mission trips to foreign countries all the time as a boy. He had been taught at an early age that there was no plan that was more significant for his life than that of God's. The nights at times had been fear inducing. The chants, the screams, and the sounds of the wild animals eating whatever was available. It was terrifying and amazing at the same time. He wouldn't trade a minute of it.

Lane could not imagine that God had planned for his life to be anymore than a solo flight; there would be no Mrs. Gates for him, and that was fine by Lane. It was God's path; his way had always been the only way for Lane, but now he seemed to question the Creator's logic in this circumstance. What good could possibly come from putting a woman with as tortured a past with someone that seemed to not be able to think about anything but how good her lips tasted on his. This had to be some kind of a mistake on his part. Maybe he had misread the wishes of the Creator. Lane was aware of the games that the enemy could play with God's people . . . he had been told through prayer, supplication, and fasting; his path would be set, and it had been true. God revealed his path. He had told Lane that it would not be an easy path. That there would be trials . . . that in some ways this would be the hardest mission he had ever been on.

Lane was a member of secret organization that was called The Truth. The idea was to bring the word to the world. The members had to remain secretive; after President Santana had been elected, he outlawed religion of any kind. He said that it caused too much trouble. That the radical behavior of certain religious groups had brought about too many heinous crimes. That too much blood had been shed in the name of religion.

The Truth had fought long and hard to keep Freedom of Religion in the constitution, but in the end not enough Christians stood up. The down fall of Christian freedom, had been all too subtle . . . It began with other religious organizations complaining about prayer in the schools. The groups complained that it was not fair to have the Christian beliefs forced down the throats of their children.

Soon after the religious groups started to complain about the Ten Commandments being in the courthouse . . . They complained that pieces of all religious groups' documents should be allowed to hang on the walls of the courthouse, because it was a structure that represented freedoms of all groups . . . however, in light of the documents that were on the walls presently it only seemed to be concerned with the Christians' freedom.

Soon the air waves weren't allowed to play anything with Jesus' name in it. A man from another country had been down visiting America and was trying to find a radio station. When he heard a few stations with Christian songs on them he became angry and called the radio station to complain. The manager did not like his attitude and had told him to leave the country if it had made him so unhappy. At that point things got worse as the man decided to bring a lawsuit against the radio station. Soon it went from freedom of speech to freedom of listening. If someone didn't want to hear it; then it had to go.

One stone being thrown after another and before long the ripples had gotten out of control.

At first the other religious groups had been happy until the Christians stood up. Unfortunately, it had been too little too late. The president passed the law . . . . There would no longer be Freedom of Religion. The president was quoted as saying "The Constitution is just a piece of paper." Some people followed that logic, some people were angry, and some just didn't care . . . but in the end regardless of the side any member of society was on, the end result had been the same . . . freedom of religion was abolished . . . and with it other freedoms were taken as well. No one could see that coming. Now the land that had once stood for freedom in a land of democracy that was built for the people by the people on the statutes of God by our forefathers had dissolved into bitter nothingness.

Lane shook his head as the last of the memory swept through him. He had thanked God for The Truth so many times. The numbers of people that were being touched by God's holy word was growing everyday. But it was hard to get The Truth out with the threat of jail looming over everyone's head. In some states the penalty for being caught worshiping carried a stiffer penalty than murder or rape . . . the president had reasoned that hate crimes stemmed from mindless beliefs in an unseen spiritual being. He further reasoned that it was that kind of blind trust that was dangerous. Serial killers were born from the pages of the bible. Men and women reading the words maybe misconstruing its meaning, but the result was the same; people were losing their lives. The president was adamant. It was that kind of mindless following of the unknown that could no longer be tolerated if the country was to once again be the power that it had once been. So being found in any form of worship would result in the same penalties as premeditated murder.

With the population moving further and further from the moral integrity that spirituality had encompassed, hate crimes had sky rocketed. That explained why Jordan could look around and see the country regressing.

"Backwards on the evolutionary chart", as some scientists had been quoted saying on the news reports. The idea that men and women came from apes had often made Lane laugh, but the moral fortitude that the country seemed to illustrate made them take on more and more of the primate's characteristics. How could things have moved this far into the proverbial toilet? Lane knew that without God the world would be lost but this had been beyond his imaginings.

Jordan had been right in some ways and trying to convince her otherwise would be like talking to a wall. Women had been very poorly affected by the lack of spirituality. Men had no guide . . . without the Holy Spirit to guide them on there way, to tell them to love their wives as Christ loved the church, courting seemed to revert to a caveman reality. Women stayed alone, or were treated like their only significance was held in their ability to breed. Some men did not treat their wives in the same way, but it was obviously not very popular.

Men and women alike had become immoral in their marriage as well. Marriage no longer held an unsaid sacredness. It was now anything goes, and diseases were spilling over into every economic gender, and ethnic group. There were no boundaries.

Jordan had been what was known as the terminator of the under ground. Her organization often worked hand in hand with The Truth to bring about justice, but Jordan was a freak accident. She is what happened when a recruit did not listen to the organization's views on a higher power. Having to dictate the fate of other people, mingled with the training a recruit received, could be overwhelming without a higher power to humble them.

* * *

Jordan walked for a long time down the highway before some one picked her up. An old man with an unfriendly scowl on his face was headed in the same direction.

"Where you headed, little lady?" He asked as he kept his eyes straight ahead.

"Up the road." Jordan's smile covered her disapproval of the old timer referring to her as little lady. She climbed into the old blue clunker; an old sixty something model Ford from what she could gather. The smell that permeated the cab caused tears to sting the corners of her eyes. The fumes came in through a crack in the elongated-oval-back-window, causing her to gag a couple of times. She inwardly chided herself for being so childish. It had to be better than walking for God only knew how long. So she would keep her complaints to herself, and the old man would come to no harm by her hands as long as he kept his hands to himself.

Never letting her guard down, Jordan scrutinized the old man's every move. She was ready for anything. The old timer had gray hair and tiny bead like pale blue eyes. His face was grooved with age and he dressed like a farmer. His mouth had the stain of dip running from the corner to just beneath his chin. A cup holder protruded form his door and held an old Styrofoam cup. Tissue tinged with a brown juice, Jordan could only imagine was spit, spilled over the edge. Jordan winced her disapproval and turned her head to try and get some air from the crack in the window.

"So what's your story little lady?" The man asked with a wink. His blue eyes glistened in the moonlight.

"I'm not your little lady, and my story is none of your business old timer. I asked for a ride not conversation. If you would like to stop I'd be glad to get out, but don't call me little lady again." The warning edge in her tone was not lost on the old man. He simply kept his face forward, and sped up slightly.

"There is no need for fear old timer I won't hurt you. I just need a ride to the next town then I will be out of your hair." Jordan turned back to the window after it seemed that the old man had visually relaxed.

"That's fine little . . . err . . . ma'am." After the words left his lips he seemed to want to take them back. Jordan could not explain the feeling, but it seemed that the old man could incite some of the same feelings of warmth and safety as Lane.

"Thank you . . . the name is Jordan." She smiled, but only slightly and again turned to face the crack in the window.

"That's fine Jordan. I am Gabriel. You can call me Gabe." The old man informed her with a smile as again the same almost undetectable twinkle filled his translucent blue eyes.

CHAPTER 14

Jordan could not get the old man out of her mind. She had guessed it was about midnight when the old timer . . . Gabriel . . . happened by. Shouldn't some one his age already have been in bed? Her grandfather used to kid about going to bed with the chickens and getting up with them. Though he was making a joke it had been his routine for as long as Jordan could remember.

Poppa Cecil she used to call him. He was truly the last of the chivalrous men. It just seemed to die with him. That was her mother's dad. Jordan loved him. He was strong, with a quiet self assurance that seemed to filter out onto all that was around him. People felt safe around Cecil Schooner. It was that type of love that Jordan had not found since his death.

Every man that had come into her life only loved her for what could be gained by her presence. Her father only loved her so she could be like those wolves on Junior's seat cover, paying homage to a moon that would never lend anything but its light; no warmth like the sun, just a faint iridescent glow. Was that enough? To give loyalty to something that would lend only a temporal light and nothing more?

Jordan could not trust that. She had to stick to what she knew. Men were pigs . . . pigs, that were better off dead, and the best man she had ever known was gone and those times were gone with him.

Men did not treat women as treasures anymore. The way that Poppa Cecil had treated her grandmother . . . She was his treasure. She was his life . . . they did not have a lot of material things but the way that the two of them were together made their lives seem full . . . like all that they shared was all anyone would ever need.

Jordan sat at the foot of Poppa Cecil's hospital bed, as her grandmother bid him farewell to this life . . . It was almost too painful to watch. Jordan stood there holding on to the covers of the bed gripping with all her strength, she was so sure that she would be lost in the moment forever if she did not hold on.

Jordan's grandmother moved from the chair and knelt on the floor beside her husband's bed . . . Jordan could see it now . . . her grandmother's frail frame . . . the woman was eighty five and her hair a salt and pepper mixture that was kept cropped close to her head in a neat perm. Her fingers were mangled with arthritis that plagued her whole body . . . but in that moment there was only one position that would do . . . she had to be on her knees . . . she had to beg . . . she had to pray for him to never leave her . . . she could not be here alone. Without him . . . it was more than she would ever be able to bear, and in the end her prayer had been answered . . . In the end, Jordan's Poppa, being the gentleman that he was . . . allowed his love, his life, the woman to go first. Jordan's grandmother slumped to the floor with a heart attack and soon after came an intruding buzzing noise . . . the monitor was boasting its horrendous truth, Poppa Cecil was gone. Tears bombarded her cheeks, as she gasped and ran instinctively to her Poppa and then to her grandmother.

Jordan started to scream for the nursing staff to come and help, but the effort had been too little too late. They were both gone. The only two people that made an otherwise ugly life seem livable had exited her world, leaving her behind to brave it with her mother. Jordan could not imagine how she would survive it all without the wonderful trips to her grandparents for the summer.

Jordan shook the memory from her mind . . . that time was a million years ago now. Women were no longer revered in such a way as that . . . now they were sex objects, work horses, and baby factories. All women had been taken right back to the middle ages. The night life was filled with women that refused to be thrown into that life style . . . but the alternative seemed even more horrible. Jordan could not decide which was worse . . . being married to a man that treated you like garbage . . . beating on you while parading other women into your home . . . or being the woman that was was put on display in other women's homes. Jordan would be neither . . . both in her opinion were degrading. As long as there was a breath in her body she would fight for a different way.

Jordan believed in the values that Black Heart Revenge stood for. She would stand behind them as long as she lived. She just had to show the organization that she could change. She could be the type of person that valued human life. She just had to find human life that was worth being valued. The world was full of people taking and not giving. Walking all over women and not just women . . . what about people like Gabe? He was a good guy right? Why did he not have more? Why was he out at midnight in an old truck filled with fumes? Why could someone like him not have more? Maybe she deserved her plight, after all she had done some horrible things in the name of what should be. She supposed that some losses were acceptable on the road to change. But Gabe, and her mother, what had they done that was so wrong to this horrible world that the two of them had to live without even the bear necessities of life.

Jordan closed her eyes as the thoughts faded . . . What was she doing? There was no time for trips down memory lane. Hadn't she been paying attention? Look around you girl. She thought . . . You know without someone to guide them they will never make it out of this oppression alive.

With the last thought scorching its truth through her mind she ran through the little town toward her brother's house. She had to lay low. Jordan was under no delusions . . . . She had committed murder, like it or not her sister-in-law could have reported her. Jordan kind of hoped she had, that way the police would not hassle her loved ones about a crime she had committed; in a perfect world her sister-in-law would have stuck to the plan . . . a plan that she was not even aware of . . . one where her sister-in-law would tell the police that it was self defense. But in the end even Jordan knew that it was not a viable claim. The way that she had slaughtered her brother, the beast had taken over and almost cost her the life of her precious niece . . . Jordan was sure that fact alone would have sent her sister-in-law into a 'tell all frenzy' if for no other reason than to be free of Jordan . . . to feel safe.

Jordan had to get to the house unnoticed. But it would not be easy. Luckily, combat training had taught her the art of invisibility.

She would be able to be right under their noses without alerting them to her presence. Only another agent would be able to detect the existence of a fellow agent in the room, and even then it was sometimes impossible.

Jordan slowed her pace to a light jog as the old house come into sight. As she had suspected the house was wrapped up with FBI agents, and the local police force. She looked around for any recognizable faces. Some of the guys in the bureau worked under cover as contacts for Black Heart Revenge. Jordan knew that they would be able to see her M.O. (motive), stamped all over this. The others would probably not suspect anything. The agents affiliated with the bureau that did suspect her involvement would be unable to say anything; anonymity inhibited it . . . secrecy was everything for the bureau, if an agent presented a problem it would be handled in-house. There would be special units dispatched that would know specifics on the rogue agent; finding the agent would not be a problem.

Jordan knew there was no need for fear on those levels. Jordan's only problem now . . . had her brother's wife turned her in? The FBI would definitely be able to detect that this was a crime of passion, a hate crime. Who ever killed Jr. knew him.

This was no random killing. Who ever killed Jr.; not only wanted him dead, he or she relished it. Jordan had to admit it had been somewhat satisfying. She was starting to understand that the rage that was ever present within her was only fed by the kill. The anger and frustration . . . the years of torment . . . that she and her mother had endured in this house, seemed to multiply every time she came near the evil structure.

Jordan hated this place. Inside of her lived a yearning for its destruction. She wanted to tear the place down board by board and set fire to the splinters as she danced around the memories that died in its flames. All of the members of her family that had contributed to its ugliness were now gone . . . but the hunger to tear it down to feel the blood of any evil person that helped to build ports to hell's abyss; like the one that stood before her now was still alive . . . still burning within her, calling out for justice with every breath she took. That same hunger that burned holes into her spirit was tearing into her now. She could not wait to find her next victim. What would it take to quiet the demand for blood? It had to be this place . . . the fact that it was still standing. Maybe if she did tear it down and burn it completely she could move on from all of the anger and hate that flamed through her spirit like a raging inferno.

One silent footstep after another she walked up to the back of the house. Then with relative ease she scaled up the metal pipe that ran up the side of the house, used for the house's gutter-system. She was careful to watch for prying eyes when she found none she continued up to the roof of the house. Successfully reaching the top, she crawled with her arms bent and legs sprawled behind to stay as low as possible so as not to be seen. Finally, she made her way to the chimney. She had not seen any smoke coming from the roof of the house and knew that there was no fire lit. She took the grappling hooks from her side that were attached to a thick black rope, and attached them to the side of the chimney. She then attached the harness around her groin, and waste. Soon she was hanging upside down; descending the chimney's length.

"Mrs. Buckley please think . . . if you could think of any enemies that could have done this awful thing to your husband. Is there anyone? Bad business deals . . ."

Jordan listened carefully as the agent gave the usual spill. How many times had she heard this? She loved to be at the scene. She wanted to see the refreshed look in the beat down eyes of the woman now freed from a life of slavery. It never seemed to get old. It was the same scene every time . . . the woman that was the embodiment of broken, stolen life, was standing in front of the FBI agents trying desperately to keep her eyes from revealing her happiness. Usually a week or two after the husband's corpse was found the woman was already planning ways to spend the insurance money.

Jordan loved that part the most. It was truly poetic justice. Jordan could remember the times that she had orchestrated the perfect alibi for the woman. Constructing the perfect death for the man . . . the plan had always gone off without a hitch.

Jordan would make a phone call telling the man that there was a hit put out on his wife so he would need to take out insurance on the both of them. The man believed it for two reasons . . . one he was the one that had run into Jordan . . . he had orchestrated the plan from the beginning. He believed that he was having a chance meeting with a hit woman. It was his idea from the beginning. The other reason, Jordan told the man that her business was quite simple she did not collect payment until the job was complete and the insurance claim was collected.

If the husband took out insurance the wife would not be pinned down with greed as a motive. As usual the poor excuse for human existence, the woman, just went on living their lives each day one thankful unbeaten breath at a time. Being careful of her every word as her sister-in-law had. It was pitiful to watch.

Jordan almost could not wait the usual thirty days that it took for the insurance to go into effect. But she had to, she had to be disciplined. The wives of her victims had been through enough without leaving them penniless on the mercy of the world.

So Jordan made the call, waited a month, staking the victim out, planning accidental meetings, collecting any information that would make him more vulnerable to her attack. It was like taking candy from a baby. With the morals of the nation in the toilet, it wasn't like she had to throw herself at her victims. The police had named her the 'John-Slasher'. It had been completely laughable. She was called that because she had the unsuspecting man meet her at a sleazy hotel on the outskirts of town.

Finding a new victim was always easy enough. A few nights at the local bar listening to the saddest story there. Married men were truly the scum of the earth. They were always at the local bar trying to get with whatever woman that would have anything to do with them. As crazy as it seemed the men that wanted to cheat weren't very picky. They had to die. Jordan was doing their family a service. How long would it take for their lifestyle to catch up with them? How long before they brought diseases home to their wives? Not to mention the especially morally repugnant scum of the earth . . . the true head cases that were so full of lust that they would go after anything even their own children. Jordan could spot this type from a mile away. Usually, she would just sit and listen to the worthless piece of trash talk to women in the bar. It started innocent enough, they would just spill all the poor me stories that they could muster onto the poor bar tender for the first fifteen minutes, then soon some woman would sidle up next to him as if he would be the end to all her problems. Soon the couple would make their leave at which time

Jordan would exit the bar and follow them from a few car lengths back. After spending the night crawling all over each other soon her unsuspecting snake in the grass victim would head home. Finally, after waiting for the lights to go off in the house she would rummage through the trash, or whatever resources that were readily available like the glove box of the car. If Jordan got really lucky, the smug jerk wasn't afraid of being caught, because he knew that like every other woman in the God forsaken universe, that had lost their mind, she would put up with whatever they had to dish out just to have a man in her life. Jordan could not see why they felt their only saving grace would be a man in their life.

Jordan would nose around in her victim's personal life until she had enough information to hang them with. The less personal the meetings were . . . the better Jordan liked it. Just as any other cheating buffoon that was led around by his hormones, her victims, would hide in closets or in the bathroom to talk to Jordan. She had called the number and started a conversation with the men pretending to be interested in them. She would put herself out as a girl of the night life that was trying to get in touch with a 'John', but she was all too happy to carry on a conversation with the man instead. She did not have to keep her pretend identity for long. Most of the men found it to be very sexy that Jordan was pretending to be someone she was not just to get to know them . . . as she put it.

The men were practically begging for the meeting. She kept them hooked by feigning shyness on the subject. Men loved thinking that they were in charge, and the idea of meeting a woman that had met them at a bar and was attracted to them, but was too shy to just come out and say hi or ask for their number . . . not only that, but had gone through the effort of creating a chance meeting—it made the man feel desirable . . . lending to his need to be in control, the change in the victim was so complete that Jordan could sense it even over a phone line. She would soon let her 'line of work' slip out into the conversation, and before long the man was all to ready to score some easy cash. He would be begging Jordan to kill his wife and practically at the insurance office the very next day. After weeks of laughing at his mind-numbingly-stupid jokes, and acting like a wanting woman she would finally 'shyly agree to meet him at a local hotel . . . She claimed it was his pushing for them to be 'together', that had dissolved her inhibitions . . . she pretended to find the man irresistible, that she would never even consider meeting with someone . . . sleeping with married men was completely out of the norm for her. Jordan found that sticking to some of the true attributes about her personality made the character that she created for the benefit of the victim more believable.

She could not imagine what it was about him in particular that was clouding her senses but she just had to know, she lied. And with that the meeting was made, the insurance was in effect, and she was mere moments away from ridding the world of another immorally-disgusting-creature.

Jordan kept up the pretense even into the sleazy hotel where she came out with a robe covering up everything. She relished the image that the victim made as his eyes would change from uncertainty to smug assurance . . . as he sauntered over to no doubt talk her into disrobing. The minute that he did he would be left just like the others . . . a corpse outlined in chalk. The whole set up lending to the false assumption that the authorities made; the man had been killed by a serial killer dubbed the John-Slasher.

Jordan steadied herself as she checked her position in the chimney; the last of the memory faded. She wanted to be alert especially in her present circumstance. As intoxicating as being at the scene of her crime was there was no room for mistakes. Even the scene of her brother's death, the one person that she had waited a lifetime to watch die at her hands . . . Even now, as she could hear her sister-in-law, feigning the impossible depths of her husband's loss . . . Even as Jordan could feel the same that-a-girl smile sleek across her lips . . . she knew that she had to stay in the here and now. Maybe now, more than ever, because this one was personal and this one could be the one that would lead to her capture. This was her family and like it or not there would be no way to cover her trail . . . Jordan would be the number one suspect.

CHAPTER 15

Jordan waited in place until she heard the last of the detectives leave. She almost lost her composure when Lieutenant Garrison threw the piece of paper into the chimney and it landed just under her feet. She had righted herself not long after she got to the bottom of the chimney. She knew she wouldn't be able to stay upside down until the FBI completed their investigation. That and the possibility, of the need for a speedy get away, kept her on her toes at all times.

Jordan lowered her feet and collected the paper between the sides of her shoes as quietly as she could. Soon with some effort she had the paper in her fingers and was unfolding it.

> Meet me at the park on the corner of First Street, at midnight.
> Don't be late need to give you valuable information.
>
> Garrison

Jordan put the paper in her pocket as she steadied her body with her free hand. She could not dwell on what Garrison wanted right now. She knew he was aware of her presence because they had trained under the same recruiter at the academy. A fact that lent them incites to the other's habits in the field; in training, recruits would pair off and spend long hours together, knowing what your partner would do was essential, because partners would work together in the field . . . If she and Garrison for instance did not know what the other was thinking or would do in any given situation it could make an already dangerous scene disastrous. The ability to read each others thoughts and actions could be a blessing and a curse . . . a curse, because it would always make it hard for the two of them to evade the other. Good thing for Jordan, Garrison seemed to be on her side as usual, though looks could be deceiving.

The art of being invisible was no easy task. She had to pick a place no one would look. Sometimes that meant next to impossible to gain access. Like having to scale a building and climb on to a roof top then gain access to the chimney after the FBI had time to check it. Then descend on a harness attached to a grappling-hook made for mountain climbing, all without making a sound or touching the sides of the chimney. If Jordan had touched the sides of the chimney lose debris may fall and alert the detectives to her whereabouts. There was no room for mistakes. Keeping in shape, remaining agile, was a must. You only had one shot. After that either you would be safely at the bottom of the chimney listening to the inhabitant's conversation or at the business end of a police issue fire arm. The police did not bother Jordan, she could disarm them with relative ease; it was the other agents, not including her partner, Garrison obviously magnified her desire to be careful. Jordan knew she would not be able to out maneuver a team of agents; especially a team of agents trained by Black Heart.

Jordan unhooked her harness and hung it over a nail in the chimney. She silently stood on one foot then the other after she heard her niece and sister in law, leave the room. Finally she had both feet safely planted on the living room floor. She made a quick mental sweep of the room then disappeared into the shadows and waited for Erica to reenter the room.

Erica was whistling some happy tune as she came back into the living room. Jordan crept up behind her as a satisfied grin lined her lips.

"No!" Erica protested Jordan's unwanted advances.

"Shhh!" Jordan started as she cupped a hand around Erica's mouth to silence her.

"It's me, Jordan; I am here to talk to you. If I let your mouth go you have to promise not to scream. I don't want to scare Penny."

Erica then nodded that she would be comply. Finally, Jordan released her then walked in front of her so that they would be face to face.

"I need to talk to you. I know that I scared you earlier with what happened with Penny. But you have to know I would never hurt her. I had just attacked Jr. and killed him. Erica I was at a heightened sense of awareness. She grabbed my arm. I didn't mean to scare her." Jordan said as her eyes pleaded her case; unshed tears brimmed stinging the backs of her eyes.

"Scare her? Jordan you had a blade to her throat! You could have killed her." Erica spat the words out angrily.

"I know. I'm sorry. I don't know what is wrong with me. I have so much rage bottled up inside of me." Jordan was sitting on the couch with her head in her hands now.

"I love Penny you have to know that." Jordan allowed her hands to fall from her face and tilted her head back to face Erica . . . she could feel the hope burning a fever-pitch path through her soul, hope that her sister-in-law would believe her . . . hope that she would be able to convince them to join her and let her train them to be able to care for themselves in the future; to never have to be at the merciless hands of anyone like her brother again.

"Jordan. I have no doubt that you love her. I can see it in your eyes she reminded you so much of yourself as a child. You have to realize that all of that ended when you killed her father. He is no longer alive to hurt her. We will be safe now. Really, you can go and if you don't mind we can stay here and live a long happy . . ." Erica was stopped short. She wanted to explain that she and Penny could thrive in the old house with Jr. gone. Now she could raise Penny in the manner that she had deserved . . . the way that she had always pictured raising a child . . . with love and acceptance . . . without fear.

"No!" Jordan heard herself shout the word. Jordan stepped back and faced the opposite direction for only a moment to collect her racing thoughts. Then turning to again face Erica, Jordan cupped her hands over her mouth in a praying hands fashion, and then allowing them to fall away from her face she stepped forward. She allowed a small reassuring smile to caress he lips, and then tenderly placed a hand on Erica's shoulder. "I mean no. Look Erica I came back so that you both could come with me." Jordan watched Erica as everything about her mannerisms seemed to scream that Jordan was being absurd.

Erica retreated from Jordan's unwanted touch. Had Jordan lost her mind? Erica could not begin to think of taking her child into such a life. She had stood there in Jordan's old bedroom and witnessed first hand what Jordan wanted to teach Penny. No that was the last thing that Erica would allow her daughter to become tangled up in. That kind of life was not for the two of them. They were quiet people . . . they loved life. Erica and Penny had gone to church and learned of a love that was without boundaries. The love of God was so great that it transcended every bad that had ever been done to either of them. Sure Erica had loved Jr. in the beginning, she did not want him to die, but she had prayed for God to either straighten him up, show him a better way, or to take him out of their lives forever. It was his will and Erica was happy.

"What . . . ? Jordan you can't be serious." Erica's voice was starting to betray her now. The fear that she was trying to keep at bay was seething in every word that fell from her lips. "Jordan she needs stability. You can't seriously think that we can roam the countryside with you. What about the way women are being treated? Have you thought of that Jordan?" Erica looked from Jordan to the long hall that led to her child's room.

"Calm down Erica, you are making me nervous. You stink of fear." Jordan's eyes cut over to Erica on the last word. "What do you think I'm going to do to you?" Disgust dripped from every word. It made Jordan sick to think that Erica would consider living in the home where the two of them had been beaten . . . and not just the two of them but Jordan and her mother as well. Maybe Jordan had been wrong about Erica. Maybe Erica did not want another life. Maybe she was satisfied with the one she had.

Erica moved closer to the hall one step at a time. Her eyes were filling with tears and her limbs were quaking with fear.

"Erica, do not make me chase you. I can catch you and you know it. I want my niece to learn how to take up for herself. If you want to live this way, then that is up to you. That girl is a different story. She's my niece. I wont stand by and let her believe what she has been through is the only way." Jordan dropped her head and sighed. She knew that Erica was going to make this difficult. She did not want to hurt Erica, but she loved Penny and she refused to sit by and watch her only living relative, a female at that, grow up in a world that had no respect for women . . . as some kind of victim. Penny had to be taught how to defend herself; otherwise she was no more than another helpless woman with a target on her head.

Jordan knew the odds. Penny had already been exposed to the life . . . that alone increased the chances that she would end up in the same lifestyle . . . like her mother married to some evil tyrant that would mistreat Penny and any female child that she may conceive.

Erica could see the determination lining Jordan's features. She knew that she would never be able to fight Jordan in a combat situation. It was then that Erica understood that Jordan intended to take her daughter. Erica had to do something . . . but what?

"No Jordan! You wont take her. I wont let you." Desperation flamed through Erica's body as she ran for Penny's bedroom.

"You don't have a choice! I'm taking her with me. I'm going to train her to fight like I do. I'm going to give that girl the chance that you are too afraid to give her." Jordan barked the warning edge on her comment placing an exclamation on her claim.

"No Jordan you want to turn her into a killer! She's a child." Erica cried as she fell to her knees. "Please Jordan." Tears fell from Erica's eyes as she blocked the door to her daughter's room.

"Come with us. I will train you too." Jordan's words were on the verge of begging as she looked down at Erica and took her hands into her own.

"I can't." Erica objected.

"You can't or you wont?" Jordan accused.

"I can't." Erica got to her feet and stepped away from the room. Jordan wasted no time. She ran to Penny's bedside.

"Penny . . . Wake up!" She said as she shook the girl's arm. Penny rubbed her eyes.

"Aunt Jordan . . . ?" The fog of sleep had not yet fell away; as the grogginess made itself known in Penny's gruff voice.

"Yes come on there's no time." Jordan urged as she began pulling the covers back, exposing Penny to the slight chill of the room Penny shivered and pulled the covers back into place as agitation lined her features.

"Where are we going?" The question was more of a whining complaint, as Penny again tried to pull the covers from her aunt and cuddle beneath there shielding warmth.

"Just come on, I will explain everything on the way." Jordan urged as she pulled the covers from around her niece again. The game of tug-a-war was beginning to grate on Jordan's patience.

"Where's mama?" Penny wined.

"She's around. Just come on Penny!" Jordan screeched. Penny pulled away from her and crawled to the wall. Jordan could see the years of abuse color her face with fear again. Fear that she had never wanted to be responsible for. Without another word Jordan spun around and left the room.

CHAPTER 16

If the visit to her old home place had taught Jordan anything it was that she could no longer deny what she was. She had to embrace her calling. It was her destiny to rid the world of the scum that threatened to destroy; the very men that would take from the women of the world, reducing them to nothing. Why should she deny it anymore? It was apart of her instincts. It was ingrained in who she was, what she did, and quite frankly what she was good at. She was a killer and she was going to embrace it. The only thing that separated her from a regular serial-killer was the people that she loved. That was no longer a problem. Penny and Erica had both abandoned any idea that having Jordan in their lives was a positive thing . . . and how could she blame them really? The scene that unraveled at her old home place had not exactly been the most desirable of situations. How could she trust herself to be around the people that she loved? She at least owed it to them as well as herself to keep her distance, at least until the anger that bled into all that she touched was satiated.

It seemed to Jordan her path was set. No longer having to worry about keeping her anger at bay, she could truly diminish the masses of unwanted garbage plaguing the face of society. Before she had been bound by an oath to keep those that she loved safe, to ensure a better future for them. Now she would only have herself to be accountable for. She knew that her mission was important, and she would still be clearing the way for future generations; making a better world for them to raise their families without the threat of oppression, but now she would be unbound, free to move swiftly without being responsible for the wellbeing of others. What would the organization think? Where would she go? She had always put one foot in front of the other with only two things in mind, the best interest of those she loved, and her revenge on men for the oppression they had inflicted on all women. Jordan had no idea what she would become. No longer having the people that she loved to be her center, and not having the stability that the organization provided her with; was an unsettling thought at best and terrifying at worst.

The organization made her stable, but Jordan truly had no other choice. All of its members had to follow the rules. The rules were not to be broken ever. If at anytime they were broken, the member that had done so would be eradicated from the organization. It was the one fear that each member held in the back of their mind. The fear of not only being erased from the organization, but that all you were would be obliterated. In short you were pulled to the side and the ugly truth was explained; the organization could make it look as though you never existed. They were willing to keep destroying people a member was associated with until there was no one left to ask questions. Jordan had witnessed the company eradicate whole families in order to reach the desired outcome . . . to make it appear that the individual never existed.

There had been only a couple of rogue agents that had tested rule breaking. One was not only eradicated from the program, but had been assassinated. There was talk of his death, but the team leaders swore to having no knowledge about the cause of death. Jordan knew there was no truth in their claims. Black heart Revenge was always there, always around the corner, under the surface, manipulating the outcome of every situation . . . and always knew exactly where their members were. Jordan knew her time grew short, each rule broken brought her closer to the end. No longer did she care to be a member, she was only being fueled by revenge now. She did not care if she had to die. She only cared that she took as many disgusting men with her as she could when she went. Each man that paid for his sins at her hands brought a smile to her face. Each name another notch on the list of people that Jordan felt owed her in some way. After all, she had to do what she was good at. If the CIA wanted to call her a loose cannon and refuse to fund her anymore she would step out on her own. Who needs them she thought as she ran through the woods toward the road.

Jordan had never taken a penny off of the men she had murdered before. It had been beneath her. She was killing with a purpose . . . she had a cause. The lives of the women they had so profoundly affected demanded retribution that someone stand up and take action. She had to. But now she would have to change her rules and strategies a bit. Erica's response had taught Jordan women did not care about there circumstance as much as she had believed. Why if given another way would they not take it? Even Penny who had always seemed to be one step from following Jordan out the door when she left would not go. Why did they choose to rot in the same awful muck that had always been? They were choosing to remain in a house that held nothing but hate and anger for generations. They were choosing wrong, but it was their choice.

Jordan had planned it out so carefully. She would kill her brother and free her sister-in-law and niece, then they would watch the old den of dead-dreams burn to the ground, finally they would leave it all behind . . . Jordan would teach them the art of self defense. Jordan laughed sadistically as she played her story book version of bliss over and over in her mind. Had she lost what was left of her mind? Had she really believed in it all that blindly? It was truly humorous.

Well no more, for now on the world would be staring down the barrel of a different Jordan, no more would she hold back. Each time she killed, careful to not get caught. Let the world know it was her. Jordan couldn't care less. At least then there would be a woman in the media with an actual backbone. She would continue doing what she had been good at with one change . . . conscience, be damned. Nothing would stand in the way of her cause. Who or whatever stood in the way would equally suffer her wrath.

Jordan continued on her pace through the dark woods as she mapped out the logistics of her new operation. Gone was the girl that had been changed by an alley way and the CIA, in her place stood a black heart's revenge in its truest form. She would do whatever it took to survive. Take the money off the corpses of her victims, steal their cars and burn them when she had made it to her next prospective victim. If the government wanted to see a loose cannon she could deliver the goods without an effort.

On the outskirts of town, not two miles from the city limit sign a heap that could be found under a rock; fittingly delved "The Pit"; set in the base of a mountain. A florescent sign blinking a tacky shade of pink, boasted that the place was open. Trucks and cars of every make and model littered the parking lot. Jordan shook her head and inwardly laughed as she growled under her breath.

"Well now let's see what will climb out from under this rock." Long since had she shed her usual M.O., of feigning a wrong number, it had proved to be quite frankly a waste of time. While she had time to kill she could think of people that were more deserving . . . so she ducked into the restroom and changed into her usual woman of the evening attire and soon she was sitting at the bar scanning the place for her first victim of Jordan puffed on her cigarette to blend in with the usual crowd of the hole-in-the-wall beer joint. She hated the taste. Jordan had never been one to drink or smoke but she hid the fact well when she was in character.

Jordan scanned the place taking in all of the decor. Red and yellow curtains with white tassels were neatly pulled to either side of the windows. A long piece of clear tape dangled from the roof in each of the four corners, ending in a cylindrical shaped housing where Jordan imagined the rest of the tape substance was being held. Fly carcasses lined the length of all four flytraps. The walls were littered with old photos. Jordan looked at a couple of the photos and soon gathered that the owner of the bar was a fan of football; almost every photo depicted a football team in different phases of success . . . one photo showed the team at the play offs while another had the team at the rose bowl, but all the photos were of the same team. Blood red table cloths stood out in stark comparison to the fake-cheap-white flowers used as decoration. Black-hard plastic bench seats bordered the room at each table ending at a makeshift stage with less than eight feet of space. To the side of the stage stood a pitifully kept karaoke machine. An older man with graying hair and a protruding belly held tight to a microphone and was bellowing his rendition of Don't want to close my eyes, by Arrow Smith . . . Jordan wished inwardly that he would have left the effort to Steven Tyler.

Jordan continued her scrutiny of the small structure. There seemed enough space for a mere forty or fifty people, but was well packed beyond that number. An older woman with a bleach-blond wig sat in the corner of the bar. Her too dark ruby lipstick stood out in stark comparison to that of her pale skin. She puffed on a long cigarette while she played with the hand of her much younger suitor. The epitome of all that Jordan hated, the man sat with his back to the window. His legs were splayed in front of him and neatly crossed as he half concerned himself with the older woman's affectionate caresses. Turning back to the woman, the man allowed a half-hearted smile, and then excused himself from the table. Jordan noted the blue-jeans and wife beater that he wore with obvious distaste for his choice in wardrobe. She turned her attention back to the bar as she watched him approach in the mirror that spread across the wall behind the bar. A wicked smile crossed her lips, collecting herself she lifted her glass of water to her lips and sipped contentedly as if she was not expecting the man's approach.

"So sugar what's your name?" A gruff voice sounded. Jordan turned to the man as she feigned shock. He had clouded blue eyes and streaked gray hair that was not as disheveled as her usual victims. In his right hand he held tight to a beer can that was sloshing all over the bar in the mist of his drunken stagger. Smelling as though he had wore more beer than he had drunk, the man held tightly to the bar while pulling himself with a great deal of effort up onto the barstool sitting next to Jordan.

Jordan fought back the urge to wince her disapproval. She had to keep up the pretense.

"What do you want it to be?" Jordan purred as she turned back to the bar scum. She tossed her hair back and blew the smoke into his face. Then stood to her feet while flicking her cigarette to the floor and stepping on it.

"I don't care what your name is as long as you are in my bed before this night is through darling." The man countered in a slur while he holding on to the bar for support.

"Well then cowboy, what are we still hanging out here for?" Jordan asked as she batted her eyelashes and pulled on the front of his wife beater. It seemed to her they could at least be sporting enough to make it hard to pick them out of a crowd. But at the end of the day the scum seemed to crawl out from under the same old one-size-fits-all rock.

They rounded the corner of the beer joint. The back of the joint nestled lazily in the bottom of the mountain. Jordan thought it was not a bad place to die. Jordan pushed the man against the wall. She then pressed her body against his allowing him to feel all that she was offering. In an effort to feign desire Jordan pulled at the man's shirt.

"Whoa little girl!" the potential victim said with impressed humor playing across his thin alcohol soaked lips. "You in a hurry? You like to take control huh? Okay I can dig it."

"You talk to much, sugar." Jordan growled as she pulled up her dress exposing the sheath at her thigh. The man looking stunned, pulled back from Jordan's advances. During the exaggerated movement he struck his head against the wall.

"Ouch!" He complained. "The name is Jake." He added as he started to move away from Jordan's unwanted advances. Jordan pushed Jake back against the wall of the bar again. With a loud thump Jake splattered against the wall hitting his head again his eyebrows furrowed in agitation.

"Listen sugar . . . I don't know what this is all about, but I'm not into all that . . ." Jake was in the middle of a long unwanted explanation about his idea of how a lady should behave when Jordan hung her head back. She braced herself for the sweet serenity that would accompany the cold steal sinking deep into his flesh. The moment was just as orgasmic as she had imagined it would be. She listened to the gurgled attempts at breathing and could feel his warm blood splatter her face and neck. Slowly she looked into his eyes.

"Jordan, baby, and I would be careful about what you were willing to let in your bed . . . never mind." With her last words she stepped away from him and wiped her blade off on his pants leg as his body melted down the wall to the ground. The feeling that accompanied his death had been overwhelming. It had even over shadowed the fact that she had only managed to collect thirty dollars off of his worthless body.

". . . You wont be accepting any candidates in your bed . . . . In the near future." Jordan looked around as she collected all the things of value from his corpse then with ease she cupped her hand around the roof of the old honky-tonk and was on top with little effort.

She crossed the roof then leapt to the ground just in front of the motorcycle her latest victim had driven to his death. Grabbing the handle bars she stood up on the bike then kicked her foot down as the motor roared to life. Soon she was cruising down the highway in search of her next fix.

CHAPTER 17

Lane couldn't believe the path that the Almighty had put him on, but what was more unbelievable than that was that he was remaining strong in his resolve. After praying and fasting Lane could only hear one resounding truth . . . that Jordan was his path to take. He had no idea how either of them could ever improve the other. Even so he could not stop thinking about the way her touch seemed to electrify his blood and the way her lips melted what was left of his nerve.

Lane looked around the bar where the yellow police tape marked the remnants of a crime. One look at the surroundings and he knew without a doubt it was Jordan's handiwork that had closed the place. Lane winced as he looked at the blood that stained the wall and the grass outlined by the white police chalk. All that was left of the man that had been unfortunate enough to make her acquaintance now outlined in chalk and loaded in the back of a Hurst to be examined by the coroner. Though, Lane somehow doubted the investigation would reveal anything more than what was already suspected. The media was alive with images of faces that had fallen prey to a woman . . . and even that was in question. A large question mark covered a photo devoid of a face.

"Who is she?" The news caster exclaimed in a peppy voice. "Anyone with any information that could put an end to the atrocious murder spree should come forward." A number had scrolled across the bottom of the television that morning as Lane waited for the lieutenant to ready himself to leave. It was not unlike a member of The Truth to be assigned a crime scene during a murder investigation that involved a rogue agent from Black Heart. The Truth would simply set one of their own in place as a social worker or preacher that was assigned to help out with profiling, or moral support. What ever the officials needed was the supposed reason for The Truth's involvement; in reality the member was involved merely for information. Any findings that could prove useful to Black Heart would be passed on.

Jordan had driven as far as her thirty dollar loot would carry her. It wasn't far outside of the town where she had killed the man that the high had started to wear off and she was feeling a dip in the emotional roller-coaster she was on. Nothing lasted forever she mused. She felt as though she was soaring when she felt the cold steel of her blade slicing through the flesh of her victims and could see the crimson flow before her. Unfortunately it was a very short lived high and soon she would need more and more to calm the beast inside of her that cried out for more.

Jordan felt so lost. How could she feel that way? She was doing the world a service . . . wasn't she? After all she only killed the scum that destroyed the lives of others. It's not like her victims were chosen only for their gender. No she was specifically choosing the men that fit the profile. Usually sporting a wife beater(a white tank top) and hanging out in places like the pit, looking for another woman to calm their aching loins. Their needs . . . . It sickened her. Men are lowered by nature it's in their nature to conquer as many women as possible before they died. Meanwhile there was an innocent woman and child that not only waited for their next beating, but also the possibility of the scum-bag bringing home a disease that could claim their lives. Some of the scum that she ridded the earth of would even go out and have unprotected sex with trashy women they met in the nastiest hole of a juke joint they could find then come home and force their lust on their own children.

Jordan had to end it. The world was going to hell in a hand basket and she was going to do what she could to turn things around. To protect the children and whatever women that was left that wanted better. All the women in the world could not be like her sister-in-law. There had to be those that were left that wanted more, a justice, a reckoning, or a revenge that would repay them for their trouble. She didn't care all would be welcome. She would teach any woman that wanted to learn and female children for that matter. Knowledge was power, and it was time that the female gender had the upper hand in that arena . . . far too long the deck had been stacked against women. Jordan had her mission and it was the most important thing to not only her but females all over the world; though they may not be aware of its importance right now. At some point the evidence of her sacrifice would manifest itself in a staggering way . . . in a way that no one would be able to deny the outcome. Because Jordan just knew that all of the women of the world would be affected in a positive way by her quest for their freedom; after all every journey had some dips in the highway leading to success, right? And hers would be no different.

Lane turned away from the bar and faced Lieutenant Sanders, as he ran his hand through his hair. With a weak quiver in his voice he finally managed to say
"How long has it been since this happened?"
"Eight and half hours best we can figure. Same M.O. as the others seems to be the same killer; still no leads. Whoever is doing it doesn't seem to have any flaws. I've been in this for twenty two years son and this is the most meticulous killer I've ever seen."
"Or not." Lane mumbled under his breath.
"I'm sorry?" Lieutenant Sanders' face contorted into stark confusion. He was nearing the end of his career . . . this was not the sort of thing that a man like him wanted or needed. The man seemed tired his gray eyes glazed with the over worked shadow that had claimed what was once a vibrant young idealist. Now though Lieutenant Sanders just prayed for quiet so that he could relax. Lane had listened to many of the Lieutenant's stories as he readied himself that morning. Lane felt as though he knew the man. Lane could not blame the Lieutenant . . . he had given twenty two years of his life to the department and God only knew what the man had had to see. Now his last few months on the job were proving to be the hardest. A lesser man would just take an early retirement and let it be someone else's problem. Not Lieutenant Sanders, he was nothing if not thorough and he loved his city. He still managed to somehow believe in its ability to thrive . . . even after all of the things that he had seen. Somewhere inside he still held out hope.

"It's nothing I was just saying I hope you catch the person that did this." Lane said as he inwardly asked forgiveness for the lie. How could he tell the Lieutenant that he knew exactly who this was.

"Thanks I'm sure we will it's only a matter of time before she messes up." Lieutenant Sanders soothed as he patted Lane on his massive shoulder.

"She . . . ? I thought you said you have no leads Lieutenant." Lane's head snapped to attention at the Lieutenant's words.

"No son it is my way of speaking off record of course. It is only my belief."

"May I ask why?" Lane was puzzled by the man's declaration and he did not mind admitting a lot impressed. He looked around again trying to take himself out of the "know" as it were . . . he looked through fresh eyes. He was trying to capture one shred of evidence that might suggest that the killer had been a woman, but other than the fact that Jordan's brother had been killed and the history that lay in the shadow of his death . . . there just hadn't been anything that would tie the two murders in a way that could remotely suggest that not only she was at fault . . . but that the murderer was a woman.

"Well for obvious reasons son, all the victims have been men with no set age range. All the victims are wearing standard issue wife beaters. The only thing about our latest victim is either our killer has broadened her motives for killing or she just doesn't care anymore and any man will do. I've seen it all before son." The Lieutenant was eyeing the area intently while rubbing the back of his neck as a slight confusion traced his features.

"May I be so bold as to ask why the M.O. seems to have changed sir?" Lane's question was more for conversation than anything.

"Of course . . . You see the guy that she killed this time was Larry Jennings . . . sure he's a drunk, but he's never bothered anyone. He keeps up the graveyard grounds and slips in here every now and then for some company. Other than that there's just no reason why a serial killer that's usual M.O. encompasses cheaters and beaters, would . . ." Sanders lifted his hands and let them fall to his sides in frustration. ". . . Would turn this corner . . . I don't know. It just doesn't make sense son. It's scary . . . before I could follow the lead easily. I could look at the map and follow the course that she was on and just about tell by the next local dive and getting the demographic of the establishment who her next victims might be . . ." Lieutenant Sanders stared at the outline only a moment longer and then turned his gray eyes that seemed somehow wiser to Lane, in his direction and continued. "I had hoped that the same line of reasoning would not apply here, but to tell you the truth . . . it looks as though it's the same as always . . . they start out careful then soon the hunger for fresh blood over shadows their desire not to get caught. Pretty soon they leave a spree of dead bodies in their wake . . . no longer are they able to comprehend reality. Nothing will ever be able to satisfy their hunger for fresh blood. Unfortunately, for the victims and the killer I'm a patient man. Thirty Years of marriage to the same beautiful woman has taught me the value of patience." Sanders said and then allowed his features to relax into an easy smile that spoke of the sadness and hope that were mingled up in the same situation.

"That is good sir. I will let you know if I hear anything. I just can't imagine what it will take to stop her." Lane bantered as he feigned ignorance on the subject.

"God . . ." Lieutenant Sanders said as he looked at Lane. "She will stop son don't you worry the Man up stairs will see to it. He has a plan for all of us." All of a sudden in that moment the Lieutenant did not seem so burnt out . . . Lane was a missionary that talked to God everyday, heard His voice . . . and it was taking an old police officer to remind him of his mission. Lane dropped his head and silently asked God to forgive him.

"Thanks, I really needed to hear that." Lane allowed a weak smile to play across his features.

"No problem son." Lane smiled at the Lieutenant's final words and started to walk off.

"Hey."

"Yeah?" Lane asked in response to the Lieutenant's prompting.

"Be careful out there son. Even a good, loyal dog, has been known to turn on its master." Lane shook his head and walked off as he pondered the Lieutenant's meaning. He finally came to the conclusion that, the Lieutenant could see that, Lane knew more than he was letting on.

The Lieutenant watched as Lane rounded the corner of the old bar and shook his head, then looked up at the sky.

"You better be with that one Lord. He's going to need it. This woman he is chasing is full of rage. I'd hate to see one of yours get hurt by one of Satan's."

"All things work for the good for those who are called according to my purpose." The words were almost audible. The words were part of a verse that came from Romans in the bible. Johnny Sanders knew that the Lord dealt with his people where they were at. That is why it is very important that His people keep their minds full of good things. 'Do not plan for evil entertainment'. He told that to his Sunday school class often. He taught teenagers and loved it. Johnny and his wife Jeanie had only been able to have one child . . . Meagan. Jeanie had developed endometriosis, cancer of the lining of the uterus, and had to have a hysterectomy . . . but they had enjoyed raising Meagan and had taken great pride in taking her to church and showing her God's plan for her life. Meagan now taught elementary school and was the youth director at the church she attended. Johnny and Jeanie were the proud grandparents of three boys and one beautiful girl. So in the end God had blessed their home with more children than either of them knew what to do with.

"Amen Lord." Lieutenant Sanders conceded as he took one last look at the crime scene then headed to his police cruiser.

CHAPTER 18

Jordan sat outside the slight beer-joint just outside the small town. Tulsa county three miles she sighed to herself. Jordan had stopped at a gas station and had managed to clean as much of the blood as she could off of her dress. A wonderful shade of Burgundy had made what was left of the blood completely undetectable. She would soon have to find more clothes and a place to get a hot shower and a meal for that matter. She no longer felt comfortable being around other people. The moment she came in contact with another person the beast cried out for their blood; giving reason after reason that the individual did not deserve to be allowed to live. Jordan focused on her surroundings once more and decided first things first . . . she would allow the beast to satiated for the moment then she would find somewhere to get that hot shower and new clothes.

So little time so many useless-waste-of-skins to rid the world of. She was running low on gasoline and her patience was not holding up too well either. She could almost see her blade running through the next man's flesh. She stepped from the bike after unfolding the kickstand. Then stepped out onto the road and crossed over to the honky-tonk where she heard the music blaring through the thin walls. Two women stepped out draped over a drunken man. All three staggered together. Jordan wasn't sure exactly which one was stabilizing the trio. She could see that it would not take much to upset the flimsy balancing act that the three was barely keeping intact. She watched with as much patience as she could muster, and almost started to walk into the beer-joint that had a picture on top with a big-busted woman wearing only skimpy shorts, a tank top that revealed her mid-drift and a gun-holster, that was equipped with two silver-studded six shooters. The lady appeared to be someone that Jordan could have respected if not for the obvious degrading she allowed . . . not only through the shameless attire that she was wearing but also the fact that she was poring drinks for a man. The neon letters read simply 'Holsters'. No doubt it would have a western motif. Where did people come up with this stuff?

Jordan shook her head as she looked back at the trio about to get into the car, and listened to the urge inside her.

"Get into the car. Three for one . . . look at those trashy women. They are part of the problem. It is trash like them that gives the world the right not to take women seriously." As each word pored through her subconscious she became angrier. Soon the desire to see their eyes close in death overwhelmed her senses. It was then that she devised a plan.

"Hey cowboy." Jordan called, as she feigned drunkenness. Each word carefully slurred for authentic effect. "You care to add another goose to that gaggle?" The words almost made her puke. Steady she told herself. Soon the pay off would be worth all the groveling. She sashayed toward the hick and his bimbo waiting for the answer she knew she would get. All men were greedy. They wanted all they had and all they could get. Sure he would let her in on the party. The only problem was the trash on either side of him. Were they drunk enough to care? Maybe they were sisters or friends that just liked to play sexual games. The thought repulsed Jordan. How could women lower themselves to such a degree? Some might look at her as trash she guessed, but at least she knew what she wanted. At least, she thought for her self . . . walked through life with her head held high. Maybe she had a few skeletons in her closet, but most of those were obtained in an attempt to rid the world of crap like the three drunken pieces of garbage standing before her.

"Oh, hey little darling. You know you can join. I love a full hen house. Climb in." The guy threw her a intoxicated wink, and tipped his hat. Jordan looked at him a moment longer as she took in his goatee and mustache. He had on the usual wife beater that seemed to bring the rage within her to life.

"Kill him . . ." The beast within demanded. She trailed on down to his blue jeans that snaked down long legs and ended on top of snake-skin boots. The right pocket of his jeans bulged with his wallet, while the left held the imprint of his dip; which explained the dark grotesque tar stains that covered his teeth, and the protruding red-darkened gums, that usually accompanied years of dipping tobacco. Jordan mused. How far would she have to go to get him where she wanted him? She didn't know, but surely the stakes would be higher with his companions in the way. Of course, they would be at the business end of her blade too, but until it all played out she knew she was in uncharted territory. She had never killed a female before.

Jordan felt utter rage for the opposite sex. There had never been a second thought given to any of her kills, not since the man in the alley. Her training had changed her perspective. No longer did she look at it as murder. Now it was simply a service being rendered to the women of the world. How would she feel about killing the two women on the man's arm in front of her? Sure the same voice that cried out for vengeance against the men of the world seemed to be thirsty for their blood, but where did the beast end and she begin? Would she be able to live with their death? What if society had some how changed them? What if she killed them and then she read that they were innocent? They could be school teachers or mothers out for a good time. Women lived in oppression enough without Jordan adding to it. Now she was the judge and jury for all mankind? Who did she think she was?

"Kill them!" The voice hissed through her mind. Jordan grabbed her head with her hands and started shaking it from side to side.

"No! Go away!" Jordan growled to the unrelenting urging of the beast.

"Looks like she has had more than any of us Earl." The blond to his left said through a deep southern draw. Jordan looked up at her. The woman stood swaying against the man she called Earl. Yet again Jordan couldn't figure out who was the stabilizer among the three of them. The woman had big hair that stood way up on her head. She had blue eyes and fire engine red lips, she wore a tank top and skin tight blue jeans. She mauled the gum that was in her mouth. Popping bubbles and smacking out each word.

"Come on Lilly. I ain't holding up nobody's head while they throw up." The other woman said. She had an equal amount of gum that was equally mauled in her mouth. Her shoulder length brown hair, swept to one side. A bit on the chubby side, with a beautiful face adorned with too much make-up. Large loop earrings protruded from her ears, and matched the gold necklace that dipped low on her neck ending almost at the same scandal-less point as her low riding blouse.

"Oh, come on girls. The more the merrier." Earl ground out then spit a long stream of tobacco out in front of him.

"Yeah the more the merrier." Jordan purred as she started toward the three. Her mind was set as she reached them she walked up to the brunette who she knew would be a bit insecure because of her weight. Even though Jordan noticed that the brunette was the more attractive of the two women. Her hair had a mild wave that gave somewhat of a whimsical quality to her features. She wore blue-jeans that were just as tight as the blonde's. Her blouse dipped low enough to reveal ample breasts. Something about the woman did not register as the type that would normally keep company with the blond and Earl . . . Jordan could not shake the feeling but the voice's ceaseless demand that she spill her blood as well continued.

"So what do you say, beautiful? One more gonna be a problem?" She asked as she moved her index finger along the edge of the brunette's jaw line. Immediately the woman's features came to life.

"No not at all." She drawled. "Maybe just what the doctor ordered." The woman stared into Jordan's eyes. Her face was lit with booze and flattery for the compliment that she had received.

"Or the mortician . . ." Jordan said under her breath as she circled around behind the trio.

"What was that?" The blonde asked suspiciously.

"I said you ready?" Jordan lied as she sidled up next to the blonde. Slowly she rounded in front of them and traced her hand down the length of the blonde's arm.

"You work out?"

"A little . . ." She said with a nervous smile. Jordan could see that the ice princess was warming up to her advances as well.

"Both of you are stunning. Let me show you exactly what I think of you." Careful not to pay too much attention to Earl, she knew that she had him at hello. The trick was to convince the two dingbats on his arm that she was all about them. After a few more, well placed compliments the trio soon became a quartet.

Jordan opened the door up for each of the women and gave the drunken fool a light peck on the cheek as she climbed into the backseat. She had no intentions of having her back to anyone. So she used the opportunity to seem like she was being chivalrous to position herself perfectly, in the backseat on the driver's side, that way she had total access to each person in the vehicle. She made quick inventory, then sidled up next to her first unsuspecting victim.

"So what's a beautiful woman such as you doing in a hole in the wall like the Holster?" Jordan asked slightly using the most common place rehearsed compliment in her vocabulary. The attractive brunette batted her green eyes and flashed a big smile through her chocolate lip stick.

"Its all there is in this town. You should know that honey. The whole town is a hole in the wall." The woman was chattering uncontrollably about the town and how boring it had been.

Jordan barely heard a word that came out of the woman's mouth. The beast with in her roared out "What are you waiting on, a written invitation? Do it!" She could feel her own pulse quicken as she watched the life's blood beat against the arteries in the woman's neck. She licked her lips and then caressed the handle of her blade.

Jordan placed a hand over the woman's mouth. Her eyes seemed as though they would bug out of her head. The brunette started to flail against Jordan's unwanted advances, but was no match for Jordan's training and powerful grip. Not losing her grip of the woman's mouth, Jordan feigned passion sounds as she straddled the woman.

Jordan looked into her eyes and whispered "Shhhh." Then in one fluid motion she slid the blade across her throat. Jordan waited as the woman's body stopped convulsing the last throes of death. She moved back to her seat, and then laid the woman's limp form against the car door.

"She's out." Jordan announced to the other occupants of the car drawing deliberate attention to her. "Maybe you can give me what I want." She said as she pushed her hair back and patted the seat next to her.

"You girls starting without me?" Earl asked as he peered in the rear-view mirror. "Hey I wanna play too ladies." Earl gave a short laugh and then an approving shake of his head at the idea of women being together in his presence.

"Oh, hush and drive Earl. I'm just gett'n them warmed up for you." Jordan eyed Earl's reflection in the mirror as she winked to him as if they shared a private joke.

"Wooeee, girl you ain't like no other girl I ever saw."

"No Earl I don't guess I am." Jordan said as she shoved the blade through the seat into his back. The gurgling sounds of the two of them dying filled the air.

"Why?" Earl gasped.

"Because . . . I ain't like any girl you ever seen before. Remember Earl? Didn't want to disappoint you . . ." Jordan said with a mocking cadence as she emphasized the word "ain't" for Earl's benefit; she pulled her blade out of the back of the car seat and then sliced it across his throat.

Jordan couldn't have planned it all better herself. Earl had pulled over to the side of the road shortly after the blonde climbed over the seat. Jordan wasted no time taking her out. She had no intentions of touching either of the women in a sexual manner. Killing them was one thing, they deserved it, the two of them couldn't have asked for their fate more, if they had come right out and told Jordan to kill them.

Jordan pushed her door open and walked up to the front seat. She pulled Earl's lifeless body out of the car and then with a struggle she was able to free his wallet from his back pocket. She opened the other car door and gathered everything of value. Then opened the gas tank and pushed a long piece of material down until it reached the liquid inside like a wick. She pulled a lighter from her bra and caught the material she had ripped from the seat covers, chosen because of the stiffness, it would move freely into the tank. Jordan knew from her father and brother's side business as mechanics that the older vehicles did not have the screen used to block the tank; keeping it from being siphoned like that of the new cars.

She moved quickly into the woods for their shelter and waited until the vehicle was roaring with flames. Whoosh, it lit and then at once the vehicle was being tossed into the air like a rag doll. She stood frozen to the spot. She could see the occupants inside were being ravaged by the flames. Jordan thought soon there would be nothing left of the trashy trio.

CHAPTER 19

The wind whispered through the trees. All around the sounds of crickets and other night life sang to life as they issued their warnings... Lane was well aware of the relevance of that threat. He had been at the business end of some of the earth's most frightening creatures and lived to tell the story... creatures that made an easy meal of a man.

The darkness was almost tangible under the forest cover. The moon's effervescent glow unable to penetrate the thick roof that the tree tops lent to the forest floor, giving an eerie, other worldly effect to the surrounding area. The feeling took Lane back to another time. A time when he was miles from civilization, in a land over seas, where he watched his parents bring the word to the people of the Cadotion tribe.

The land had been beautiful, but the nights were trying. More times than not the Cadotion people had fallen ill to various germs that the vermin population carried. Some of the illnesses were curable while others left countless dead, such as malaria. Lane's parents had never faltered in any event. He stood by as a child taking in all of the efforts made by his parents to teach the Cadotion people how to better care for their supplies such as water, and food... but also attempted to carry the word to the tribe. It was their mission to bring the gospel of Jesus Christ to the people across the seas.

"Otherwise some may never know of Christ's love..." Lane's mother's words rang out in his mind. "It is up to us to bring these people to the Lord. That is 'the great commission.'" She would always remind Lane of the importance of the mission.

Lane's mother had been a beautiful and tender woman, gentle with all that she had come in contact with. The memory of both his mother and father often left Lane anticipating the time when he too would be in the arms of the Father. Forever, to live in the light of not only his parents but of the very One that had created all things. The thought was more than he could put words to . . . but in the end that was the mission . . . to find not only words but the perfect words that would successfully convey "the great commission", John 3:16, For God so loved the world that he gave his only Son that whosoever believed. Would not perish but have everlasting life . . . So "the Great Commission"(Matthew 28:16-20), was in short, to tell the world of that great love.

Lane's feet pounded the earth. He had to find Jordan before the police did. He could feel desperation mount with every one of his heart beats. Surely he had lost his mind, after all the person he sought to protect seemed to kill with the fervor of a hungry lioness protecting her young. Of course she needed to be caught. The last thing she needed was protection from him. So why did he now find himself hopelessly trailing after her. It seemed he had abandoned all logic. How long would it be till the police caught up to her, and if they did what of him? Surely there would be consequences to his actions. He was breaking a law. He had to be. Aiding and abetting, or messing with an ongoing police investigation, surely there was something that could be done to him for his actions. He just could not seem to focus. He just had to find her. It was more than following the call of the Father. The desire to keep her safe . . . was a mission of its own.

The intensity grew within him, alive with need. He could think of nothing but how desperately he needed to protect her. The whole concept seemed foreign to him. In the logical portion of his thinking the part of him not cramped with the web that her beauty seemed to entangle him in, he could see how irrational it all was. It couldn't be more insane if he were trying to offer solace to a tarantula that was stalking a fly. Yet he could think of nothing he wanted more than to have Jordan safe in his arms.

Lane could sense he was not far from catching up with Jordan. He was no more than a few miles behind judging by the skeletal remains of the old car that was still smoldering from her usual M.O . . . Kill now, burn later. That thought lingered in the recesses of his mind as he became completely engulfed in the "burn later".

Lane knew he had to end all of this. Somehow, someway he would have to stop Jordan's killing. Either she would have to come to know the Master and allow His love to bring about the change in her life she so desperately needed . . . or she would have to meet with the cold steel of his own weapon. Lane in no way relished the thought of having to end Jordan's wrathful state by bringing about her death and sending her soul to live in torment with Satan, but he knew the Master had been specific.

It was not Lane's choice, he was simply a vessel. He had one chance to prove to Jordan that all men were not haters of women. If he was unsuccessful he would be forced to stop the needless killing of God's children.

"Please God allow your servant to do your will." Lane murmured as he stood listening to sounds on the wind. He could feel his honed senses prickle as he felt eyes graze his skin from above.

CHAPTER 20

Jordan felt Lane's presence as she did before but, unlike before the desire to be away from him was overpowered by the desire to be near him. She knew it was the same low burn within her that always became a raging inferno. The hissing voice screamed out for Lane's blood to be spilled. More than that though, this time the desire was more than before. The voice was insistent, angry, and even needful.

"Kill him!" It screamed through her mind. Then some where inside of her psyche, she became the victim again as the beast within locked her away in a forgotten chamber of her mind. No longer, was it standing on the sidelines, waiting at every opportunity that Jordan would afford it to kill; it now had a foothold and was gaining ground all the time.

Jordan was no longer there. Now the beast within seemed to wear a Jordan skin suit, as she remained locked away. It using all of her skills and stealthy-grace, swung up into a tree. It stood crouched like a mountain lion waiting to pounce on its prey. Now, Jordan's body, with the demon monster inside, had Jordan on auto pilot, darting her eyes from one side to the other with a glass, dim lit animalistic glow, filtering from their green haze. The beast listened and waited patiently for the perfect opportunity to strike.

Jordan did not exist in this moment, though she could taste the honeysuckle on the air, and hear the crickets screaming their disapproval, of the invasion of their homes, and see the tangible midnight blanket that fell around the forest. She was being held captive in her own mind, a prisoner of war encapsulated in her own body; she could do nothing more that watch and wait. Peering out from her own eyes, as if they were window panes of a familiar old house; helpless to stop what she knew the beast meant to do to Lane.

Jordan screamed, a soul wrenching cry, from inside the unyielding walls of her own mind, but some how knew the sound did not make it outside of her mouth much-less to Lane's ears. She wanted desperately to warn him of his fate. She had held hands with this beast for far too long, and now she and Lane both, would pay with their lives. She knew what it would take to satisfy it. But, never had she seen the beast within so determined to feel and see the life blood drain from anyone as it did Lane.

Hate pulsed through each of Jordan's heart beats, like the distant drums of a tribal war dance. She felt helpless, locked inside of her own mind. She screamed to take control, for the beast to loosen its grip on her senses. Freedom was not hers, now she too was its unwitting victim, along for the ride. She had no other recourse, but to sit idly by, as she watched through the 'windows of her soul', as people commonly referred to the eyes, as the beast ripped her only companion, her only friend, the only person that had ever shown her even the slightest bit of human kindness, to shreds.

Anguish bit down into her tortured mind threatening to extinguish her very life's breath, and oh, how she prayed for it to be so . . . that in that very moment it could be possible that she would cease to exist, and that she would somehow be spared the horror of watching her only love fall prey to the beast.

* * *

Lane could feel Jordan, but something wasn't right. He felt something he was not used to feeling, when he was chasing her in the past. Danger, fear or what was it? He couldn't quite understand his apprehension, but he knew something begged him not to make another step. He could feel a constant nudge of disapproval . . . urging him to not continue in the present direction.

The calm, still voice, within him, was like a breath. Like a soothing part that was always with him, but this time it seemed more insistent. Lane recognized the voice. It was the master.

"Don't go." The wonderful blissful voice grew within him, and started to change. It became more insistent, burning with more intensity than anything he had ever felt before. It was gnawing at him, demanding, fierce . . . but he had to find her. He had to get to her. The detective on the scene was smart; he would waste no time catching up with Jordan. He had years of training under his belt. Lane could sense the man's determination, to solve the case, and he knew that his own time to find Jordan was running short.

* * *

The beast crouched on the branch. Reigning in all of its senses, and Jordan's too. Waiting as it watched, intently from above. Each step that Lane made, the beast could feel the rage for blood intensify. It was keeping a grip on Jordan, while it watched for the exact moment to launch its attack on Lane. It would have been no easy task for one of the lower level demons. But, for hate it was simple. Hate grew in its host each time the host acted in an unforgiving way. Hate's evil tendrils would grow and ebb further around its host claiming all that was left of the host's humanity. Until finally it became the host. Jordan's streak, of unforgiving acts of revenge, had managed to solidify hate as a formidable enemy; not only to Jordan, but to the only man she ever loved or trusted.

Now, here in the blackness of the inky night, that was so substantial it almost seemed to be concrete, her body acting as her tomb, she would crouch helplessly inside, and have to witness 'Hate' destroy the love of her life.

"Jordan I know you're afraid and I can feel that whatever . . ." Lane waved one hand around in the air for emphasis, and then continued. ". . . this thing is . . . that has control of you right now, it is strong. Maybe to you it feels . . . too strong to fight." Lane paused, praying silently to the Creator of all things for wisdom and strength. Lane knew he would need more than any strength he possessed if he hoped to conquer the beast, that held Jordan at bay, and threatened his life, and her very soul. "Concentrate on my voice Jordan; I know you have been hurt. I know that you have been disregarded but this is not the answer. Hate . . ." Lane paused again, yes that's it . . . and then, he quietly thanked God his Master again for the answer. Lane, allowed the realization, like a slow dawning, to creep into his senses, and the overwhelming truth, to claim every part of his reality, because there was no denying, how much strength he would need. Lane closed his eyes, and called upon his two old friends to join in the battle. Love and Mercy, then with every fiber of his being he called upon his faith in God, and stood still.

"Jordan I know you are there and I know you are angry. I know that you have done many horrible things that you can't seem to find your way back from, but God loves you . . ."

At that moment, before Lane could utter another word, the creature sprang to life as it landed on Lane's shoulders, dangling Jordan's legs around Lane's neck, as both hands had a firm grip on Lane's head. The creature had to silence Lane. It could not stand in the presence of the word. It had to take the upper-hand in the only way that it knew how . . . blood shed. Because, it knew that in the presence of the truth, it could not stand. It would lose ground fast.

Lane was not surprised; he was walking in the Creator's wisdom. Every move the creature made was only matched with an easy counter move by Lane.

In an age-old-dance, of good verses evil, Jordan's hate filled body, and Lane's body filled with love and mercy coming straight from the throne of God, moved like shadows on a dimly lit wall. Blow after blow, Hate could not get the upper hand; it was no match for the love and mercy that the creator was infusing Lane with.

Finally, in an act of desperation the demon cried out in Jordan's voice trying to distract Lane. And, at that moment, Lane took his spiritual eyes off of the creator, and let his guard down. Hate lunged at the opportunity, as it stabbed Jordan's six inch blade just inches from Lane's heart.

Lane's eyes went wide, as the pain skidded from the point of impact like a sunburst. Jordan's eyes glowed a fiery dark red, as Hate hissed laughter in its venomous tone. Her head fell back, as the demon savored the feel of its foe dying.

"Where's your creator now angel?" Hate taunted Lane.

Lane's visage was one of astonishment. He was perplexed by what the demon was talking about . . . sure he had felt different all of his life, and he had an amazing connection to God, but an angel? That was absurd, right?

Lane thought back to his mother and father, as he tried desperately to remember anything that his parents had told him. Lane knew that he was adopted; his mother had died in childbirth . . . that had been no secret. He had asked his adopted mother on many occasions, what had made his mother die, but in the end she had only told him there were difficulties, and it sometimes happened that a mother or child and sometimes both could die during childbirth. Lane couldn't recall anything that would indicate his mother knowing that he was anything other than a human child.

"Hope? Pshh" the demon hissed. "You think a demon, as powerful as I am, can't recognize any entity that comes from your Master!" The demon spat the last words as if they burned coming off its tongue.

Lane tried to ignore the demon; the pain moved through his body . . . he cried out to God for protection. Lane fell to one knee and bowed his head.

"That's right, pray to me your new master." Hate hissed as it stalked from side to side, making Jordan have the appearance of a sumo-wrestler, about to attack. Lane's eyes shot up at that moment, as power radiated white from all his pores, and his eyes.

"Silence, demon, in the name of Jesus Christ of Nazareth I command thee, you will leave this child now!" Authority resonated from every syllable of Lane's command.

The demon screamed out in anguish as it distorted Jordan's face. Finally, with one last attempt at taking the upper hand, Hate used Jordan's voice again.

"No, Lane, your killing me!" The demon tried to use all of its power, to play on Lane's sympathy again. Lane held up his hand, as more power roared from the throne of God, in a drowning thunder a voice like many waters spoke through Lane.

"Hate, I command thee to be quiet and to leave this child. NOW!" The voice spoke with such authority that it could be none other than the Creator of the Universe.

At that moment, Jordan crumpled to the ground in a limp pile. Lane sank beside her, as his body tried desperately to recover from the amazing power, which had surged through his veins.

Lane could feel his mind, as it seemed to spiral in a tunnel, which soared through a long distance, and then all at once there was light. In that light, was hope and mercy . . . he could feel them so strong, as they pulled him along . . . further and further, as he rose toward singing and warmth. Finally, he was there . . . he was in the place that he was going. In his being, there was a sudden knowing . . . a realization . . . He felt at one with all things. He was astonished, by the beauty of the place, he was standing. He knew that he was standing in heaven, but more than anything he was amazed at the two entities standing before him. He never knew what they looked like, but he would recognize his old friends anywhere . . . Love and Mercy . . . and here they were in angelic form. Beautiful, magnificent angelic beings, stood before Lane, as they smiled at him; Comfort and joy, filled him completely. Both beings were bathed in a glorious light that encompassed them from head to foot. Flowing robes, a blue that Lane had never seen or could even imagine stood out in stark comparison to the effervescent glow of white light that filled the space around them. Lane looked on in astonishment as he continued to take in beauty like he had never before known; no place but heaven could have been the keeper of such elation, hope, and boundless perfection . . . he had made it. Lane was home.

CHAPTER 21

Jordan pushed her aching body from the leaf-litter of the forest floor. Slowly, the scene that had played out moments before breathed across the canvas of her soul.

"Lane?" The name slipped through her lips, with equal parts desperation and love. Love . . . ? She caressed the word with her mind, holding it, allowing it to cool the fires, of the aftermath, that hate's destruction had stretched out across her core. It felt good . . . to feel. She could feel love's soothing medicine pouring out on the deepest wounds of her past. Like a balm or salve, love erased the festering emptiness that had for so long been filled with a toxic demon spawned from her own un-forgiveness and hate. A demon that was fueling fires of strife and discord throughout her soul.

Gradually, Jordan allowed her mind to open up to the carnage that hate had left behind . . . each time, digging its poison talons deeper into her twisted psyche. Refusing, even the slightest attempt Lane had made at showing her affection. But now . . . in the mist of the darkest day of her life . . . she could feel a newness making its way through her. Pricking, at the darkened canvas of her soul, were a million points of light ushering her away from the past.

As Jordan, stood admiring this new feeling she became aware of something beyond the warmth making its way through her . . . bit by bit, she took in the form lying a few feet from her, and again she allowed his name to slip past her lips, only this time it became a tortured cry. "Lane?!" Jordan gently, pulled at the long strands of hair that were matted to his face with sweat and blood. And, suddenly, a fear like nothing she had ever known, more powerful even, than what she had felt as a small child hiding in her closet, waiting for her father's tirade to cease. This fear was born of loss; a loss that even as she knelt down beside his unmoving body, Jordan could feel its fingers taking hold, erasing the hope behind its murky shadows.

Jordan knelt there, caressing his muscular chest, as her eyes pooled with unshed tears; she felt her fingers begin to tremble. Tenderly, she lowered her head to his chest then with the meekness of a child she stretched her body out beside his. She had nowhere to go. The demon inside her was gone. Lane's Creator had made sure of that, and without its insistent lust for blood shed, she did not have a clue where she would go from here.

She lay there holding on to the only being, that had ever cared for her, as if he were her life raft. She couldn't go back. No, not after all she had encountered through Lane's love. He had cared for her. He followed her into places that no being, especially a being of light should ever have to witness.

But why? Why would he come? Why did he care for her? What had Lane said? That the Creator loved her? Even more than Lane had loved her? Jordan was astonished at the thought. Even in her darkest hour she felt sheltered and safe in Lane's presence. So how could this Creator, of Lane's have a love, even more powerful than what she had felt radiating from Lane?

Slowly, hope wrestled its way around the shadows, cast by fear, as Jordan came to her knees.

"Creator, um Lane's creator, are you there?" Jordan's voice was thick with unshed tears, and she could not imagine how anyone could understand her. She cleared her throat and was about to make her voice more clear, but suddenly, she felt an overwhelming desire; to be still.

"Jordan, I give to you a new name . . ." A gentle voice, caressed across her soul; in it Jordan could sense a mountain of love and wisdom. But, Jordan could not be sure where the voice had originated from, and she had only just begun to understand trust, and even that was limited. She was still uncertain that this creator, of Lane's was real, or some dreamed up, figment, of his imagination.

Jordan turned around and grabbed for her weapon, as she crouched over Lane's unmoving form, preparing to protect his body if that's all she would have left of him. She would bury him and somehow find her way back from the drowning remorse that threatened to cut off her very breath.

"My child . . ." The voice came again. Though, it seemed to be everywhere, and nowhere at the same time.

"Who's there?" Jordan's voice trembled. Never had she felt fear in the face of a foe, seen or unseen. She would always stand her ground, it made no difference. This was different, though. The voice that she heard now was one of authority, and compassion at the same time. It incited fear born of respect and peace, all at once. She wanted to draw closer to it, to soak it up, to learn of it. She wanted to hide from it, and run to it.

"I am." The voice caressed her desolate soul, like a balm it soothed at the jagged tears caused by the past.

"Are you Lane's Master?" Jordan questioned, as she remained crouched over Lane's body.

"I am the Creator. The Alpha and the Omega . . . I am. I give you a new name. No longer will you be called Jordan. For now ye shall be Faith Charis. For it was through the faith that you learned to have in Lane's love against all odds, that you have come to be healed. Charis is a symbol of womanly beauty, charm and inspiration; this is to remind you of the way that I see you. I love you with a mighty love. You are my child and I am your Master; now, and always." The last words came and Jordan fell on her face as she cried out for forgiveness. She begged for Lane's life. She understood in that moment what her grandmother had meant, as she stood at the end of her husband's death bed, and said that she could not be here without him. Jordan pulled at Lane's body as she cried for God to give her another chance. She begged God not to leave her in this place without him, not to leave her here alone.

CHAPTER 22

Lane stood facing Love and Mercy. He was filled with so much love and understanding. He in that moment knew the whole story. His mother had told him the story in Genesis six about the giants of old being the offspring of angels. He knew in that moment with complete awareness and understanding that his mother's fate and his had been decided at the hands of his father's greed; his father's desire to have his mother. It was not rape. Lane was not born of rage. To the contrary his mother and father had loved each other very much and Lane was a product of that love. It was just that Lane's father had allowed his knowledge of what their union would mean to be clouded by his desire to be with her. to love her. to hold her. In the end it was that greed that had not only cost Lane his mother, but his father as well. Unable to bear the loss of his beloved, Lane's father ended his own life.

Lane's father was not exactly an angel but just as Lane was a direct descendent of the fallen angel's bloodline. His father was Julius Arden, born in 1957 to Jake and Louis Arden. The bloodline could be followed all the way back to some of the legendary giants of old. Julius was an impressive seven foot three. Lane too was of enormous stature, he was six foot nine. All of the history was poring through his mind as the demand to know came, like the desire to know and knowledge lived simultaneously in the same instant.

His mother was Emily Haden, born in 1963 to John and Sarah Haden. She was a short woman of five foot four inches tall, with a grace and beauty that rivaled most of the women in her surrounding neighborhood. She had golden blonde hair that fell to just above her hips and lay in spiral ringlets. Her eyes were the color of a spring sky; just as blue. In them there was a love that spoke of forever . . . she loved the Lord with all of her soul and chased after His teachings with a fervent need.

His mother and father were married and soon after Lane made his entrance into the world . . . but his mother did not survive the birth. Lane was twelve pounds and six ounces at birth and was born breach. His mother hemorrhaged too death soon after his birth. There was nothing that the hospital staff could do to stop the blood shed. They had no way of knowing that Lane's mother's body would be unable to afford the birth. Times were very different. The medical field had not made the leaps and bounds into new advancements at that point, so the knowledge of the medical staff was very limited.

Lane had been promptly placed up for adoption, and The Truth had seen to his affairs. Because of the delicate conditions surrounding his birth, Lane was adopted by members of The Truth. John and Susan Gates, the couple was stationed in the Codotion village at the time and was asked to return to the states to get the paperwork taken care of. The couple had never had children of their own and had accepted Lane with open arms. He was named Tristan Lane Gates. The Gates loved Lane very much and decided that they would explain the story of his birth when he was older, but the two had been killed in a plane crash on the way back to the states, when Lane was a mere twelve years old.

The Truth had sent Anderson to bring Lane back to the states where he had been staying with the Tribes spiritual leader until his parent's return. Anderson was delicate in all the attempts he made at explaining not only that his parents were deceased, but that they in fact were not his parents at all, at least not in the general sense. In the sense that they had given all to care for him, and taught him about God, and imparted all of the wisdom shared between the two of them that could be taught in twelve years of life, they were definitely his parents.

Lane had a strong relationship with God, even at twelve and it was that relationship that had brought him through.

Lane looked to his friends Love and Mercy as a knowing came over him. These were the two that had brought him through every battle. They had given him comfort and stood by his side against many an enemy, but never until this moment had Lane known that they were actually angels. He was amazed by the thought. He had so many things he would of asked the two of them in this moment . . . he laughed at the feeble thought that his human mind would of embraced. He had the answers to every question and there would be no need.

Love and Mercy stepped forward as they took him in their arms and pulled him to them. He could feel the love of all those that had gone on before him and when he pulled back from the embrace he knew why . . . standing there to his astonishment was a cloud of witnesses. All of those that loved him that had served the Lord with all of their might and in the mist of them all stood his precious mother. He knew it was her. He just knew.

Lane's mother stepped forward as she held a translucent hand to his cheek and began to caress his face. The love that he felt coming from her only paled in the light of the Creator's love. In that moment he could only imagine what he might have done had he not already bask in a love that was stronger. He could only imagine that it would be more than his being could hold. He looked into her eyes as he lifted his own glowing limb and placed it to hers. She came to him with ease. This was her son. The one that she had held beneath her heart for so long and could only see him from a distance. She was so proud of him. Lane could feel that too. Like everything else it was a knowing.

"It is not your time." His mother said in a hauntingly beautiful voice. "You must return. She needs you." She smiled and then gestured for him to bend to her kiss. With every ounce of love that she had kept tucked away in the secret chambers of her heart that existed only for God and her son she kissed his cheek and whispered her love . . . but he knew.

CHAPTER 23

Jordan stayed glued to the spot. She held on to Lane's lifeless form as she scanned the area. She could sense that a presence was approaching. She rose to a crouched position and held her trusty blade a few inches from her chest just above Lane's abdomen. She had forced herself to free it from Lane's chest. He was gone, but she would not allow anyone to take him from her. So with all of the strength and courage she could muster she blew out a hard breath and allowed the tears their freedom . . . she pulled the knife from his chest as scream born of loss and desperation slipped through her lips.

"I'm sorry that this has happened to you Jordan, but you know that I can't protect you unless you come with me now." Lieutenant Garrison's voice came through the trees just beyond the perimeter where Lane's body was laying.

"I can't leave him Garrison. This is my fault." Jordan sniffed back the inner turmoil that threatened to drag her down under its extreme weight. "I have to make this right."

"You can . . . come with me. I will turn you in and you can go thru Black Heart's change process. Let this go. You are different now Jordan. I can sense it in you." Lieutenant Garrison moved a little closer but was careful to stay where Jordan could read his intent in body language. Small traces of sunlight were cascading thru the foliage, at the top of the canopy made of the tree tops bending in toward each other. "You have to move on Jordan. The bureau tried to get all of us to accept that there was a higher power, that we were not in control of everything . . . this is why, Jordan. This very moment is why you need to understand that you can not fix everything. It is not your place to rid the world of all the evil that exists in it. There is a delicate balance that only God knows how to keep in check." Again Garrison moved even closer. This time he held out his hand offering it to her.

Jordan looked up at her friend; her co-worker . . . was that what she really thought of him? Where had the days gone that she was able to think of him in that way? How had she lost her way so profoundly? She thought about that. Yes she had lost her way. She had fallen into the same garbage that she was trying desperately to stop. She thought about the way that she had treated her sister-in-law. She would have treated Erica no better than that of her brother to get Penny, her niece, out of that house. When did she become the final say of how everyone lived their lives? She was becoming a tyrant. The word breathed across her soul as she dropped her blade and stood to her full height. Jordan stepped closer to Garrison and then all at once she fell into his arms and began to weep.

"Hold it right there!" The command came from Lieutenant Sanders. He had been following close on Jordan's trail and had found the smoldering remains of the vehicle out near the highway. By his calculations Jordan was on foot and should not be too far into the woods. He investigated the vehicle a little more and with the icy chill of the late fall afternoon the car could not have been out for more than an hour. He crouched down to take in the footprints in the frozen patches of the grass . . . just as he thought. She was on foot and if his instincts were not failing him then she would have stood just beyond the tree cover. She would want to witness the blast. Returning to the scene of a crime was something that most serial killers could not resist.

"I said put your hands in the air where I can see them." Lieutenant Sanders barked out the order again.

"Lieutenant Garrison . . . I'm a Lieutenant in charge of special cases with the government. I have been sent to take in Jordan Buckley. I am going to show you my badge." Garrison gently set Jordan to the side and lifted his hands into the air as he nodded to Jordan to do the same. Then he slowly eased his right hand back to his chest. "I'm just going to get my badge." Garrison looked Sanders in the eyes so that he could read his intentions there. "I have been in charge of an elite force headed up by the government designed to capture rouge agents, like Miss Buckley here." Garrison said as he lifted his badge out from in the inner pocket of his suit jacket and nodded his head in Jordan's direction. "Miss Buckley and I trained under the same instructor on the force, but she did not heed the advice of the bureau to seek spiritual enlightenment. That mistake ended in Miss Buckley going out on her own and resorting to vigilante justice. The academy does not approve. I will turn her in and she will be made to pay for her transgressions." Garrison watched the Lieutenant hoping that any part of his story was resonating well with the guy. He had to get Jordan out of here and back to the bureau where he could protect her.

Lieutenant Sanders looked over the badge and slowly handed the document back to the other officer. Then he lowered his fire arm.

"I'm sorry but this is a Beulah county investigation as well. We are agreed that this little lady needs to be locked up . . . but where . . . seems to be another matter." Sanders smiled at Garrison as he started to loose his handcuffs from around his belt.

Garrison gave Sanders a once over and then nodded his approval. It did not matter which one of them took Jordan in. All that mattered was that the process got started so that Jordan could be put through the judicial system and then her death could be faked so that she could get her surgery and finally be set to straight. Garrison took the handcuffs from Sanders and told Jordan to turn around.

Jordan dropped her head as she started shaking it and apologizing for what she was about to do.

"I'm so sorry, but I can't do this. I don't deserve it. Can't you see? I'm a monster." Jordan side stepped Lieutenant Garrison and moved behind him she swiftly grabbed his gun from its holster and then stepped out away from the two men. "Shoot me or I'll shoot you!" She screeched the command at Lieutenant Sanders. "Stay out of this Garrison." She warned.

"Jordan don't you understand it doesn't have to be this way." Garrison pleaded as he took one step in her direction.

"Stay back." She growled . . . "Don't make me shoot you." Jordan leveled the gun to her own head. "Fine I'll shoot myself." She cocked back the hammer as she leveled Garrison with a malevolent gaze.

* * *

Desperation was not an emotion that Jordan was used to, but since Lane had fell to the ground and not moved; it was fast becoming the only emotion she understood. She looked from Lane's lifeless form back to the two men in front of her. Both were determined to stop her . . . that was evident. Each man had his own idea of how that could become a reality. That too was evident.

Garrison wanted to put her through the organization's idea of rehab . . . that meant losing the one thing that had always stayed the same no matter what—her reflection in the mirror. She didn't have a good explanation for why it meant so much for her to keep the same face in the mirror. Maybe it was because she resembled her mother so much. It was the only time that she felt as though she had not truly become what she saw in the eyes of her victims . . . the eyes of her niece and her sister-in-law. It was when she looked in the mirror that she saw her mother and not Jordan the monster that killed in the name of justice. Was that even true? She couldn't decipher between what was real and what was imagined anymore . . . the lines were becoming hazier all the time.

Then there was Sanders, the small town sheriff that was great at his job and loved his town with all of his being. Jordan could only imagine the axe that that man had to grind. How dare she come into his perfect version of Utopia and bring this kind of unmitigated chaos into their mist. She could only imagine the countless man hours that he alone had put in to insure that not only the community but who ever lived at the Sanders nest would be completely safe—oh no he was not about to turn a blind eye. Jordan was sure that his idea of stopping included either a bullet or an eight by twelve prison cell.

Neither of the men's idea of 'solving the problem' was a desirable solution for Jordan. This could only end one way. She had to be gone . . . really gone. Not the agency's version of gone, but dead.

CHAPTER 24

Lane was stirring as his mind took in all the sounds of the surrounding forest. He could hear the birds singing, and of course the crickets and frogs were still giving their angry warnings. He could also hear some voices a male and . . . he could hear Jordan, but who was she talking to?

Lane sat straight up as he heard the ear splitting sound of gunfire. His heart slammed into his chest as he rubbed his head and then allowed his hand to drift further down his anatomy to where the six inch blade had been in his chest just inches from his heart and his lungs. One direction or the other and . . . Lane allowed the shutter that had been playing over his shoulders and neck to take hold of his entire body. It was then as he was thanking God and thinking about all that had happened to him that he started to remember the strange dream. That's what it was right? It had to be a dream. He wasn't really in a place where his old friends that always helped him in every battle had proved to be . . . angels? And what about his mother and what had she said? That Jordan needed him?

It was at the last thought that Lane began to remember the sound of the gunfire that had tore him from his unconscious state.

"Jordan!" Lane allowed the word to free itself from his lips and then gave himself over to the desperation of the moment. He adjusted his eyes to his surroundings and it was then that he noticed the two male figures standing over the female body. But no it was not just any female body . . . it was Jordan's.

Lane forced himself to his feet and tried not to give into the blackness that threatened to claim him. He could hear the man's voice talking to another voice that was coming from a radio. What was the voice saying? That the examiner was on his way? Why did they need an examiner and what would he be examining? Lane continued slowly toward Jordan's body as the reality of the moment slammed into him like a brick wall. The force of it almost brought him to his knees.

It was Lieutenant Garrison that noticed Lane first. He turned to him and at that moment he was on the radio again ordering an ambulance be dispatched to the area. Something about another victim and a knife wound. Lane stopped listening as he fell to one knee and pulled Jordan's head into his lap.

Lane took in the still features of her beautiful face. The perfect color that he had always thought her complexion to be, her silky dark hair that hung to her waste in soft waves now rapped itself around her waste and mingled in with her arm that was lying in an awkward position. Lane moved her arm to the front of her body by pushing it forward with one hand and then pulling it until it lay just in front of her breasts with the other. He then noticed the loose strands that fell over her eyes . . . her closed unmoving beautiful deep green eyes . . . he pulled the strands free of her face. It was then that he saw the wound on her chest. Just to the right of where her heart lay was the starburst pattern of a blood splatter. How odd . . . he thought. She was so still and she seemed to be so peaceful in this moment. For once she wasn't planning or plotting or running from demons that she would never be able to outrun because they existed inside of her and not on the outside where it would be much easier to draw a line in the sand and do battle. No it was the demons that existed in one's heart that caused them the most anguish not the one's that stood toe to toe and face to face with them.

* * *

Sanders watched intently as Lane cared for Jordan. It was then that it dawned on him that their battle may not be over. Sanders leveled his gun on Lane and waited for any kind of confrontation to ensue. He had underestimated people in the past and had paid dearly for it. His partner had lost his life during a routine traffic stop. At first the stop had seemed normal enough; the car had pulled over to the shoulder of the freeway and cut the engine. Sanders approached the vehicle from the left side, the driver's side. The driver was riffling through her purse to find her identity, but as she did he could hear the passenger yelling profanities at her. Sanders asked the man to watch his tone and please allow the woman to show her license, registration and insurance and then they could be on their way. About the same time Sanders noticed that his partner was pulling his cruiser in behind his own cruiser. Sanders could feel that he was starting to physically relax at the thought of backup, even in an ordinary circumstance where nothing seemed to be amiss it had been drummed into their heads to wait on backup.

Johnson was a young rookie on the force but he showed a lot of potential. Sanders enjoyed working with the kid. At the time Sanders was only twenty five and he had been out of the academy only three years. He had floundered a little after high school not really knowing what course his life would take. It was not until he had witnessed a robbery and had felt out of control because of the circumstances surrounding the event that a friend of his had been enrolling in the academy and asked would he like to join as well.

"Hey man they have two more slots. Not trying to rush you on the decision, but what are you really doing?" His friend had a point and it wasn't long after that he had joined and graduated at the top of his class.

Sanders could still remember that day as Johnson approached the vehicle on the same side, the driver's side. Johnson had told Sanders that he would stand there with the couple while Sanders checked their information. As Sanders started back to his cruiser to call in the information he heard the couple starting to quarrel again. Johnson did what any other police officer given the same circumstance would have done . . . he asked the couple to save the argument for later.

The woman turned to her husband and screamed at him . . . something about how all of this was his fought. The man grabbed the back of her hair and rammed her head into the stirring wheel. At that moment deputy Johnson pulled his revolver and told the man to get out of the vehicle. He was under arrest for assault. The man started stepping from the vehicle slowly in what seemed at the time an effort to comply with Johnson's orders. It would prove later that it had all been a distraction technique. While the gun was trained on the man, the woman opened fire on the deputy. Sanders shouted into the radio to send back up that an officer was down. He called in the license number and it turned out the ideas were fake and the car was stolen. The two had been on a spree of robberies all up and down the coast, but all of that just did not matter. What was done was done and Johnson had paid the ultimate price for the underestimation. The woman had never been the victim. In fact it turned up later after the two suspects were caught that she was not only not the victim but that she was the master mind of the whole operation.

* * *

Lane sat still holding onto Jordan for dear life as he peered up at Lieutenant Sanders. "I'm not going to do anything to you. I know that you did what you had to do. I had a knife in my chest remember? I understand that Jordan gave you no choice." It was then that Lane's lower lip started to quiver and he dropped his head to her head and started to whisper into her hair. "Why?" He cradled her for a long time and then he allowed them to take her as he went with the EMT and paramedic team that was giving him medical attention.

Lane could feel the defeat of it all weighing him down. He felt like a failure. He had allowed his personal feelings to cost Jordan her life . . . just as his father had done with his mother. It was both of their own selfish desires that had dictated their actions. Sure his father had loved his mother. But in the end it had not been enough had it? He had married her and it was his love that had killed her. Come to think about it he too had been apart of his mother's death. Hadn't he?

If only he had listened to the Creator, and kept his no no and his yes yes. Why had he allowed his own personal desires to cloud his judgment? Now Jordan would live in torment and it was his own fault. She had thought she knew hell, but that was only a fading glimpse of what was to come. The place of real torment would cast heavy shadows over the abused existence that Jordan had been forced to suffer. It was always the same. Every person in the past that Lane had witnessed to had always said the same thing . . . almost as if it were in some sinner handbook. "I'm already living in hell. Believe me I won't notice." Satan had lied to them all and Lane could not begin to fathom how to make them see the truth. This life no matter how bad only paled in comparison to the torment that awaited those that did not seek refuge in the light of the Father's love . . . those that did not accept the truth . . . that Jesus Christ was not only the Way, but the only Way.

CHAPTER 25

Garrison could not believe his ears or his eyes for that matter. What had Jordan said that she would rather be dead? Dead . . . he could not imagine what was going through her mind but based on the events that were playing out in front of him he was certain beyond a shadow of a doubt that she was not thinking straight. He had to think, quickly. She had the gun trained on Sanders, and then she turned it on herself.

Time seemed to stand still as Garrison tried desperately to think; it was then that he remembered the gun, that the academy had issued him, as a last ditch effort. It was a special weapon that had been designed by one of their top invention technicians. The chamber was loaded with a capsule that slowed the heart rate until it was undetectable to the examiner's heart monitor. It also lowered the body temperature, by only a few degrees. The body temperature would only drop mere increments at a time, stopping just above that of normal room temperature as not to cause suspicion. Trained personnel may eventually find it disconcerting that the body temperature had not changed . . . if they had had the body in custody for longer than the agency had intended. The pill also had other amazing abilities that would give off the appearance of death . . . but one of it's most considerable abilities was it caused a coagulation of the blood, simply put, it stopped bleeding. It also had chemical properties that worked with the melatonin, produced by the pineal gland, which is responsible for changing the color of the skin. The pill would change the color of the skin to a slight grayish pallor, which is usually depicted in death.

To anyone outside of the bureau, Jordan would appear dead.

Stepping forward, Garrison pulled the gun from the inside pocket of his suit jacket. In an instant he had trained the gun on Jordan and fired. There would be no time to waste. The gun that Jordan held tightly to her own skull was not carrying miracle capsules, but deadly steal that would all but relieve Jordan of her head. Jordan's eyes flew open as the capsule entered her body, and just as quickly she was staggering. Then after a few failed attempts at trying to fight off the mind-numbing effects of the capsule, she crumbled awkwardly to the ground.

Garrison allowed the examiner to perform all of his usual tests, to check for any signs of life and once the examiner was satisfied that she was indeed gone . . . Garrison was allowed to take her body to the academy. Garrison had made it clear that the academy was the only true family that Jordan had ever known and that it was only fitting that they see to her affairs. Sanders and the examiner both agreed and by then Lane was already in the back of the ambulance on his way to the hospital . . . so he was not there to protest. Not that Garrison thought he would. What would Lane do with her body? It was not her dead body that Lane was concerned with. Garrison had come to learn about the organization that Lane was affiliated with, they were invested in something far more important . . . her soul.

Watching Lane plummet headlong into the anguished abyss was not easy, Garrison would have to bide his time. He wanted to let Lane know on the scene that Jordan was not dead, but he could not risk it. It was partly his grief that lent to the authenticity of the moment. Garrison was not at all sure that if Lane knew the truth of the situation . . . especially given his affinity for the truth that he would be believed if he tried to fake his anguish. Unfortunately, Garrison had no choice but allow Lane to plummet head long into the sorrow that was sweeping over him, and he could not throw him even the slightest bit of hope. Later he would have to somehow catch up with the poor guy and explain everything, but unfortunately that would have to wait. Now it was all he could do to sit back and allow the coroner to do his job.

Garrison could feel his heart pounding in his chest . . . as though each beat was a threat to bound from his chest and lay at the feet of the men in front of him. He could only imagine what Jordan's reaction would be to her new environment when she finally came out of her drug induced state. He knew all to well that there would be no escaping his impending date with destiny. He would have to be the one there to walk Jordan through everything. The bureau would insist on it . . . but the reality was he had no intentions of abandoning Jordan. He just was not looking forward to the fight that would ensue when she woke to find out that she was in the one place she had vowed never to go . . . The Garden . . .

* * *

Jordan felt as though she were in some sort of psychological cocoon. Everything in her mind shouted to her limbs to move . . . just move. Still there was nothing. She couldn't even protest when she heard Lane saying that she was gone and how it was his fault that he had failed her. She wanted to tell him that it was his love and insistence to show her the truth, of her situation, to make her open up her spiritual eyes, and take extreme inventory of the monster she had allowed herself to become, it was that determination that had in the end made her want, no crave more. But she could not move.

The two men had stood their talking for a long while and finally Garrison had convinced Sanders to let the investigation, now that it had truly been resolved, fall on the capable shoulders of the bureau. Besides, she had heard him reason, the bureau was the only true family that Jordan had. Jordan wanted to laugh. The agency had taught her to protect herself, that was true and she would even go as far as to say that it was probably that ability that had given her the confidence she needed to no longer walk through her own life, as some sort of outlawed shadow. But family? The idea was almost laughable. The bureau was family, to no one . . . least of all Jordan. No, her family was buried in the Cedar Hill cemetery, just on the outskirts of the neighborhood that she grew up in. Her family was a little girl that looked like her mother, but embodied Jordan's wild spirit. Her family was a tall stranger that strode into her life and righted all that was wrong. And now her family was no longer apart of her life. All of them gone and it was all her fault.

Panic gripped Jordan. She did not want to go with Garrison. She knew that he meant well, that the agency would have a fake funeral, because they had already successfully faked her death, but she had no desire to go with him. She just could not lose anything else to the beast. Already it had cost her so much. The trust of her niece and her sister-in-law, her ability to trust others, it had taken a chance at a new life with Lane, and now it would take all that she had left . . . her uncanny resemblance to her mother. Looking in a mirror, for Jordan was a bitter sweet experience. She loved to see her mother's green eyes and long dark hair. The graceful lines of her face, but on Jordan the image lacked something. Her mother's eyes held a peace . . . something that Jordan had always failed to comprehend. How could her mother look so peaceful; when she lived in a battlefield? The only explanation her mother ever gave, only managed to confuse Jordan even more.

"Love Jordan. God's love." Her mother would say as she lifted her head, slightly and held the end of Jordan's chin, to insure she had her full attention. "Joy always cometh in the morning, baby." She would add and then as always continue on with the task of being at Jordan's father's beck and call.

Jordan missed her mother now more than ever. She longed for her mother's optimistic way of making Jordan feel whole again. No matter the circumstance, her mother had always been strong for her children. She extended that love and comfort to Jr. as well . . . even after he too started to make demands and a few times became violent. Jordan's mother loved them both and Jordan would do anything to be cradled in the comforting warmth of that love now.

Jordan tried to listen, as she let the revere fall to silent, in her mind. She had to know what was going on. She wasn't sure why she was unable to speak, or move, but she was certain it was something one of the white coats (as she called them) back at the bureau, had designed. No doubt, Garrison had shot her with some sort of dart that would alter her, in order to give off the appearance of death. Now she could only bide her time until it wore off, because she knew all to well that whatever the substance, she had coursing through her veins, it was powerful and no amount of struggling, on her part would serve as an antidote.

※ ※ ※

Lane stood, barely able to breathe. He had no choice but to put one foot in front of the other. Life was not life, without doing the will of the Creator. He had accepted his role, a long time ago, and the time that he had just spent in the arms of his mother, and his old friends, Love and Mercy had only proved to solidify his beliefs. He had but one mission in this world, and that was to bring all that he could into the glowing light of the Creator, so that there, they could accept the truth . . . Jesus is the way.

Lane shuffled forward as he allowed the medic to guide him onto the Gurney. He would go to the hospital, so that they could tell him what he already knew . . . he was fast becoming healed of the knife wound that had been inflicted by Jordan, while she was overtaken by the beast. Then, after he was released he would find a quiet place and beg forgiveness for his failures, and then he would allow the peace that always came from God to fill him, because it was only then that he could move forward, in the knowledge that came only from the throne of God, his master, the creator of all.

CHAPTER 26

Sun streaks danced across the room, and fell onto Jordan's face, as she allowed her eyes finally, mercifully, to flutter open. The smell of lilacs and honey suckle, always honey suckle, seemed to be in a serene place, filled her senses. She bolted to a seated position as the horrible truth made its unrelenting way through her, she was in the garden. Instinct brought Jordan's fingers to her face. She half expected to flinch. She didn't know how long she had been asleep. The last cognitive thought she could remember having was of calming herself in the ambulance that was taking her to the bureau. She had allowed her mind to focus on the good times, as few as they were; that she and Lane had shared. Then she could remember she had wanted to protect him so desperately from the lies that were spilling from his innocent lips. The lie that he was to blame for her death; but she couldn't move, she couldn't talk. She could only listen to all that he was saying and though she knew that every word was miles from reality she could only listen. The idea dug a pain filled trench through her mind, as she continued to examine her face and body for differences, which could be detected by touch. None seemed to be detectable. As far as she could tell she still held her mother's features. Calm pored through her nervous system, allowing the edge to be chipped away from the growing stress within her.

Jordan moved slowly, intently, to a seated position as she took in her surroundings. She hated this place. Too many times she had had to bring some poor unsuspecting fool, that had not made the cut on the first or second go around in the field, into this place, and each time it seemed to be the same; each member always left the garden appearing to be different on the inside, but there was more. There was a part of them that seemed to be missing. Maybe it was their identity. That was the only thing that Jordan could imagine it to be. How could a person go their whole life looking in the mirror seeing one face, and then wake up one day and not recognize the image that peered back at them in the mirror? How would she ever be able to come to terms with losing that much of what made her, Jordan? After all, Jordan had been sure that it was that one trait, her mother's image indelibly calling to her from the mirror, which had kept her from becoming all that the beast had desired. Her mother's image permanently painted into the canvas of her face that had called to the places in her very soul that were inherently good.

Jordan walked to the room's edge and there she noticed her image. She allowed her shoulders to slump as she took in the site she made . . . Her mother's voice filled her senses as she continued to stare at her face. She allowed her hand to caress the contours of her jaw. To her satisfaction no changes had been made. She allowed her mother's voice to carry her back in time. She was standing in the kitchen of her old family home, watching her mother work feverishly to satisfy whatever demand Jordan's father had made from his makeshift throne, the recliner that nestled right in front of the floor model television. It was Sunday afternoon and he was watching a football game as usual, demanding his supper. He made no effort to help her mother, not even after he gave up drinking and no longer continued in the nightlife that had claimed the best of her mother's existence, in a sham of a marriage.

"You can't sweat the small things Jordan. You worry too much about things that you can not change. My beautiful daughter, when will you understand that control is all an illusion? The reality is that God is in control. You have to submit to that reality, and then you will truly be happy; but not until." Jordan closed her eyes as her mother's words faded.

Jordan allowed her image to wash over her as she tried desperately to capture one more uttered syllable that her mother had spoken. It was then that she noticed something else. She was no longer wearing her usual gear. She was in a loose fitting gown that was white and made of cotton that was as soft as satin. There was nothing frilly about the fabric. It was very plain, and something else she had no weapons.

The room had nothing but a bed and a white sheet with one simple white cotton cover and a cotton pillow. The room was surrounded by windows that she could tell were bulletproof. The panes of the windows were so thick that they had to be bulletproof. The room seemed to be in the middle of a forest; because there was plant-life all around, except in the room itself . . . the plants were on the outside of the room running the length of the windows. At the top of the room was a type of ventilation system that Jordan imagined to be a way of allowing the smell of the plants to fumigate the room. Jordan reasoned that the allure of the plants was to be some sort of calming affect on the person in the room. Jordan found nothing calming about the room, to her it was a prison; and until she could be proven otherwise she would treat it as such.

Jordan walked the edge of the room allowing her fingers to carefully feel under the window seal for any abnormalities in the walls. She crossed the distance from the window to her bed as she purposefully sat on the edge and allowed her eyes to take in the room searching for hidden cameras. She knew that there had to be some sort of device that would allow surveillance of the room. The facility would have a way of keeping track of the person that inhabited its structure . . . there had to be a way that they could keep track of the prisoner's activities, that would be the only way to know for sure the progress or lack there of, that was being made with the prisoner concerning the tactics used by the bureau. In order to change the unwanted behaviors being exhibited by the individual being held the bureau would have to watch the prisoner very closely.

Jordan tapped into the most basic of her instincts as she allowed all else that bombarded her mind to fall silent. She had to know where the enemy was. She had to determine a way out of her prison. And she had to do the one thing that had been pushing her since before she left the shadows of the leaf-littered floor of the gloomy, forest. She had to tell Lane that it was all a lie. He was not to blame. He had not failed her. In fact it was his love that had brought to life something inside of her that she had believed did not exist, because before meeting Lane and experiencing his pure love she was certain that her heart was dead. She was sure that she was the truest form of what it meant to be a black heart in search of revenge. But now, all that mattered was telling him that she was alive and that no matter what happened to them from that point made no difference, because she was completely in love with him; and that could mean only one thing. Her heart was neither dead or black, in fact it was more alive than she had ever felt it to be. She knew that because as she stood looking in the window of her makeshift prison she hadn't only seen her mother's indelible image peering back at her, for the first time she saw something more . . . she saw the peace that had marked her mother's eyes. The peace that had evaded Jordan for so many years, and had left her desolate and dead; a peace that was now inside, washing over every part of Jordan. She didn't understand it. She just knew that for the first time she understood how her mother could be in the middle of a war-zone and not be in turmoil; because as Jordan stood in the one place on earth that she had never wanted to wake up in, she did not feel fear or loneliness. She did not even feel anger or rage. She felt nothing, but a peace that defied logic . . .

* * *

Garrison stood in the media room watching Jordan as she took in the cell that she had been placed in. He was not looking forward to the confrontation that he was in for upon stepping into the room. He had one thing on Jordan, strength, and that was small solace given Jordan's training.

Garrison and Roberts had been the two agents that had found Jordan in the alley. Garrison was a new recruit at the time. He had only been in the academy for three months, and in all that time he had never seen anyone that had so fiercely encompassed all that it meant to be a, black opps, agent, for 'Black Heart Revenge'.

The site of Jordan in that alley heaving, as she stood over the body of the prisoner that had attacked her, still sent a shiver up Garrison's spine. Jordan seemed to vibrate with anger. Even without the slightest clue what she was doing she had been a force to be reckoned with. Garrison had to make himself follow agent Roberts' orders. He could remember all to well that he wanted to leave, get away from whatever was driving the woman in the alley. He wanted no part of it . . . but in the end he had followed orders and he and Roberts had recruited another invaluable force for the bureau. At least, that was the way that it had seemed at the time. Now though, he was not so certain.

Standing in the wake, that was the destruction Jordan had left behind her, Garrison could not find one good reason not to walk into the cell and end it all. And unfortunately, if Jordan gave him a reason that was exactly what he would do. He would put a bullet between his friend's eyes and continue with his day as if nothing had changed ... because that was the way of the Black Heart organization.

CHAPTER 27

Lane stood up and thanked the nursing staff. He felt sorry for the seasoned nurse that looked a little flustered. The in-route, radio traffic had indicated that Lane had been stabbed just inches from his heart. The staff had set up a trauma room, and waited anticipating the patient's arrival. Now though, the patient was sitting on the trauma room, bed without a scratch on him. The medic could not explain it. Already he had gone over the report three times and he had even questioned the EMT that had accompanied him on the call twice; but nothing made sense. The medic was frantically running his hand through his hair as he methodically called back the vital signs to no one in particular.

Lane patted the guy on the shoulder and offered the only bit of peace that the man would understand, or even identify with.

"Hey it's okay . . ." Lane tried to make eye contact with the poor guy. "I'm a fast healer." The guy just absent mindedly nodded in Lane's direction as he again tried to pull enough evidence together, that would save not only his tarnished reputation, but his license as well. Lane was not worried about the guy, because he knew he would bounce back under normal circumstances, humans always did . . . they were resilient like that; but this was not a normal circumstance. Fortunately, for all concerned, Lane was a messenger of God, and all loose ends would be tied up. God would erase any evidence that had made Lane seem above human. So in the end the members of the medical field that had been involved with his treatment would be protected. Lane smiled at the guy as he watched the Master work yet again. The man blinked and then gave Lane a lighthearted smile that spoke of years of experience in the field.

"Looks like you are doing better." The medic nodded in Lane's direction. "They got you all splinted up, huh?" Lane smiled at the guy as he noted the sling that was on his arm, which had not been there moments earlier.

"Yeah, false alarm . . . turns out nothing was broken. Guess I need to be more careful where I put my feet." Lane laughed lightly and then turned his attention to the nurse that was now cleaning the room and no longer trying to fit the pieces into a puzzle that would never fit.

Lane shook his head slightly and then smiled at the ceiling as he allowed his thoughts to go beyond the ceiling tiles and into the place that he had been only hours earlier, but now seemed a lifetime ago . . . He silently thanked God for not only His wisdom, but His mercy. Everything God did was for His people. Lane had a front row seat to that one all consuming truth, and he would not give it up for anything. It was in the light of that truth that he would be able to move forward and leave behind his failures . . . that he would be able to leave Jordan's memory in the past and walk in the path that God had for him and not look back.

As the last thought caressed his mind and became a soothing balm to his ailing heart, Lane turned toward the door and exited the hospital. He would have to find a hiding place . . . somewhere that he could spend time alone with God and allow His truth to wash over him. Only God could identify with loss. After all He too loved Jordan, she was His child, but more than that. God had done something that would forever seem impossible by the standards of man . . . He had given the most precious thing He had ever created or known, all of eternity had been searched and He had been the only One that was worthy to die for all of the sins of the world, God had sent His only son to die in man's place so that He would never again have to be separated from man. Lane could only imagine the remorse and intense loss God must have felt in doing such a selfless thing, just to have it return void in times like this with Jordan. His precious daughter had denied His only son's sacrifice and had gone to a place of torment that would far exceed anything Jordan or any other human could have imagined in their darkest of nightmares.

* * *

Lane ran through the woods he was heading to the only place he knew of that he could be alone with his Master and not be interrupted, a place that he could meditate and not only talk to God but listen to Him as well. Lane was going home. Not to the cabin in the woods, but Lane was going back to his roots, to the place where he had been raised after his mother died. Lane was going to the 'Truth', the organization that had taken care of Lane and taught him all that he would ever need to know in order to bring Truth to a lost and dying world.

Lane was certain that his mentors would know what to do. He had to go to them because he had to confess his failure to them and allow them to pray with him so that he could move forward. Lane was certain that he would need all the prayer that he could get, because though he was certain that he would find peace in God's presence, he had never felt so far from it in all of his life. There was a gap that stood between him and that peace, a devastating ravine with jagged edges, and he had to find a way to build a bridge that could span the distance, a distance that seemed to go on forever. Because, Lane had never felt so confused, if Jordan was gone and he had so profoundly failed her, then why did he still feel her presence with every beat of his aching heart?

Lane could not rest until he reached The Truth, there he would find all of the answers to all the questions that plagued him, including the most confusing question of all, especially concerning his faith . . . where had Garrison taken Jordan's body? The idea that Lane would entertain such a thought was absurd. Never before had he cared so much about a human's body. Wasn't it the soul that mattered? Of course, that was what he had been taught. That he should do all that was in his power to bring the Truth to all mankind before it was too late. It was his job to bring as many as possible into the light of that truth. So now that Jordan was gone, her time of knowing and accepting had long passed. Finding her body would do her soul no good. That was the truth, Lane knew that, so why would he be so concerned with finding her body? The question nagged at him as he continued on to the Truth. The closer he got to the place that had helped him to become the soldier for Christ that he was the more he found himself wanting to find Jordan, the closer he felt to Jordan.

Lane reasoned that it had to be that the Truth was housed inside of Black Heart Revenge. The Truth was actually one of the many organizations that had been kept on staff by the operators of Black Heart, in order to help the recruits to come to terms with the anger that almost always seemed to cripple them. It took the organization little time to realize that they were over their heads with some of the recruits; certainly Jordan would have fallen into that category.

Of course, there were other religious groups that were based in the confines of Black Heart as well, but none as successful as the Truth. Lane knew that no false god could bring real peace. It made perfect sense to him. The whole idea that a person would create something and then worship it was absurd, it would be like God creating mankind and then worshiping them. At least man did move and breathe, unlike the false gods that humans would erect and then bow down to. How could anything that had been created by His hands ever have more power than He? Idols depended on man for everything, their care and upkeep, anything that an idol needed in order to maintain its condition was shouldered on the capable shoulders of its creator, man. That alone should have raised at least one red flag as to why man should not be worshiping wood and metal, right? But, man had scales over their eyes and it was up to the Truth to bring them face to face with the creator of all so the scales could be wiped away . . . allowing mankind to finally see the absurdity of their ways, and accept The Truth. That God, the God of Jacob and Isaac, the God of Israel, the God of Lane and yes the God of Jordan, of all mankind, was the one true God . . . not some pieced together wood and metal idol that had been erected by man to bring false hopes in times that seemed there was no other explanation.

Lane was passionate about his mission, he knew with every fiber of his being that time was growing short, and though he had failed Jordan and she had perished to wake in a place of untold torment; he would not fail again. He would spend time with God, and he would find out where to go next, and he would stay focused. But he had to do one more thing concerning Jordan before he would truly be able to move on . . . he had to find her body. He had to know once and for all that she was truly gone, because somewhere in the deepest recesses of his mind he couldn't let her go, and that was not at all how he should be feeling about a lost cause. He should be letting her memory fade and moving forward away from the past and into the future. A future that would be bright even in the face of the darkness that Jordan's death was certain to bring.

The Creator had moved in his life so many times allowing peace in times when it seemed to be a thousand miles away, and for some reason it made no sense to Lane he was not letting go of the mission that was Jordan, as though he felt the Creator Himself pushing him undeniably in that direction; the same as he had felt when he found her on the ground in front of her old family home, lying on the ground weeping for all that she had lost. It was the sweetest of nudges, a gentle push that guided him; Lane had come to depend on, to know the right direction that he should go. Now he felt that same familiar nudge . . . and it wasn't insisting that he move away from Jordan, to the contrary, it seemed to spur him forward, to demand that he find her and protect her from some unseen danger.

CHAPTER 28

Jordan continued to survey the room, but nothing seemed to be amiss. The bureau had certainly done their homework, at least where this room was concerned . . . if Jordan wanted to escape she would simply have to wait for the right opportunity to present itself. Maybe someone would come into the room to feed her, or to allow her to have exercise, or maybe one of the medical staff would be charged with collecting her, for her impending surgery. Jordan had no doubt that though she had not yet gone through the life altering surgery, which would take away her mother's familiar image, that she would still be forced to endure the process. Jordan knew that the bureau would make no exceptions not for her, and not for anyone. She was a rogue agent, and she would be put through the normal process. She too would be debriefed; brain washed, and then placed in any number of the religious sects that plagued the organization, just waiting for an opportunity like this, to help some lost soul find their way.

The idea of being in the room with a bunch of religious nuts, as Jordan commonly referred to them, normally would place her on edge, but since her time with Lane the idea did not seem so far fetched. Maybe Lane did have the real deal; maybe her mother had the same real deal. After all, there was some commonalities between the two of them weren't there? For instance she could see the same peace that resonated behind Lane's gorgeous blue eyes, existed behind those of her mother's. Also a patience that Jordan was bereft to understand. Both Lane and her mother had been through more than any normal person could have endured and yet their sanity was still intact. No matter what happened it never failed to astonish Jordan that both kept complete patience with the misguided souls in their world. Jordan could not be certain that all of these were traits engendered by all Christians, but at the very least it baffled her that two people from different parts of the world; their only commonality was pain, loss, frustration . . . yet both held a complete disregard for it all. Both Lane and her mother claimed Jesus Christ as their savior, and both loved others with a fervor that Jordan could not imagine possible. Even now as she could feel a newness radiating through her soul; she could not imagine going through any of the things she had gone through and loving the transgressor with complete disregard for the transgression. How did she get there from here?

Jordan moved from the edge of the bed to the floor and allowed a quick peek underneath. She had hoped for the unthinkable, that maybe there would be some sort of door in the floor under the bed leading to a way out. She knew that the idea was too far fetched. An organization like Black Heart would not train the sort elite soldiers that could move like shadows on the wall never being seen or heard, and make such a simple mistake, but hope had allowed her to believe . . . they might have made such a mistake. She felt hope jeering at her, laughing as it claimed its victory. Jordan stood and again allowed hope to drag along its empty promises to yet another dead end, as she looked again at the ventilation system that allowed the smell of the plants to lend their allure to the occupant, again she felt the pang of defeat as she noticed the iron bars that were strategically placed just inches apart as not to allow even the smallest of objects to pass.

There would be no way out. She had no choice but to try her luck with one of the staff members. The unfortunate soul that entered the room in an effort to do whatever menial task, would be faced with Jordan's determination to leave; her desire to yet again be in Lane's wonderful presence, but for the first time she had no plans to hurt Lane, no, she would tell him all that she held in her heart, and then she would never again look back. She would walk in the ways of Lane, his God would be her God, his people her people . . . she no longer had an innate desire to change the world by teaching women how to take up for themselves. For the first time she was interested in the change of only one person, Jordan Buckley, herself. An idea that would not be easy to convince others... no one from the bureau would blindly believe that Jordan had just fell into such a life-changing belief system, even the fact that she had spent countless man hours with one of The Truths most successful agents, Lane would not convince the bureau that Jordan was a changed woman. And she was certain that her image had been broadcast all over the planet by now, as one of the world's most deadly of serial killers finally brought down. How could she blame the media really? The world would be demanding some sort of a solution to the 'John Slasher' wouldn't they? And it would be up to the officials to ensure the public that the threat was finally muted.

* * *

Garrison walked with purpose to the cell that held Jordan, no time like the present. While he was not looking forward to the task at hand, he knew that he was the only one on staff at Black Heart that stood a chance at reaching Jordan. Garrison had no desire to fight Jordan. He knew that if a fight did ensue one of them would die. He also knew not to assume that just because he was the one with the gun, that he would be the victor to the spoils.

Jordan had gone beyond the usual training requirements for field agents... she was determined to be the best. She had been on a mission from the start. That was probably why most of the instructors had allowed her to slip through the cracks. Most recruits would have had multiple evaluations to make sure they stood absolutely prepared for the outside world, not so with Jordan. She had played the game well. She had made every effort to make the staff relax in her presence. Garrison was the only member of Black Heart that was allowed privy to the most inner fears and desires that made up Jordan Buckley, which considering her extreme hatred for the opposite sex, seemed a down-right miracle to Garrison.

Garrison stopped just beyond the first pane that lined the bank of windows that made up the cell where Jordan was being held. He did a quick inventory of his weapons. Something still felt amiss about going into the cell, though he knew that there was a special bond afforded only him, concerning Jordan, he still felt something in his gut insisting he not go into the cell. He knew all to well the fury of Jordan Buckley, the determination, and the skill that she possessed. Garrison had no desire to be one of her hapless victims, and he knew that anyone that stood between Jordan and whatever goal she had deemed necessary to obtain, would end up at the very least unconscious, and dead in the most extreme of circumstances. So baffled was Garrison that Jordan was no longer the Jordan that he had witnessed so many times in the past; the defender of women. the crazed killer on a mission to free the world of all its evil. In the forest the night he claimed her unconscious body, Garrison had witnessed something different about Jordan. No longer did she seem intent on changing it all. He watched her crying over Lane, begging for his life. Praying? He thought. That was what she was doing right? She was praying. Garrison shook his head at the thought.

Garrison did not have a clue what Jordan had become. The thought sent icy shivers down his spine. He had looked into her eyes that night and he was sure of one thing, someone was in control of her, someone as deadly: maybe even more deadly than he had ever known Jordan to be, but that someone . . . was definitely not Jordan. She was perplexed in some way, as though she were bouncing back and forth undecided. One moment she would kill them the next she would kill her self. She was fighting for her life or theirs; Garrison could not decide. But at the moment he knew that he would have to keep his focus and not allow anything to take center stage in his mind more than Jordan's intent concerning his wellbeing at this very moment.

Garrison tried to let the revere of that night fade away. to focus intently on the Jordan that was in the observation room. Garrison thought that just watching Jordan through the surveillance cameras was eerie. He could not decide what Jordan was playing at. Something about her face was different even now. But he knew his partner, and she was definitely equipped to play the part. Jordan was like a chameleon, transforming into whatever role best suited to bring her to the ultimate goal. He just prayed her latest goal did not include his untimely death.

* * *

Jordan allowed her eyes another quick sweep of the room, but was still having no luck finding any cameras. Then all at once it dawned on her, of course the cameras would not be in the room and besides if any organization had the technology to hide a camera so as not to be detected by a captive member of the bureau, it was definitely Black Heart. Jordan allowed a sly grin to replace the downcast defeated frown that had been on her face for most of the morning as she searched for a way out, with no luck. Finally she looked up at the ventilation system again and examined the rim of the window for grip. There was just enough. It would not take much, with the strength that she had gained in her fingertips by climbing the edges of buildings, with no rope; Jordan seemed a virtual spider at times.

Jordan slipped off her shoes and placed them under her bed just out of site. Then she pulled the sheets and the pillow from the bed and bunched the fitted sheet and the pillow under the top cover, just enough to allow for the illusion that she was sleeping. Finally, she placed the end of the flat sheet in her mouth and began to pull with her right hand as the fabric ripped into halves, that were almost equal in size and shape, and then she began her ascent up the window's edge, to the ventilation system covers. Finally, with one hand she held on tightly as she tucked a small portion of the sheet just inside the vent to cover the camera, which was just where she had thought it would be. Why hadn't she thought of it before? Was she losing her edge? Jordan shook off the thought; she had no time to wonder about her skills and whether she had properly kept them intact. Jordan pulled at the end of the sheet and then pulled it through to the other vent just a couple of feet away on the same wall. She then looped the sheet through it as well, she stabilized her body by keeping her toes curled intently on the almost nonexistent, windowsill, and then she pulled the two ends of the sheet together, and finally with some effort she tied the end of the sheet as tight as she could.

Jordan held tight to the edges of the sheet while she sat poised, her knees crouched beneath her, on the slightly dangling part of the sheet. The position she was in allowed her perfect access to the door. Now, all she would have to do is be patient. Eventually, a staff member would enter the room at the very least to check on why they no longer had visual acuity, or to tend to Jordan's needs. The thought of hurting someone that was only there to care for her, caused a ripple of guilt to pass through Jordan, something that she was not used to. But, she could not think about that now. She had to do whatever it took to get to Lane, and at this point she had not been presented with very many options. This was her option.

* * *

Garrison continued on down the corridor, past the first window, and allowed a curious peek into the room. He had forgotten to bring his radio, which would allow the control room to keep in touch with him, in case something was amiss in Jordan's cell. The bed was still against the wall, and it appeared that Jordan was still asleep. The pill that he had shot her with, back in the woods was strong, but he would have thought that its effects would have long-since wore off. He had seen Jordan with his own two eyes scouting the room for a way out. Maybe she had given up. Though the thought seemed very unlikely, he had no explanation for the fact that she seemed to be safely tucked away in her bed. The thought sent uneasiness skidding up his spine, and all through him. Again, he felt the desire to run from the cell, and not look back. But, again, he had no choice, he had to be the one to enter her cell, no one else would stand a chance. At least, he had a modicum of hope. She actually liked him and trusted him, on some level. But, after the scene in the woods, he too was probably thought of as enemy, to Jordan . . . no doubt, she would blame him for bringing her to the garden. Jordan had made it perfectly clear that she had no desire to ever be brought to the garden, but in the end, it was he, Garrison, her friend, her trusted companion, that she would feel had betrayed her, and Garrison was sure he would pay a hefty price for that betrayal.

CHAPTER 29

Lane could feel his heart start to calm a little as the compound came into site. Not your usual compound, the place was hidden from the prying eyes of the public. Actually, the place was not even a compound; not really, at least not as far as any onlookers would have believed. The entrance was strategically placed in a pub, known as Saint Patties, in the Irish district, of Manhattan, New York. Charlie, a former CIA Operative, owned the pub; he retired and opened it. He had been approached by the CIA, via John, one of his old partners. John had presented the offer in such a way that Charlie could not resist. The CIA would assume all of the debt involved in owning a business, but the ownership would as always remain with Charlie. All Charlie would have to do is allow the organization to build, under his pub. Charlie easily owned an acre that surrounded the pub, which stood in the middle of towering buildings that claimed either side of its jaunty structure.

The City counsel had approached Charlie on countless occasions trying to break through his resolve and make him sell, but Charlie had stood firm, turning them down. With the CIA, not only backing his business, but funding it, Charlie would no longer have to look over his shoulder.

Charlie soon agreed to the offer, and allowed the building to commence. The city officials would have no other recourse but to look the other way. The cover for the organization was set into place and Charlie's beloved bar was given a new sheen to an old fossil. His pub never looked better. The entrance to the compound was placed at the very same entrance as the high-stakes poker room. There was a key pad placed to the left of the door, blocking the entrance. The room was built on a turn table that spun so slowly that it could not be detected by the human eye . . . so that when the numbers were put in the key pad the position of the entrance could change without the card-player's knowledge. When a member of the organization or one of the religious groups that were housed in the organization keyed in their personal identification number, the room would spin on its axis allowing the door to the compound to revolve into place. As soon as the member was safely in the foyer leading to the compound the normal entrance to the poker room would spin slowly back into its usual place, never tipping off any of the card players inside.

Once an agent or religious group member stepped into the foyer, an elevator leading to the underground workings of Black Heart and the other establishments housed in its confines, would take the agent below. But first, the agent would have to endure a retina scan and then a bio-reading, of their finger print. No shortcuts were taken when it came to the security, of the organization. The protection of the agents and associates of Black Heart was of the highest level of concern. No one without proper clearance had even the slightest opportunity to access the inner-workings of the organization. There was actually a whole section of the bureau that was dedicated solely to the safety and protection of the agents, and anyone that obtained knowledge that pertained to the bureau was eliminated, drafted, or protected in the same manner as any other member of Black Heart.

The compound was not large in structure. There was only the acre of land that was allotted to the building that housed the organization and the religious groups that made up Black Heart, but there were other areas that had been put into place to help with the training of agents. On the outskirts of the city there was a large farm that was a cover as well. The agents would be sent to the large compound on its rolling acres that appeared to the untrained eye to be a high-tech chicken house. Here the agents would train hard, inside the structure as to not be detected by the outside world.

All the way, every mile, Lane could only think of finding Jordan. Though he had no understanding of the desire, he knew of just one place that would allow him the time and serenity to hear God's voice: he had to get to the garden. The place was used in debriefing, because it allowed for a serenity that seemed other-worldly. Though, Lane, may not agree with the cells, that were housed on the outer edges of he garden, he knew that they were not used in torture tactics. Lane did not like anything that seemed to eliminate one's freedom. It just felt wrong in some way. So much had happened to ensure the freedom for all mankind and anything that threatened the sanctity of that sacrifice should be eliminated. He did think that there should be ways to keep predators like serial killers, rapists, and child molesters, and any of the members of society, which could not function with any sort of decency, without causing harm to others, in Lane's opinion those people, should be dealt with swiftly. Though he was not at all certain what the swift act should consist of, Lane was glad to not be the judge in those circumstances. He could not imagine having to deal out punishments, which should 'fit the crime', a task he was certain did not come easily. But, the members of Black Heart . . . well to Lane that was a different matter all together. It was complicated.

How could they pull a hurting soul to the side, after witnessing them kill, most of the time, in self defense, and turn them into a killing machine, only to be surprised when that individual took killing to another level . . . the idea was hypocrisy at its worst. Still, Lane loved the garden, and he would not allow those things that were out of his control to keep him worried. God was in control and it was up to God to decide wrong from right. Thankfully, Lane would never have to be the person wielding the proverbial axe, which decided one's innocence or guilt. He was only the messenger, and for that he was grateful.

Lane had always appreciated the effect that the place seemed to have on him. The moment he stepped into the garden, he felt God's presence. The garden was not only an extension, of Black Heart, used for debriefing. It was an alcove of the Truth; a place of peace . . . a sanctuary built by The Truth, to allow its members to get in touch with their inner peace . . . and hear what God's will for their lives, truly was. The feel of the Holy Spirit was not only real, it was tangible, in the abode; and Lane needed that right now, more than ever. Especially when it seemed that his heart was aching for the impossible, it seemed he could not to take another step, without seeing Jordan, and truly knowing that she was gone . . . or maybe, some fraction of him held out hope that there was still a chance, at a future for them. In spite, of all of the mountains, that plagued the canvas of their future . . . the mountains, which seemed impossible to climb. Lane could not help but be reminded of God's word . . . with faith the size of a mustard seed, he could move mountains. That was true wasn't it? He had lived in the bright sunlight of that truth his whole life, and he of all people knew what God was capable of.

Lane thought about his own life. The idea of him being the offspring of a human woman, and an angel was beyond reality . . . it was like a story; straight out of the bible had dropped right in the middle of his life, and took root. He recalled his time with the missionary family, that had taught him all that he would need to know to bring the Truth to all people, and he could remember many stories from the bible, but the most prevalent in this season of his life came straight out of Genesis, the sixth chapter. It was a story about renowned men, of old; it went on to talk about how angels had been cast out of heaven. The story went on to say that the angels had found human women to be desirable, and had taken them, and out of that union come the giants; giants like Goliath. He could remember the stories, which were taught to him, about the bible. All of the stories seemed to be great life lessons, the kind of things that grownups used to encourage children; to show children that yes they were capable of many things. But this, this was more than Lane could have ever imagined, a story from the bible being true, okay, that was something that Lane just accepted, no problem, he believed every word of the bible . . . he always had . . . but, this was a story that wasn't just a life lesson, it was his life, it was his history. The idea nearly brought Lane to his knees.

Lane thought a little more, about what exactly that had meant. He was a descendent of the giants? His ancestors had tried to take over heaven, while being led by the father of lies, Satan, and in the process they had been cast out of heaven. And if that had not been bad enough, they had gone on to take human women, a union, which had caused those women; women like his mother, their lives.

The idea that he would do anything, to hurt Jordan; poured anger, like hot coals through his veins. How could he be so selfish? He could no more expect that Jordan or any other human woman, for that matter, could bring his offspring forth into the world, than could his mother, or the other women that had died tragically, needlessly, in the past; because of what? Selfish need . . . greed . . . what else could have possessed any man to knowingly take a woman and impregnate her, only to watch her die, during the birth of his child? Lane wouldn't do that. More importantly he thought as reality poured sadness into the mix right along with anger which was already rushing like a mighty river, through his veins; he couldn't, because even if he had been selfish enough to, Jordan was already gone . . . and that was why he had come to The Garden, right? To prove to himself, once and for all, that Jordan was gone, and she was not coming back, no matter how desperately he wanted it to be a lie. The truth had been lying on the forest floor and there was no denying what he had seen with his own eyes. Jordan was dead.

CHAPTER 30

Scant seconds ticked away like hours as Jordan readied her senses she honed in on the resonance of her surroundings; she could here the slight footfalls just outside the cell. She also knew that it was her old partner, Garrison that would be entering the room, a fact that she had not relished. Before the creature left her body she would have longed for the opportunity to get even with him, but now all of that seemed futile. Desires long forgotten from a distant past, like a beloved treat, that no longer held its usual savor. Jordan no longer cared to make anyone pay. She would only do the things that were necessary to be able to move forward in her life, a life that she hoped. No prayed. That one day she could spend side by side with Lane.

The thought in itself nearly toppled her with regret. She did not deserve one as pure as Lane. He was innocent. She deserved to rot in the place of torment that Lane spoke of. But she couldn't imagine a torment worse than being without his love. The faces of her victims, burned in her psyche, like after images. Anguish born of regret threatened to cut off her air-supply as it pressed insistently on her heart . . . it seemed to crave her remorse; demanding she look at each face and claim the horror left in the aftermath of her rage.

The pain was becoming more and more intense as the vale was being removed from her eyes. The whole time, while in the demon's clutches she felt as if she were a prisoner being held behind the steel beams of her mind; an impenetrable fortress that demanded she always be present and see all that the creature did, but never able to interject her own decisions. She could not imagine that she would have done things so differently; than that of the demon . . . Though, it crouched endlessly inside her waiting for the time when its lies had fully encapsulated her into their steely grip allowing it to pull the strings; Jordan would always know that she was at fault for the unforgivable things done to all the victims at her hands. Though, it was not her will completely that had initiated the unforgivable acts, in the end it was her anger, her undeniable entertainment of the demon in the first place that had allowed him to call the shots . . . something she would forever have to be faced with. How would she move on? Why should she? She didn't deserve any of the promises of bliss that she felt when she was lost in Lane's powerful embrace. She deserved only torment. But she was driven, by a force that was beyond her understanding. Even as, she sat perched, on the makeshift hammock, designed to support her weight, above the door and out of her friend's site; Jordan knew that she would stop at nothing to be back in Lane's arms.

One by one, individual sounds became a little quieter, the trickle of water, that fell from the irrigation system, just a few yards away, fell to silent, as Jordan honed in on the one sound that mattered . . . the approaching footfalls of her once trusted friend and partner, Garrison. The thought brought with it, a sting of sadness. They had been through so much together. Sure Jordan had no desire to come to The Garden and the old her, would have certainly wanted retribution, for the transgression, of a friend, but this was a new day, and in it came new beginnings. Not the beginnings that she had so longed, to believe were real, the day that she talked with Garrison and the other agent, as they sat on her couch, waiting for an answer; but this was a true new beginning. And she could feel all of the promises that it made. All of the promises that she wanted to believe in . . . to grab onto, and never let go . . . Jordan no longer wanted to play the blame game, all she wanted now was a new beginning with Lane, and she would do whatever it took to make that a reality. She only prayed that whatever, would not end in the tragic loss of a friend.

* * *

Garrison stepped closer to the door of the cell, and allowed his shoulders to relax a little. He had to stop being so tense all of the time. His doctor was going to have a fit, already he was a virtual walking pharmaceutical. Jordan was his friend; they had crossed some pretty rocky terrain together. She would just have to be made understand that all he had done he had done for her. He cared for her deeply. He had to make sure she was okay. The bureau had talked about eliminating her. That was what brought him out to her old family home, and the reason for his letter. He intended to warn her in the park that night but things had gone beyond wrong. And instead of being at the park warning his old friend about the bureau's intentions, he was forced to bring her to The Garden.

He was keeping Jordan, in one of the old cells that were undergoing renovation. No one at the bureau had a clue of her whereabouts except two of his trusted colleagues from the media room that owed him a few favors . . . John Benton for instance, had fallen in love with a rogue agent several years earlier; Jordan and Garrison had helped to cover up some of her more outlandish transgressions, allowing the agent to fall back below the agency's radar.

Cynthia Jacobs had been with the bureau for three years and unfortunately was not showing any signs of improvement. The bureau had just about had it with her antics as the upper management had referred to her clumsy nature. Cynthia was not born to be an agent like most of the agents at Black Heart. It had been a mere act of self-defense that had landed her in the department. Her home life had not been one of torment, her mother was only a notch above June Cleaver while her father was a railroad worker. Cynthia's father had worked all day and yet at the end of the day covered in coal dust, he always had a smile for his girls as he called them.

One day on the way home from the store to get a couple of odds and ends for her mother's meal a group of men had cornered Cynthia in an alley. Cynthia had confided all of this to John, who had later told Garrison and Jordan while begging them to help her . . . The agency would kill her and it wasn't even her fault . . . of course she couldn't tie up a crime scene that she had caused; she was no killer. There were miles of difference between good ole self-defense and murdering because it was in your nature. Yet the agency had foolishly tight-cast Cynthia into the same group as agents like Jordan. Agents that had been tortured and beaten, raped, or ignored all together until one day all of the sins of the past had culminated into a horrific scene like the one in the alley, where the man had planned to rape and kill Jordan. Of course Jordan was a killer with her track record, who could expect anything more. But Cynthia; Cynthia was no killer. She was just a scared teenager that had defended her right to survive; the right to walk home from the store without the fear of someone attacking her.

Cynthia's attackers had not been as easily thwarted as the man in the alley with Jordan. At first Cynthia had dropped her bag of groceries and ran for the direction she knew her home to be in. That attempt had proven futile as one of the men jumped in the mouth of the alley blocking the opening that led to the street. Cynthia hunkered close to the wall that was farthest from the men, and in that moment her hand happened across a sandy substance that turned out to be dried-dusty cement. Taking a deep breath, she prayed with all her might as she grabbed a fistful of the dusty stuff and cast it as hard as she could in her assailant's direction.

The cement dust hit its mark . . . the first man fell to his knees screaming profanities. The man just behind him retreated a few steps and then stopped as an angry scowl tightened his features. The second guy started in her direction again, with murder in his eyes . . . but Cynthia was on the church softball team so during the confusion she had managed to grab a handful of rocks that lay by her feet. Cynthia started to fling the rocks; smacking two of the men in the head, knocking one unconscious and the other, though he had a few bumps, and scrapes was no worse for the ware; the man scampered from the alley as he went he was screaming something unintelligible over his shoulder about crazy women.

Unfortunately for Cynthia the guy that had been rendered unconscious died later that afternoon. Cynthia was approached by the agency soon after his death. The members of the agency had not been present to see Cynthia fumble her way to safety, and had assumed her to be just another agent in the making.

Truth be known, Garrison didn't feel that John owed him anything. He would do it again. Cynthia was Garrison's friend too, and getting her reassigned to 'The Truth' had been his pleasure. It had taken some convincing to make the department understand that death wasn't the only way to ensure Cynthia's silence. There were other agencies that in all fairness Cynthia was better suited for, and Garrison had been right. Cynthia took to The Truth like it was her home from birth. Now Cynthia sat side by side with John, in the media room, helping to ensure that Jordan was given the same fair shot.

If Garrison had been caught with Jordan he would probably lose more than his badge he would be standing the chance of being eliminated as well. To say that he was thankful for John and Cynthia's help seemed too empty. Without the help of his friends he would pay the ultimate price for helping his partner. He would pay with his life.

Garrison lifted the magnetized badge, with his picture and employee number, and scanned it. Simultaneously there was a low-buzzing sound and then a popping noise that indicated the door was open and access to the cell was being granted. Again, Garrison could feel the daunting tendrils of dread skitter up his spine. He had always learned to go with his gut, instinct was everything.

"Instinct, it's a God given ability, people . . . listen to it. Don't be stupid." He could hear the words of his instructor loud and clear.

"Jordan, it's me." Garrison announced. "Don't do anything that we might both regret . . ." Garrison's words fell short as he felt the sudden grip of fabric around his throat and then a force pushing against his shoulder then the ground was rising up to meet him as he felt his mind swim . . . there was no oxygen in the air . . . a euphoric filling embraced him, calming the madness that threatened to undo him and then he was blissfully lost to darkness.

* * *

The door pushed open slightly and Jordan could see Garrison step into the room, as his shoulders visually slumped and then he was saying something. Probably a tactic to put her at ease and get her to drop her guard. She hated what she was about to do, but in the end, it was him or her.

Jordan allowed the center of the sheet to drape over Garrison's head; as it fell into place around his neck she pushed the ball of her heal into his shoulder, and then pulled up with her arms while she pushed down with her foot. Thirty seconds, she thought, that's all she had to hold on for . . . just thirty seconds and her friend would be rendered unconscious, and she would be free of the cell and on her way to find Lane.

Jordan felt Garrison struggle and she pulled up violently, trying to hold on for dear life . . . fear washed over her, not for her wellbeing but for his. She willed him to pass out. She was terrified she was going to kill him. She ticked off the seconds in her mind. One Mississippi . . . two Mississippi . . . she continued . . . frantically. . . . Let it go . . . her mind seemed to scream. God please don't let him die. Her mind pleaded even as she pulled desperately knowing that she had no choice, if she let go she would be in for the fight of her life, and for the first time she just was not sure she was up to it. She did not have the stomach for it. Finally mercifully Garrison slumped and then as she released her grip, she planted her feet and leaned back into the sheet toward the wall so that she could lower his body to the floor; so that he would not hit his head. The concern she felt for him was odd. She had grown used to the affection that she held for Lane, but to feel anything other than contempt for the opposite sex, even Garrison, was strange. The rage she had carried within her at times had seemed almost primal; but now in this new season of life she wanted to learn of compassion and love and hope . . . she prayed for peace. What had her mother said? A peace that surpasses all understanding, wasn't that it? And that is what she had felt in the forest, as she lay down beside Lane pleading with his God for his life. The moment that she heard the voice, still and calm, taking her on a current of other-worldly peace . . . that was exactly what she had felt, and she had to know it again.

Jordan lowered herself down to the floor. She cautiously stepped to Garrison and checked for his pulse, it was normal and his breathing was deep and rhythmic, he was asleep. Jordan smiled, and said a silent thank you, to Lane's Creator. Then she grabbed her shoes, and she was gone.

CHAPTER 31

Lane stepped inside the pub, as the smell of cheap wine wafted up into his nostrils. He never would get used to the smells that surrounded the night life but the pub he knew was a necessary cover. Besides he liked the owner, Charlie. He was in his late fifties, and had a thick Irish brogue. Pale skinned with short, curly, red hair, Charlie was a jolly sort and never missed the opportunity to tell a good joke. Most of his jokes were innocent enough, and Lane didn't mind stopping to listen to the old guy from time to time. Unfortunately, today he was in a hurry and he would have to wait to chat with Charlie later.

Lane nodded in Charlie's direction, and waited as Charlie smiled and nodded back. A sign that not only meant Charlie was giving a return greeting, but was also an unspoken agreement that all was well.

After receiving the go ahead Lane stepped to the wall, where he pinned in his code and waited for the wall to open. Then he stepped inside the foyer, and eyed the scanner as a red light passed across his eye, scanning his retina for proof of his identity. A monotone-voice, thanked him, and then calling him by name asked him to place his finger on the bio-screen, to be scanned as well. Lane did as asked and almost simultaneously, the elevator door opened and he stepped inside and began the descent to the compound.

As the elevator stopped the same voice asked for a destination. Lane's heart calmed as he gave his usual answer. "The Garden." He spoke the answer in a matter-a-fact tone. A light buzzing sound whirred through the elevator, then the door opened, as the smell of lilac and honeysuckle melted what was left of his anxiety.

Wave-petunia with their dark purple beauty bordered the pathway along with, orchids, and spider-lilies. A cobblestone grey and red pathway, nestled between lilac shrubs, served as a map for visitors; keeping them on the right path. Lane stepped on the path and looked around as he allowed the crape-myrtle and honeysuckle, which cascaded down the rock walls that housed the irrigation system, their usual sweet assault of his senses. A welcomed sense of euphoria set his brain at ease. He allowed his gaze to take in the other plant life and finally, he smiled inwardly, as he found the dogwood trees that encircled the fountain in the mist of the garden. That's where he was headed. The peace that emanated from the vicinity was like a balm to his tired and aching soul.

The fountain was built by The Truth, to be a replica of the Arc of the Covenant. A sacred biblical box that was thought to house the ten commandments, and stood for the power of God, during the time of the Israelites struggles with the Philistines. The fountain, golden, with a cherub on each end; in which water streamed out the praying hands, and into a surrounding pool that was edged by a grassy meadow, encompassed by a cobblestone path; was the epitome of calm-beauty. The outer border was encircled by concrete benches en-lade with intricate carvings, of swirling old English lettering, which read 'In God we Trust'.

Lane headed purposely, for the spot. He could feel the tension in his shoulders begin to dissipate as he claimed his usual bench. He allowed all the uneasiness to leave his body, and his mind to rest on the things that mattered. He would soon be at the throne of God, being still, and hearing the Master of all creation; as He and only He, could show him the way. He would soon be on the path to Jordan, because God alone knew where she could be. Lane steadied himself for the answer he was not sure he was ready to receive. He could feel Jordan so strongly as if she were right there with him. He could only pray that that meant she had made her peace with God and was safe in His arms. Because, Lane could not imagine that he would be able to survive, if he knew that she was in the torment, which only hell could bring.

* * *

Satisfied that Garrison would live, Jordan left the cell. Though she did not shut the door behind her; she couldn't understand why . . . she just felt it would not be a good idea to lock him up in the room. Like a warning sounding . . . and intuition of sorts, she reasoned.

She continued on down the path as she allowed the sounds and smell to overtake her senses. For the first time she was like a new creature, actually enjoying all that was set before her. No longer filled with anger, rather with a calm assurance that rustled across her very being, which allowed her to some how know that all was well. Jordan listened for the sound of voices, footfalls, or any indication that she may not be alone. The minute that she felt certain that she was truly alone, she felt her shoulders begin to relax. She wanted to see the place through the eyes, which she seemed to somehow only now possess.

Joy put a spring in her step as she allowed the little girl that had for so long been huddled in the back of the closet hoping to fade into the scenery, to step forward and bask in the beauty of her surroundings. The smells and beauty came together in a melodious symphony of sensual delight. Carrying Jordan on its current to places she had never dared go. She was no longer the rage filled being she had once been, but a small child basking in the purity of Lane's Master's creation. And she was certain for the first time that no matter what lies the beast had shouted at her, or the deceit that her own wounded spirit had dumped into the frayed edges of her mind, that God existed, and He was all the things that Lane had said and more . . . love and peace, grace and hope, kindness and goodness . . . and most of all mercy . . . and for the first time, in that place, with all of the tapestry of flowers woven into its surroundings and the symphony of smells, she could allow herself to believe that just maybe, she too could obtain that mercy.

Jordan smiled inwardly, as she continued down the path. Finally, she rounded a bend in the rock-wall that was laced with beautiful purple flowers that looked like fat, healthy grapes, and honeysuckle and the lightest sound of trickling water; and there in front of her, just when she thought that nothing could be more beautiful, she saw him.

Lane was in the mist of fully blooming dogwood trees, sitting on a bench, in a meditative position. His shoulders looked totally relaxed as his beautiful honey brown hair lay down his back in sprays of fine curls. His huge six plus foot frame, spoke of strength and purpose, but his face was filled with the other-worldly peace that she was only beginning to understand.

"Lane . . ." Her hand floated robotically to her mouth as she felt her knees shake. Could he truly be there before her? Was it that easy? Something inside of Jordan reached for the old untrusting person she had once been . . . it was too good to be true. She couldn't trust him. Could she? How could it be; that she could step out of the cell and walk down the path and there he would be? How could her aching soul be made whole with only the site of this man and more importantly how could he come to be in this place . . . ? How was it possible that he would know exactly where she was? Jordan wanted desperately to run to him and believe with all of her being that it was just that simple, that some fairy-tale in the making sent to her by the creator himself had been orchestrated into this wonderful moment, in the most beautiful place she was sure existed on earth. But life had never worked that way. Not ever.

* * *

Lane could feel God's peace melting through his senses taking over every part of him. Leaving him filled with joy. He knew with a certainty that Jordan was okay. That she was in God's presence and that she would be fine. God would somehow bring him through this, because that's what He did. He protected His children, He took care of things, even when there seemed to be no way . . . He made a way and this would be no different.

He quietly thanked God for all that He had brought him through, and asked for peace concerning Jordan. Strength to let her go, he still longed to be with her but he knew that his Master would take that from him. That he would set him on his path, a new path, and allow him to survive the loss of Jordan. A love that he had never been able to experience . . . A love that would if only allowed, blossom into something more beautiful than he could have ever imagined; even more beautiful than The Garden.

Lane stood and allowed his mind to return to his surroundings. As he was just about to step from the fountain area, and back into the real world where he was certain God would show him his new mission, Lane heard the soft cry of Jordan's voice. Was he losing his mind? He had just prayed for peace where she was concerned and he was certain with all that was in him that he had been granted that peace. But, now as he stood to leave he was sure he could feel Jordan's presence as strong as he had ever felt her and more than that he was hearing her call his name.

Lane turned toward the direction in which he had imagined hearing her voice, and there like an angel, Jordan stood with a long white cotton gown that descended to her calf muscle. Her hair lay in ringlets all around her shoulders and her beautiful green eyes were filled with something Lane had never seen in their depths before . . . peace.

CHAPTER 32

The room was whirring with sounds of reality seeping back in. His head felt like it was splitting into. Garrison placed both hands on the floor beneath him as he pushed against its coolness, trying to regain his footing. What had happened? He rubbed his hand against the back of his neck and allowed the last thing he remembered to sift through his mind.

"Jordan!" He whispered. Garrison wrestled with the urge to lie back down and allow his head time to stop its incessant spinning. He had let her escape, and into the very place where she was being hunted. Black Heart . . . Jordan had no clue what she would be up against. Why would she? He had brought her to The Garden, so naturally she would think that he was ordered to do so. His stomach somersaulted; what had he done?

He continued his efforts until he was finally on his feet as a slow dawning crept over him . . . he was alive; and for that matter, though, Jordan was behind enemy lines, though he had been knocked out and everything was clearly his doing, he could not help but celebrate, because the fact that he was still breathing spoke to a change that had taken place in his partner, his friend, and in that moment despite every uncertainty that screamed at him for attention, he knew that she would be okay. Jordan was no longer a murderer. Now he just had to find her, and keep her safe until he could figure out how to convince the bureau of what he already knew . . . Jordan Buckley had changed.

* * *

Lane swiftly crossed the distance between them, and then stopped just inches from her. "How . . . how can this be?" He sputtered out the words trying against all odds to understand.

"You of all people, ask me that?" Jordan's brows furrowed as she searched his face for the truth. "Is it not you that spoke of God and miracles? Now it is you that ask me how it can be true." As the words came from her mouth, tears started to glide down her cheeks . . . and again his name was a whisper across her lips. "Lane . . ." She breathed and then she was in his powerful arms. Crushing her body into his, wanting to drown in the depths of his love, a love that she could feel coming off of him in waves so strong that it was almost more than she could bear. Jordan had almost reverted to her old ways in the beginning when she first saw Lane not believing that she could trust him, but the moment that she saw the innocent shock in his eyes, she truly knew that her fairy-tale had been put together by the hands of the only One that could have made something so wonderful a possibility. The Creator, God . . .

Lane clung to Jordan and even as he knew that he could stay this way forever, he knew that it was impossible. He could feel the urging in his heart to get her away. Someone was coming, he could hear them, and he was certain that Jordan would have to had her body not been convulsing against his. He loved the feel of her, the knowledge that her grief was about letting go of the past, of that much he was certain, but he could not just sit here in the middle of The Garden waiting to be found. He was not sure what to do, where to go. But he could not stay here with her. He knew that she was wanted for murder, and society would demand its pound of flesh.

"Jordan, we have to go. We can't stay here. The bureau . . . they will be after you, and the public, well I can only imagine what they want." The thought nearly brought Lane to his knees. What would happen to her? What was God's plan for her? Did he find Jordan only to lose her again?

"I know . . ." Jordan was saying as she took his hand and started toward the entrance, the way he had come.

"No, we can't go that way. You will be seen. There's another way out." Lane pulled her along as he led her to a back entrance that few of the members knew about. During some of the renovation projects an access route had been put in for the builders, selected specifically by the CIA of course, because not just any organization would be allowed run amuck in the compound. The idea for the back entrance had been to allow the men on the crew access to the building, with a key card that was provided to them by the bureau, also the team had been sparse, so that the amount of people coming in and out would be easier to track. Two guards had been kept by the entrance during building details and were responsible for making sure the crew that entered the compound matched the faces on the badges.

Lane continued to lead the way, hoping that he had put enough distance between them and whoever was on their heels.

* * *

Unable shake the feeling that Jordan was in a lot of trouble; Garrison was desperate to find her, quickly. Running toward the entrance he could not help but think that Jordan would use the back entrance. He kept thinking at first she may think that it would be okay to just run around the compound and blend in, but now he was thinking better of it; Jordan after all was smart, and more than that she was trained . . . trained to notice things. She would notice that he had placed her in the renovated portion of The Truth; wouldn't she?

Armed with that thought Garrison decided it would be best to take a look around before leaving. What if she had no knowledge of the renovation? Maybe she did not know that there was another way out. He could hope that she would not be caught by another agent. There would be no telling what would happen to her. Finally coming to the realization that time was of the essence he headed for the back entrance; if he did not see her there he could always double back.

Garrison got as far as the Serenity waterfall when he saw Jordan and Lane standing arm and arm. He opted to stay out of site, at least for the moment, just until he could see where the embrace might lead. Hope had told him that Jordan had changed, but as a trained agent, instinct would always have the last word. He would have to be certain that things were truly as they seemed. He cared very deeply for his friend, but he had a duty to the public not to let unstable members into their mist, even Jordan.

The scene was so touching. Garrison felt as though he were watching the ending of a love story . . . Jordan stood holding, no clutching Lane and her arms were racking with the intensity of her grief. Lane was caressing her hair and then all of the sudden he was dragging her to the renovation exit. Excitement surged through Garrison. He just stayed out of site praying that the two of them would make good their escape.

Garrison was still standing silently watching and praying when he heard a voice coming from ahead of him. He had been so engrossed in the scene with Jordan that he hadn't thought about his own safety. What if anyone had suspected him as being involved with facilitating her escape? The minutes seemed to be stretched into hours as he watched the agent approach.

"Garrison, how are you?" It was James Ruston, one of the leading agents. Surely he would not be so easily fooled by any of Garrison's lame excuses.

"James . . ." Garrison started as he floundered for something, anything to say. "What brings you to The Garden?" Simple yet affective Garrison thought as he mentally patted himself on the back.

"I could ask you the same thing." James tilted his head to the side as he caressed his goatee. "I've never known you to hang out in this part of the compound." James allowed a slight smile, and then continued. "So care to explain? You deciding to go with Christianity, or is the verdict still out?" James allowed a short burst of laughter, which was anything but humorous. Garrison decided to approach this from another angle.

"I don't think I have now or ever been in the habit of reporting my goings and comings with you . . . so unless something has happened in the bureau's hierarchy, that I haven't been made aware of, Agent Ruston, then I think I'll be on my way." Garrison started toward the normal entrance, when James cleared his throat.

"You're right about the pecking order not having changed, but I'm sure that Anderson would be all to pleased, to know that one of his top agents just stood idly by while one of the department's most wanted fugitives escaped with a Truth member." James accused as he stepped even closer. "So tell me Garrison, have you ever told Jordan that you're in love with her, or do you plan to lead this miserable existence for the rest of your life? Protecting her from a distance, no matter the cost to you, and now . . ." James pointed toward the renovation exit. "Aren't the stakes a little high, even for you? Don't be so pathetic Garrison; a blind man could see that she's in love with the giant . . ."

James was continuing on with his barrage of taunts, but Garrison had stopped listening. He was not in love with Jordan, he could see that his loyalty to a friend may be misconstrued in such a manner, but he was definitely not in love with his old partner. He felt sorry for her if anything and he wanted her to have a chance. He liked Lane. He could see how good Lane had been for her. If only he could somehow stop James from running back to the higher ups with his version of what was happening; at least until he could put it into words without it all sounding as pitiful as James was managing to make it sound.

God knew he had witnessed the whole thing and he was still having trouble believing some parts of the story. So if he was having trouble with it all, though he had witnessed it how was he ever going to convince The HOD (Head of Department) Anderson, that Jordan had changed, that she should be reassigned, and for that matter that he was not a rogue agent turned against the department for some ridiculous crush that he had for his partner?

CHAPTER 33

Lane eased around the corner and looked first one way and then the other, ensuring the coast was clear. Jordan had finally gained control of herself, but he knew that she was still in a delicate state. She needed somewhere to come to terms with all that she had experienced. He knew that her possession had not been some sort of hoax, but convincing logical members of Black Heart that Jordan had not been responsible, well not entirely, for her actions would be next to impossible. He could not see that the two of them were being left with much of a choice. He would have to get them out of the compound, and back to his cabin; where they would grab a few supplies and become fugitives. He hated the way it sounded. It seemed so dishonest, wasn't the whole idea of Christianity about truth? Even the organization that he worked with was named The Truth, so how could he be thinking of doing this? Running away from responsibility was a foreign concept, but Lane was bereft to think of one good thing that could come from turning Jordan in. That thought led Lane to another, what about Garrison? Garrison could be trusted, couldn't he? It would seem on the outside that Garrison was not trustworthy, but if Lane gave it any real thought, he could see some holes in the idea that Garrison had betrayed Jordan. For one Garrison had brought Jordan to the renovated portion of the compound, hadn't he? And logically he would have turned her into the powers that be, had he not cared about her at all. Then he had to think about the way he had claimed her body on the scene of her supposed death; he had been the only agent on scene, and that in itself was totally outside protocol. So the only logical alternative that could explain his actions was that Garrison was on Jordan's side. He was doing everything in his power to protect her. The thing that worried Lane was what did his plan of connection in-tell?

* * *

Garrison did not have time for this. He was only going for the regular exit into The Garden in order to throw James off his scent, but it was no good; James was like a dog with a bone he just wouldn't let up. Garrison had to do something and fast. He had every intention of following Jordan to insure that she make good her escape, but with James demanding answers and threatening to go to the HOD, he really was left with no options.

Garrison pulled the gun from his coat pocket and pointed it in James' direction. He wasted no time with small talk, and he couldn't take the chance that James may get the upper-hand. He pulled the trigger and just as suddenly as the capsule was freed from the guns chamber, James was on the ground. Garrison drug the agent back to the cell that Jordan had been held in, and after placing the agent on the bed, he pulled the door to and started for the renovation exit again. Garrison pulled his cell phone from his pocket and called his friend in the media room and told them of the events that had taken place, though the two were well aware having seen most of it on the monitors, they agreed to watch for anyone and keep any members of the agency away from the renovated portion of the cell; at least until Garrison had time to sort all of this mess out. Garrison returned his cell to his pocket and continued toward the back exit.

Garrison was almost to the door when his cell phone started to vibrate. The screen lit up with Lane's number, which Garrison had, just as he had all of the other agents and missionary personnel that worked inside the compound. It was important that each member be able to contact one another incase of an emergency. Garrison clicked the green send button and listened before greeting the caller. "Hello?" Garrison tried to keep the shock out of his tone, but honestly he had never expected to hear from the two of them again, at least not willingly.

"Garrison?" Lane's voice was laced with fear and uncertainty. It didn't match up to the giant of a man that he had had dealings with in the past.

"Yeah, this is Garrison . . . Lane?" Garrison knew who it was but for the moment thought it better to allow Lane to monopolize the conversation.

"I'm not sure what to do or say here . . ." Lane started a little shaky. ". . . but I think I'm in uncharted territory. Jordan isn't herself, or maybe she's more herself than she's ever been . . . how would I know?" Lane sighed and was quiet for a moment. Maybe giving Garrison a moment to say something, anything; he did.

"Where are you Lane? I only want to help her, I swear. It's why I brought her to the renovated portion of the cells." There he had said it and it was true. He only hoped that Lane would believe him and allow him to help.

"Garrison . . ." Jordan's teeny voice filled the line. I'm scared Garrison." She stopped to allow some time for her to get control again as the sobs had taken over. "I wanted to know if you could help us; tell us what to do?" Jordan braced herself for his answer. She had always been able to count on Garrison, hadn't she? Even in this he had risked everything to bring her to the renovated cells to allow her time to prove that she had changed, and allow him the time to plead her case before the HOD. But surely he had to understand that the bureau would not help; not this time, no, they would at the very least insist on her being recycled. Which would mean plastic surgery and jail a fake death, and she would have to do what she could never again do . . . kill.

"Jordan, listen to me; you have to go with Lane and you have to get as far away from here as you can. I want to meet with you though, before you leave I mean. Do you remember the place that I told you to meet me at on the scene of your brother's death?" Garrison waited hoping that Jordan would remember him writing the note and tossing it into the chimney telling her to meet him at the park. He could only imagine that Lane wanted to take her back to his cabin and get some supplies, but what Lane could not understand is that the bureau would look in specific places . . . places that they would assume she would go to. Though, the bureau may not know at this point that the two of them were involved, emotionally, they would know that Jordan would go to people that they assumed she trusted. Lane was one of those people, and unfortunately James' presence was only further proof that he was one of the people that the bureau had assumed she would contact. The good thing was that each member was given a secured line, which even the bureau was unable to trace or tap into. It was the only way to protect each agent from falling prey to enemy spies.

"Jordan? Did you hear me?" Garrison was prompting her for an answer as he slid his card down the indicator strip, to exit the building. A loud whirring buzz sounded and then the door opened.

"I heard you. I will meet you there at six." Jordan said and then hung up abruptly. Garrison only hoped that she would meet him there and that they would not attempt to head back toward Lane's cabin. She had hung up and he hadn't the time to explain the dangers of that decision.

Jordan handed the phone back to Lane and sniffed a few times. Then she pulled herself up to her full height and looked straight into his eyes.

"Garrison wants us to meet him at the park near my old family home. We can't go to your cabin; we have to meet him by six. I can't explain it, but he and I have worked together a long time and I could feel . . . that he . . . I don't know it's hard to explain . . . I guess that he was telling me something without saying anything. I know that that may not make any sense, but it's the only way that I can explain it." Jordan looked deeper into his eyes praying that he understood, because even though her resolve had mounted; at this point it was not ironclad and she would never be able do this on her own. So unfortunately, no matter the danger, or the trap that Lane's reasoning may lead them into . . . Jordan would follow, because she had no other choice. She loved him and she couldn't imagine ever again being separated from him.

CHAPTER 34

All the way to the park, every step of the way, Garrison eyed his surroundings; being ever mindful of the possibilities that existed. He could not take the chance that he might be followed. James showing up at the compound had been no accident, he was certain of that. He had to be more careful from here on out. His initial thought had been that the area he had chosen would be safe because it had was out of the watchful eye of the other members of Black Heart; it was that oversight that had inadvertently placed Jordan in danger. He knew from experience that James Ruston was not in the habit of involving himself in other people's lives, no, he always thought of number one; so he would never have come looking for Garrison unless he had been sent by one of the higher ups. He had let his guard down once . . . but it would not happen again. He had to stay two steps ahead of the bureau, and if James' involvement had told him anything; it was that the bureau would settle for nothing less than recycling, a possibility, he was certain Jordan had already considered.

Lane crouched low just outside the park pacing first one way and then the other. He did not like this, he felt like an animal being lured into a trap by dangling food. He could not shake the feeling that the park was just a little to high profile. Cloak and dagger was a bit far fetched for Lane, but even he could think of a dozen more suitable places to have met someone, especially considering the extraordinary circumstances they were all facing.

Jordan stood close at hand; she too seemed a little on edge. She was crouching low to the earth as well; as she watched for Garrison. A low whistling-type-humming noise came from a few hundred yards to the north west of her. Jordan smiled; it was the train noise that Garrison had tried to teach her while they were in combat training. Only he would know the significance of the noise, and only he would use it at a time like this. Even Lane was undeterred by the sound; he had no clue that it was her zany partner, alerting her as to his presence. She still had never learned how to make the sound, but she could even now remember all of the great times the two of them had had together as he tried without success to teach the call to her. The two of them would fall to the ground in a side-splitting bout of laughter as they tried desperately to gain control of their composer. That alone sometimes seemed the impossible. It was those times that helped Jordan to move through the memories of her past long enough to focus on what the bureau had to offer her. Unfortunately, their time together had not been life-changing enough to stop the hate that filled her broken heart and mend the pieces of the jagged-angry edges that pricked at her soul. Anger that spurred her forward into the streak of revenge that had inevitably claimed her life and given her over completely to the demon.

Jordan cupped her hands over her mouth and in her best attempt tried desperately to repeat the sound; she failed miserably of course, but she was certain that not only, would her partner be on the edge of insanity with the attempt at trying not to laugh at her, but he would be made aware of her presence.

Garrison stood in some reeds, that ran the edge of the pond where the ducks gathered and tourists would feed them with the foodstuff bought at the entrance to the park. Over priced food was the city's way of covering any new renovation projects for the park. Garrison listened intently as Jordan made the attempt at the answering call to his train whistle. He had to remind himself that this was a very serious mission and falling into a fit of laughter would not be a wise decision. He had chosen the call, because it was the only way to alert Jordan that he was indeed in the park; short of just standing up and shouting 'I'm over here' which he could not very well do; he had no other choice. Both he and Jordan had been taught to forgo any emotional outburst when on a mission, so it was a safe bet, while

Jordan maybe dying inside she would not sacrifice the mission to let it show.

Lane sat dumbfounded, what in the name of all that is holy, was she thinking? Did she want to alert the whole park as to there whereabouts? With the sound of the awful noise he had just heard her make he thought their chances would have been better, had he just stood up and told all that was interested just exactly where they were hiding. He opted not to get into it with her, at least not for the moment, but he did at least cast a disgusted look in her direction, which was not lost on Jordan.

Jordan stifled a giggle, and then pointed her index and middle finger at her eyes; she pointed at Lane, and then gestured for him to follow her. She circled around; heading in the direction of the pond, staying low to the ground all the way. Finally, Lane could see a figure in the shadows ahead. He grabbed her arm, pulling her protectively back toward him. She placed an understanding hand over his and then nodded that she too saw the figure. She mouthed, 'Garrison' and then continued on toward the shadowy figure.

* * *

Garrison finally feeling certain that he had moved beyond the childlike urge to fall to the ground and roar in laughter, started toward the sound he had heard. If you could call it a sound, he thought in amusement . . . it was more of a low growling combined with a sick whooshing sound. He had almost made it to where he was certain the sound had initially generated from, when he heard a low gasping sound. He stopped and tried to see anything out of the ordinary. After a full minute of hearing nothing; he continued on. He had just stepped to the edge of the park, and was about to move into the open, when he saw two men; one stood in front with a gun trained on Jordan, while the other was just raising up from what looked like Lane's body, which was collapsed in a heap on the ground.

Garrison waited for a few beats which seemed to take forever; he hoped to be able to make some sense out of what was going on before he tried to lend a hand in any way. His initial gut feeling was that this was members of the agency, that had followed either Jordan and Lane or him; but as he listened he realized it was not the agency at all.

One guy was rubbing his brow with his gun, moving about in nervous fits and jerks. The other guy seemed to be in charge and was saying something about Lane and Jordan being FBI; not even close. Garrison held his spot, hoping for an easy way to handle the situation, after a moment or two he came to the realization that he would be presented with no such opportunity, and opted for the element of surprise.

Jordan was trying to keep her focus, but the thug had hit Lane over the head with his gun, hard. The bone-crunching sound was sickening even to a former killer, such as her. Now Lane's body lay in a heap at her feet and she could not even check on him.

"Who are you with?" The one in charge, at least that's the way that it seemed, was demanding. "Who sent you? FBI?" He scowled at her. Jordan took in the heaving man. Not quite the stature of Lane, but not many men were she thought. Still his bulging biceps and strong profile spoke of strength just the same. His blonde hair swirled to one side of his head, causing the man to shake his head to the right every so often in order to maintain his site. Jordan was becoming irritated with the attempts made by the man and longed for a razor to end both of their suffering. Black dress pants combined with a white button up shirt and black tie brought his style together in a success meets ruggedly handsome fashion.

"We're not here for you. Whatever you are doing has nothing to do with us. So please just be on your way so that I can check on my friend. You may have killed him." The last word caught in Jordan's throat as she gulped back a strangled cry.

"Not here for us . . . you gotta be kidding me lady. Sure you're here for us. Who else would you be here for at six in the morning?" The guy stood awaiting an answer as his displeasure showed in the lines of his face. "Look you best start talking lady. I'm running thin on patience and I got things to do." The Bronx-sounding-brogue in which he spoke lent even further to his frightening allure. It was funny how before when Jordan was possessed by the demon that she would have not cared; just dealt with the guy as though he were a roadblock, but now she felt almost vulnerable.

"Sir, I don't know who you are . . . or for that matter why you're out here at six in the morning, but I assure you that my reasons for being out here; have absolutely nothing to do with you. I am on the run . . . that is my friend and I . . . we're on the run together." Jordan said as she prayed that the truth would gain her some brownie-points with the huge man in front of her wielding a gun.

"Shut up!" The man screeched angrily. The other guy was a mess literally; he had stringy black hair, a torn t-shirt, and faded jeans on. His eyes were nearly bugging out of his head. Jordan guessed he had been taking some kind of drug, from the looks of it probably crank. Just to the edge of the road, a black van stood with the side door open and what looked to Jordan to be a shower curtain covering the back window. Two large brown and gray bulldogs were tied outside of the van, both poised for the attack; a low growl emanated through clinched teeth, but either dog would be unable to make good on their threat to attack. Both of the hounds pulled feverishly at the large silver chains that were held fast by silver clips cinched to broad leather straps encircling their necks; hoping for freedom.

Jordan pulled her attention back to the one in charge. He still stood his breath heaving, as he tried to grasp for control of the situation. At that moment the other guy turned away lost in a fit of laughter.

"Shut up, you idiot, are you trying to get us caught? This is probably some of your doing anyway." The guy with the gun growled. "You and your stupid . . . lets get some hookers, nonsense. Had we stayed here and not ventured out, at least until the coast was clear . . . we wouldn't be in this mess now." He cast another disapproving scowl in his not so trusty cohort's general direction, and then continued. "You filthy animal; just look at yourself, it's your addiction that keeps us in the trouble we're in. If you weren't my cousin . . ." The guy let the last words fall, as he turned his attention back to Jordan.

"Now you listen . . . I don't know why you . . . and your friend . . . came to be here, in this park this morning, but lady this is your unlucky day. See we work for James Ruston, the boss of a drug cartel, and well it's just that we can't let you go. You have seen too much, and besides that . . . now you know too much." Frustration lined the man's face as he was clearly uncertain about what his next move would be.

As the last word left the guys gritted teeth, Garrison jumped from the edge of the woods and brought his gun down, hard, on the back of the guys head. Jordan seized the opportunity, and swung around catching his crony in the jaw, with a roundhouse-kick. Upon impact, Jordan heard a sickening-crunch and then the man's body dropped face-first to the ground. The other guy, the one in charge, that Garrison had banged over the head with a gun, fell in a heap, to the ground beside his cousin. Garrison was all business at this point. He looked at Jordan and pointed at his eyes with his index and middle fingers. He indicated that she should back him up. Jordan grabbed the gun from the fallen boss, and then checked the other guy for any weapons. Then without further delay stepped behind Garrison and started a wide low circle keeping close to the ground. Stopping long enough to check for a pulse on Lane's unconscious form. She allowed a moment to thank God that he had once again saved his life. She headed around the van. Garrison followed her lead and kept to the opposite direction. After being certain that the outside of the van was clear, Garrison circled around to the back of the van where Jordan was crouched.

Jordan pointed up at the van window and signaled to Garrison to open the curtain so that she could look in the van's interior. Garrison obliged her; and Jordan just as quickly jumped to her full height training the gun on the inside of the van. Jordan gasped; lying on the floor of the van was tons of drugs, an assortment really. She could also see to the side two women lying on their sides huddled together to stay warm, and fast asleep; both women were dressed in what Jordan had assumed were their street attire. One had a short mini-skirt on with a long sleeve pink jacket that cut mid-drift and tied around her waste, covering a slight black sports-bra. The other woman had on leggings, with a low-dipping top that ended just above her navel.

Jordan cast a knowing glance at Garrison. "Call it in; but what about Ruston's involvement?" Jordan's brow furrowed as she allowed the question to take root even for her. This wasn't good. Of that she was certain, but it couldn't be ignored. It was obvious that they had inadvertently come across a drug scam; and worse than that it was involving one of their very on, James Ruston.

"Are you sure?" Garrison asked as he touched her arm. He waited for a beat and then looked deeper into her eyes. "Follow my lead; I have an idea."

CHAPTER 35

Jordan stood poised, a picture of fear and beauty; baby's-breath cascaded down the back and sides of her hair, littering the curls that fell clumsily to her waste. She wore a long white gown that fanned out at the shoulders and then gathered at her bicep, the sleeve ending in long bouts of lace hanging in jagged edges to her wrist lent to an eighteenth century allure that gave the dress just the right smack of eccentric appeal. The bodice was form-fitting, dipping ever so slightly at the bust-line, while silk plunged to her waste and like the lace of the sleeve, the skirts of the dress hung in jagged edges to her ankles. She wore white silk flats that reminded her of ballerina-shoes without the blunt edge of the toe. Her green eyes glistened with unshed tears; the remnants of unleashed guilt, Lane guessed, as he took in her beauty from a front row seat of the amphitheater.

Jordan was having a hard time letting go of the past. Maybe time was all that she really needed. Lane had called in the crime-scene, back at the park. Anderson was already investigating James, for some allegations, made by a few of the agents, at the bureau. Though he had come up empty, he had put James on trailing Jordan and Lane; hoping that he would get comfortable and sloppy at the same time, incidentally revealing his dealings with the drug cartel to Anderson's spies. Anderson never dreamed that Lane and Jordan would happen upon Ruston's cohorts while trying to keep Jordan safe from the reproach of the bureau.

Anderson sat next to Lane now, watching Jordan as she was being inducted, into the Truth; he sent a knowing smile in Lane's direction, and then sat back in his chair enjoying the way things seemed to just work out at times. The judge had been filled in on all of the details concerning the murders, committed by Jordan; save one: the fact that Jordan was possessed at the time. An idea that would not sit well with a supreme court judge, so in the end it was decided against; and in its stead, Anderson and Garrison gave another explanation; one that a man of the judge's education, would deem plausible. Jordan had showed signs of insanity at the time of the murders. Unfortunately, to their discredit, Garrison and Anderson had been so busy with other assignments; that they had failed to follow up with Jordan, they had failed to debrief her, and place her in a containment cell until she could be evaluated and plans could be made for her medical attention. Garrison had finally made the attempt at the end, which was why there was video footage being shown of Garrison bringing Jordan into the bureau. He also had kept the footage of Jordan escaping, which could show that some change had definitely been made in Jordan's psychological standing. The men argued that had Jordan still been homicidal at the time of her escape, she would have killed Garrison without a second thought.

The judge deemed that in light of all that Jordan had done to bring the men involved in the drug-ring to justice; that she would be given leniency. He ordered that Jordan be remanded to the psychiatric ward for no less than three months; where she would be thoroughly evaluated, before being released into Lane's custody . . . where she would serve out the remainder of her probation doing community service. The judge reasoned it would help Jordan to feel that she was giving back; he further stated that in his years of being a judge, the most common issue with rehabilitating criminals, was the criminals returning to the life that they once knew . . . the cause he reasoned was simple, guilt, and lack of knowledge. Most criminals had no other course of action, because they were not educated to do a trade. Knowledge he argued, was indeed power. He further stated that while studies did show that some criminals had chosen their path, most often the path had chosen the criminal. The man was very passionate about education being the key that unlocked the future for any member of society; no matter what their status may be.

Lane could hardly believe how beautiful Jordan looked in the long white gown; chosen for its symbol of purity. Women and men alike wore the same color when being inducted into the Truth. The color was to represent the purity of one's soul; it had nothing to do with whether the individual was physically pure. The Truth held tight to the belief that Jesus was sent to wash clean all of the sins of the world; no matter what they were. The garment was to show that the individual wearing it had a type of spiritual circumcision, in which the person had accepted Christ and he had taken away all the bad things that littered their soul: things like murder. Nothing was impossible with God, a fact that Lane was completely aware of; as he again took in the raving beauty of the woman before him. She would be considered pure by the world's standards, wouldn't she? She was indeed untouched by a man; but Jordan had been touched by the cruelty of the world and that had stolen away a purity that was of a much higher value, spiritual purity.

Jordan stepped forward as her name was being called. A man with long silver robes, chosen for wisdom, gestured her forward. Lane had told her before the ceremony what to expect. Lane had explained that silver, was as the bible put it best, like a crown of wisdom on one's head. So the elders of the Truth would always be seen in silver when they were at induction ceremonies. The man had a sash around his waste, drawn taut to keep his robes from falling open. Lane had explained that the blue was a sign of riches, but not in the usual sense . . . not rich in the way society had judged a man to be rich. The Truth judged riches in wealth of knowledge, and in closeness to God. This was never judged in one's age, Jordan could see that was true now as she noticed a male and female sitting adorned in silver robes with blue sashes, and neither could have been a day over eighteen. Jordan could not help but be awed by what that meant, the obvious sacrifices the two must have made to achieve such a high honor, was bewildering.

The man cleared his throat, and only smiled as Jordan jerked to full attention. He laid a kind hand on her arm, and lightly squeezed while mouthing you are fine child.

"Jordan Marie Buckley, do you swear to uphold and live by the laws and statutes of the Truth? Do you further promise to never do harm to another individual, and to make it your goal in this walk of life to bring the Truth to all man? Do you intend to never abandon the importance of the Great Commission, to tell all of the lost children of the world of one Jesus Christ and the sacrifice that he made for all mankind on the cross at Calvary?"

"I do . . ." Jordan said as her lower lip started to quiver. And she did . . . she would honor Christ for all the days of her life, not only for the sacrifice that He had made for all mankind, for her; but for lending to her one of the most precious of all His creations, Lane.

Jordan turned to the onlookers as she was presented to them a sister, in Christ and Lane could see that she would always keep the promise that she had made this day, because once again he could see that Jordan was crying. Tears streamed undaunted down her beautiful face as her whole body shook, but more than the tears, greater than the sum of all that made up Jordan here today on the stage making the pledge and crying, was the peace that registered in her normally stone-like features. Lane's eyes misted over as he sat in awe of the Creator of all, once again mystified at how he could bring everything together; make a way where there seemed to be no way.

How precious a gift, Lane thought; to give your only Child for the sins of all mankind, and then to be ready and willing to take away the tears of the world if needed in a moments notice . . . Lane smiled at the idea for a moment longer, and then thought about Jordan's tears, tears of happiness and peace, He could not help but wonder if those too would be removed in heaven. After all the bible had said He would wipe away all tears.

CHAPTER 36

Crystal blue water, untouched by pollution, canvassed the valley floor spreading lazily around the mountain ravine. Animal calls died on the morning air giving way to the promise of yet another beauty-filled day. Jordan stepped out of her tent, the one she shared with her new husband, Lane. Finally, she thought as a lazy grin crossed her lips and she patted her flat tummy trying to ward off the insatiable hunger pangs she was feeling lately. She guessed it to be all of the wonderful nights she had spent in the arms of Lane. Magic she thought, that is exactly what it was; two people giving themselves wholly to one another, evaporating into the other and becoming one . . . she couldn't think of one good reason she had not given into his attempts at making her his wife sooner. The nights spent with him, were nothing less than magic. She never imagined that two people in love bound together by matrimony, a gift, she was starting to understand, from God yet another way He showed His children the magnificent love that only He could give, could find so much freedom in binding themselves together in a union that would engrave their souls with the other's love and commitment forever.

"The union between a man and woman represents the union between Christ and the church", Jordan could remember the words of Anderson as he performed the ceremony only a few weeks earlier. She shivered as she thought how close the ceremony had come to not happening; her life with Lane could have never been. So many issues loomed between them even after Jordan was released from the psychiatric hospital early.

Jordan had stayed in the psychiatric ward as ordered and was as cooperative as she could be. The doctor was a Christian as well, which in itself was a miracle; Jordan had started to see a commonality with scientific minds and not being able to accept the beliefs held in creationism. Most people that were scientifically minded had some trouble with believing the ideals of Christians. For instance how a man could go forty days without food, or the same man be put to death in the most brutal of ways only to rise again on the third day and return to a magical place with streets of gold; well it was a lot to process for someone who seemed to or at the very least thought they had all of the answers.

The psychiatrists in charge of Jordan had been different though, and to Jordan's delight he had believed her when she explained all the horrors of her childhood. She had told him how the demon had come to be in charge and taking over, she had taken full responsibility for entertaining the demon in the first place, but she only wanted someone outside those that had witnessed it all to believe her. The idea that it was only in her mind was unsettling, though the members of the Truth fully believed in possession they did not perform exorcism, not in the general sense, they would simply pray for the host and sometimes if things were bad enough the host would be contained in a cell of the garden where the individual would be kept under close surveillance in case the demon were to prompt them to hurt themselves. Harm to one's self or others was never allowed and against their better judgment until the prayer vigil were successful and the demon left the hosts body, the Truth would opt to keep the individual sedated and in extreme circumstances restraints had been used.

The doctor in charge of her case listened to all that Jordan had to say and prayed with her. He offered his sympathies for all that Jordan had undergone; and then conveyed to the judge that he simply did not see any reason to hold Jordan in the facility any longer, fact was Mrs. Buckley was the picture of mental health. He explained to the judge that the insanity that Jordan had experienced was only temporary, due to the stresses of her childhood and the judge ruled that Jordan should be immediately remanded to the custody of Lane.

After being released to Lane, Jordan could see that the two of them were starting to become closer; but Lane had always seemed to keep his distance. Finally, one day Jordan had to know why. Before, when Lane was chasing her through the woods, Lane would pull her into his embrace, and kiss her, Lane would always chide himself for having left his mission, which she now knew was bringing her to Christ, but since then Jordan had learned so many things about the Christian faith and the statutes that the elder had made her promise to uphold; a promise that Jordan had not taken lightly . . . so she had studied the faith in detail, hoping that she might be able to understand all that it meant to be Christian. The struggle, the blessing, and every nuance that Lane and the others of The Truth had to endure in the journey of their faith. In doing so Jordan had learned that Paul was sort of one of the founders of the faith and that he like her was a murderer and yet he had led many souls to the faith. Paul had said in Corinthians, in the bible that a man and woman could be joined in matrimony if they were equally yoked. Jordan had asked Garrison what it meant to be equally yoked. He had directed her to Anderson, who had explained that it is when two people are in unison in all their beliefs and ways. Another way that God had proved His love for man; in telling man to be equally yoked He knew that it would make the bonds of marriage easier, as marriage in itself can be trying, there is no reason to add to the challenges. Simple things, Anderson had explained, can cause enmity between two people. Such as what types of foods to eat or where they would live . . . to more pressing issues, such as how to discipline a child . . . Anderson went on to say that he had seen too many marriages dissolved for similar reasons.

Jordan thought about all that Anderson had told her about being equally yoked and she couldn't imagine what would be holding Lane back. They were definitely equally yoked, they were practically mirror images of each other. They loved the same foods, both loved to travel and just wanted to live in whatever mission field God chose for them. One day after trying to analyze their relationship for the hundredth time, Jordan decided to just ask Lane what the problem was. She found him talking to a group of children that were playing with a frog. Jordan smiled at the site that he made, the tender way that he had with children, and then she felt a twinge of guilt. Here she was determined to get Lane to make a lifetime commitment to her, but how could she? Her father's beatings had left Jordan barren, unable to conceive children; she could still remember the remorse she had felt, and then the anger that had soon replaced it, had become so rock solid no wonder the demon had been able to take over. How could Jordan ask Lane to make such a commitment to her, when she could not offer him the one thing that she could see he wanted, children? Jordan started to walk away, when Lane grabbed her arm and looked into her eyes; his blue gaze drained all of the resolve to let him go as she allowed him to whisk her away to a more private area where they would be able to talk.

"Jordan, is something wrong? You look . . . I don't know . . . I guess, sad." Lane prompted as he pulled her against him and rubbed her back, caressing away what was left of her concerns. She could settle for this couldn't she? His friendship, wasn't that all that mattered? That the two of them could be together, that was all she really wanted. She could not ask anything more than to be lost in his embrace and reminded that all was right in her world. So why was the desire to be more, to have more with him, always present?

"Hey, you okay? Tell me Jordan; no secrets remember?" Lane insisted as he released her and looked deeper into her eyes. "I don't know what I want . . . I mean, with us . . . I feel like I want something more. A deeper connection maybe, but sometimes you make it clear by your actions, the way you pull away, I mean, that you don't want the same things that I do." Jordan shifted her weight, all of the sudden uncomfortable under the scrutiny of his gaze. For the first time she wanted to be anywhere but near Lane. She started to walk away, when he grabbed her.

"No, not this time, Jordan." He said as he pulled her tight against him. "I love you. I know that you have to feel that." He soothed.

"I know you love me in a Christ way, I get that and so do I . . . you I mean . . . ugh . . . why is this so hard? I love you too in that way, but I love you . . ."

Lane placed a hand over her mouth and then replaced it with his lips, only lightly caressing hers with his own. When he pulled back there was a look of utter defeat that stole Jordan's breath.

"Its time I was honest with you, Jordan." He said as Jordan felt the chill of dread make an icy trail down her spine. He pulled her along with him into a shaded cove near the water's edge. "I'm not what you think Jordan." He shifted his weight then lowering himself to the ground, allowed an exaggerated sigh.

"You are what I think, Lane. You are a good man; loving and kind. You love God and you saved my life." Jordan's eyes pleaded her case along with her words.

"That's just it . . . that's only half the truth, Jordan. You have to hear me. I'm not just a man. I am more than that." Lane captured her right hand as he caressed the fine veins that etched its surface.

"Its okay Lane, I understand, you don't love me the same way that I love you. Just say that and stop making this so hard." The fear that lay in the deaths of her eyes was agonizing to see. Lane almost turned away, but he had to tell her, she deserved to know the truth. He should have told her from the beginning. Things should have never gotten this far between them.

"Jordan, listen to me . . . I'm not only a man . . . I'm an angel. We can never be. Our union would destroy you, can't you see. I love you too much to allow that. It would be selfish." Lane was almost begging now as he searched her eyes for understanding. He didn't know if he had the strength to walk away from her if she insisted they be together. For the first time, Lane could almost understand his father's inability to walk away from his mother.

Jordan jumped to her feet and started to make good her escape, but Lane was there just as quickly. "How'd you do that?" Jordan asked as fear raced through her body.

"I told you, I'm an angel. Rather I am a descendant of the fallen angels, of the giants of old. How do you think I healed you in the forest? How else could I have healed so fast when the demon, that had possessed you, stabbed me?" Lane did not want to be so blunt, he wanted the time that it would take to make her understand, but there just wasn't any. It was now or never. "Jordan if we marry and you conceive, you will die; just as my mother did." Lane confessed as he waited watching her lovely face go from fear, to confusion, and then back to understanding.

"But that's great! I mean not that your mother died while having you . . . actually that's horrible, but that it's the only reason you are staying away from me . . . and to think my father actually did give me something . . ." Jordan allowed a small cry as she moved into his arms, and then she continued. ". . . the ability to be with you."

Now it was Lane that didn't understand. He pulled Jordan back as he ran his thumbs under both of her eyes wiping away her tears.

"I don't understand." Was all he could manage to say. His throat was thickening with the tears he would wait to shed, for the loss he was feeling, until after Jordan had left him. He didn't understand. How could she be happy at a time like this? But he would take solace in the fact that she could be happy and not torn apart as he was fast becoming.

Jordan could see that she had lost Lane, so she put her hands on either side of his face pulling him down so that the two of them were eye to eye. "I'm barren. I can't have children, Lane. My father . . ." She gulped, as she tried to regain control.

"We'll adopt." Was all that Lane could say as he pulled her into his arms, and crushed his lips to hers; it was a kiss that promised passion and happiness no matter what joy the past had taken from them, because in that moment, Lane could see that they were indeed equal in every way that mattered. God had made each of them for the other, complimenting each thing about the other in a way that fully allowed them to be one.

* * *

Jordan stood taking in the sites that made up the Cadotion habitat as she allowed the memory of her and Lane's wedding to wash over her. The place for the ceremony had been set; no other place on earth would have sufficed. The garden with all of its lavish greenery and flourishing floral tapestry was already the image of serene beauty . . . any couple would have borrowed from its gorgeous imagery to create the same lavish wonderland that was nestled in the middle of The Truth.

Anderson was asked to be in charge of the service, due to his deep personal connection to both Jordan and Lane. Garrison stood in as Jordan's man of honor, while Gabriel one of Lane's close personal friends from The Truth stood by Lane's side as best man.

No real attention was paid to exact color schemes or music or guests lists. Lane and Jordan did not have much family and what family Jordan did have in Penny and Erica had died at least for the moment due to Jordan's erratic choices. In the end the ceremony had been very small with only Jordan, Lane, their two witnesses and Anderson officiating. Jordan wore a simple t-length dress that was made up mostly of eggshell-colored silk and small strips of lace that etched the seam of the garment from the shoulder and following the same lazy pattern to the tip of the skirts. The neckline of the dress fell gracefully in an oval pattern that only modestly hinted to the treasures beneath. Her shoes were a simple pair of open-toe sandals that kept with the simple yet elegant eggshell shade of her dress. Her hair fell clumsily down her back in loose ringlets; the front of her hair was pulled back and tied loosely in the middle of her head with a turquoise ribbon that Lane had insisted on.

Jordan stood proud, the only woman in the mist of all the men that meant the most to her, as she allowed her eyes to drink in the picture of strength and faith that Lane embodied. He too wore a simple eggshell colored tunic that was chosen from the Cadotion tribe's apparel. The garment rapped loosely around Lane's body and was held closed with one of the turquoise belts lent to him by one of the elders of The Truth. Jordan had insisted on the color; saying that Lane was indeed royalty because he would always be her king.

The couple stood in the middle of the serenity area in front of the cherub fountain . . . the dogwood stretched lazily this way and that encapsulating the circle they made. The purple hue of the crape myrtle announced their presence with other-worldly beauty that paled slightly to that of the spider-Lilly and babies-breath bordering the red and gray cobblestone-walk that drifted lazily around the fountain's edge. The irrigation system trickled lending to the relaxed aura as exotic birds cried from their perch with their ghostly protests.

Jordan gazed admiringly at Lane; taking in all of the things that culminated into Lane being both beautiful and powerful. The long sweep of his unkempt honey-golden-brown curls that cascaded down his back like shimmering gold, his towering stature, and chiseled features all lending to an angelic yet Viking-like quality. No one but Lane could possess angelic beauty and the exaggerated rugged-danger-look of the Viking men and have it come together as pure perfection. All the things that would hold her attention for the rest of their lives; right there for her to bask in. She could hardly allow the belief to take root that she could tie herself to this man, this angelic being for the rest of her life, and beyond . . . that one day in a place that she could only now imagine they would walk hand in hand on streets that were made of pure gold and worship the king of kings forever.

CHAPTER 37

The Cadotion tribe had been more than accepting of Jordan; a new presence in their mist. The people were stunning, Jordan thought. Golden brown skin and long hair, men and women alike, pulled tightly at their nape to fall in multiple loose braids. Various forms of intricate beading were woven through the braids of the women. The younger girls wore pastel colors while the older women wore darker earth tones. The men of the tribe wore deeper colors, matching that of the forest's deep shades in order to blend in on a hunt. The elders of the tribe mostly chose as they might the colors they would wear. The tribe had a saying 'Agonnie sidatio Intally', meaning knowledge found in age, is power. Ironic, Jordan thought, most societies today would probably agree with the tribes proclamation, but how many of the world's societies actually honored their elders, as did the people of the Cadotion tribe.

Jordan had been in the village for nearly three months now and was astonished at how great she felt. If only she had understood the ideals of these people earlier, the foods they ate for instance were always fresh and never touched by the unnatural spices that other countries would put on their foodstuffs. She had been guilty of the same thing, too much salt, garlic and other spices that had been added to the foods she would eat. Jordan had never been a large person, but she could see by the results she had gained in changing her diet to that of the Cadotion people, that she was definitely being affected by her choices in menu. Her body was taking on a more lean quality. She had continued with some of her own workout regimen, with its rigorous ups and downs, but had added some of the more graceful style of Lane's workout. Both the change in her eating habits and the workout combined had sculpted her body into a combination of refined elegance and sinewy strength; taking Jordan's body from being merely in shape to being a sculpted work of art.

Jordan was enjoying the antics of her adopted daughter as she played with one of the tribes many dogs. Amelia Spring Gates; the name was chosen for Jordan's great grandmother, and because Amelia was born in the spring. The Cadotion people believed that naming a child after something that was represented during the child's birth was a good omen. Jordan had no such belief system, but she wanted to honor the people, and she loved names like Spring and Summer.

Like Lane, Amelia's birth mother had died during labor. Her father was killed in a senseless raid by a rival tribe, the Manerky. The Manerky were known for raiding surrounding villages. It was the senseless loss of Amelia's birth father and other tribe members that had caused the tribal leaders to sanction a treaty. The tribes surrounding the Manerky people would not retaliate if the Manerky would agree to live in peace; otherwise all of the tribes had agreed to band together and destroy the Manerky camp every man woman and child to a person, until the whole of the tribe was wiped out of existence. The Manerky people had reluctantly agreed to the treaty and had so far abided by the treaty laws.

Jordan brushed an arrant hair as it grazed her face playing on the wind. Amelia ambled over in her little two year old way and grinned, revealing the gaps in the front of her mouth, where she was missing her two front teeth. Jordan stifled a grin; as she took her daughter's beautifully tan body into her arms, and smoothed back her long black hair.

"Hey you . . ." Jordan said as she nuzzled her nose to that of Amelia's. "What can I do for the most beautiful girl in the world?" Jordan cooed to encourage her daughter to open up. She knew Amelia, and when she got this look she wanted something.

"Want . . . go . . . to . . . Aniahi . . ." Amelia pleaded as she allowed her hand to drift in the direction of the medicine woman's tent. Jordan cast Amelia a serious glare, which only lasted long enough for her daughter to give her another adorable toothless grin.

"Pease . . ." Amelia pleaded as she left the L out of please. Jordan again tried to maintain her composure under the scrutiny of her daughter's golden-brown face and beautiful brown eyes.

"Okay, but only for a little while." Jordan said as she patted her daughter on the back. "Stay out of the way. Aniahi is very busy. She is the medicine woman. I know that you find it very interesting, and I am proud of you, Amelia . . ." Jordan said as she touched her daughter's cheek. ". . . but you have to understand that her job is very important. She has to keep the people healthy. The medicine, combined with all of our prayers, keeps the Cadotion people well." Jordan allowed a sympathetic smile. Amelia was very smart, but she was only two. Though, she did not lead the life of normal two year old children, there were still many things to protect Amelia from. Even with each tribe member lending a hand in watching the other's children; there were wild animals that prowled at night for food, and there were sicknesses that Amelia had to be vaccinated against, and no matter how much care Aniahi, the medicine woman took in assuring that Amelia did not touch things that were potentially harmful . . . Amelia was two . . . and like any other two year old . . . she was fast as lightening to touch, or pilfer through things before Jordan or Lane could get to her, and Lane was at least in part angel.

Jordan allowed a soft laugh, at her last thought; the idea that their two year old could give even an angel a run for his money, was hilarious.

"What's so funny Mrs. Gates?" Lane asked as he approached from Jordan's back.

"Oh nothing, just your daughter . . ." Jordan said opting not to tell Lane that she thought it funny that even he with all of his abilities was just as inept as she to keep up with a two year old.

"Speaking of Amelia . . . Where is she?" Lane said as he cast Jordan a weary glance.

Jordan laughed as she extended her hand up to Lane and allowed him to pull her into his massive arms.

"She went to see Aniahi." Jordan allowed a slight giggle again and then pulled free of his grasp. "Come on let's go see if she has the medicine woman tied up yet." Jordan shook her head not sure exactly how she and Lane would survive their daughter's terrible two's.

* * *

As Jordan and Lane stepped into the medicine woman's tent; Jordan could not believe her eyes. Their daughter was seated calmly taking in all that Aniahi, was showing her. Amelia sat with her legs crossed in front of her nodding intently as the medicine woman explained, in her native tongue, all of the different herbs and how they were capable of relieving certain ailments. Amelia had learned both English and the Cadotion dialect in order to ensure her every possibility. Lane too stood spellbound as he took in their daughter's motionlessness.

"Amazing . . ." Lane gasped out as Jordan simply nodded in agreement.

"Ah . . . Aniahi, eintare, Amelia howuere." Aniahi said as she caught sight of Jordan and Lane's puzzled faces. The medicine woman allowed a smile as she encouraged Amelia to go to her parents.

Aniahi, says she is teaching me about herbs, mommy." Amelia translated for Jordan's benefit . . . Lane understood the dialect of the tribe because he grew up with his parents being missionaries to the people.

"That's right sweetie." Jordan managed to say weakly, and then she stepped forward to the woman and took one of her hands. "How do you do this? I mean how do you have this affect on Amelia?" Jordan allowed all of the puzzlement that she and Lane both were feeling to wreak havoc on her face.

Aniahi, having understood Jordan through the signs that Jordan used while speaking . . . nodded her understanding. Then she allowed her hand to wave freely around the room indicating all of the herbs, and said. "Amelia's patatio." Meaning that the path of the medicine woman was the path of Amelia, and that was why Amelia would sit for hours intently taking in all that Aniahi had to say . . . she was destined to one day be the medicine woman of the tribe. Jordan allowed the realization of what that meant to wash over her. Their little girl would grow up to be the healer of the tribe. She would bare the weight of all that meant on her shoulders. Jordan went to her daughter and pulled her tiny form into her arms, as she prayed for the ability to protect her from all that she had seen Aniahi have to face.

The villagers were normally a calm people, but any people faced with the potential demise of a loved one due to sickness could become dangerous. Aniahi had the scars to prove it. While taking care of one of the village children a father had become distraught when the child did not survive the illness and had attacked the medicine woman. Several of the other tribesmen had contained the distraught man, but the damage had been done; Aniahi's beautiful face would forever carry the scars of that ugly time. Before the villagers were able to pull the man off of her the man had hit Aniahi in the face with the tip of a loose piece of metal that was on the table; a tool used by the medicine woman to chop up the herbs. Though the cut had not been deep enough to warrant stitches it had been deep enough to leave behind an ugly scar, enveloping one half of her face from just below her right eye to the top of her lip.

As Jordan stood clinging to Amelia, Lane stepped forward laying his hand on her shoulder. Aniahi came to Jordan; placing her hand beneath Jordan's chin she lifted her eyes so that she could talk straight to Jordan's heart, as the Cadotion tribe called it.

"Allow her to embrace her path." Aniahi said in her native tongue. Jordan collapsed into a bout of tears and then nodded to the medicine woman that she would.

* * *

Jordan and Lane had spent a little more time in the tent with the medicine woman agreeing on proper times to send their daughter to start her knew apprenticeship as the future medicine woman of the Cadotion tribe. They had finally settled on late afternoons just after Amelia had eaten lunch. This would allow her the time to calm down. Neither Jordan nor Lane would have imagined Amelia sitting in the floor taking in all that the medicine woman had to say as she had, but there she was a picture of astute learning.

Jordan walked beside Lane admiring the beauty of the lazy river and the blue sky as they both seemed to go on forever becoming one on the horizon. The way that she and Lane seemed to do in their relationship; in all ways melding together until it was hard to know where she ended and he began. Jordan pulled on Lane's arm as she laid her head on his bicep allowing the afternoon to have its way with her senses. The place was all beauty and grace; set in rolling hills covered by greenery. All the colors imaginable came together in a symphony of untouched beauty.

"Well..." Lane began. "... are you ready to go get our daughter?" He cast a purposely weary glance in her direction. Jordan lightly tapped his arm as she playfully admonished him for picking on their daughter.

"You know . . . this time won't last forever . . . don't you?" Jordan asked as she became more serious.

"Yes, and believe it or not, as big a handful as our little one can be; I am not ready for her to grow up. I could chase that little girl forever if it meant never losing her." Lane confided as he looked into Jordan's eyes allowing her to see the sincerity there. "What will we do with ourselves once she's grown? I don't even remember life without her." Lane sniffed as he shook his head warding off the tears that threatened.

"Oh Lane . . . We will be together; all of us. You know that. Amelia will grow up, sure; but she will always need us. Don't you think?" Jordan asked as she stood facing Lane now searching his eyes for the truth. She was trying desperately not to succumb to the same fears, always a part of her as well . . . just a thought a way. She had to believe that their beautiful daughter would always need, and maybe want the two of them in her life. Hadn't Jordan wanted her mother? Wouldn't she even now, do anything for her mother to be here, sharing in her life . . . holding her gorgeous granddaughter, basking in her toothless grin?

"You were thinking of your mother. Weren't you?" Lane prompted as he allowed his hand to caress the soft contours of her neck.

"Yes. But how did you know?" Jordan asked as confusion crept across her face. Lane took her in his arms and allowed a contented sigh.

"Because, it's when you are thinking about your mother; that you look the most peaceful. Almost as peaceful as you look right now or when you are holding our daughter . . . I can always tell. Lane admitted as he propelled her forward by gently pushing his hand to her lower back. "Let's go get Amelia, so we can get something to eat." He said and then looked at her again as a mischievous grin caressed his lips. "I'm hungry."

Jordan laughed at that. "You're always hungry." She quipped. "Just look at you. If you weren't hungry I'd probably have the medicine woman check you out." Jordan said as she allowed the laughter she had been holding back to have the last word.

* * *

As always Aniahi was lost in her teachings and Amelia was glued to her usual spot on the floor as Lane and Jordan made their entrance. Both were careful not to disturb the medicine woman. Amelia was doing well in her studies and even now she had known things that Jordan would not, simple things really; things that though they were simple in nature were not common knowledge. Like how to take the sting out of a finger once a splinter is removed or how to stanch blood flow from a stumped toe. Amelia was very studious and would never miss the opportunity to show off her new skills. A two year old walking around at the ready to treat all of the ailments one may encounter along their day made for quite the charming site.

Jordan stood with her hands still holding tight to Lane as her head tilted to the side in awe of her daughter. Aniahi looked at Amelia as she pointed to the very spot that Amelia was sitting to indicate that she should remain seated. She told the child in her native dialect that she would need to speak to her parents for only a moment. Jordan felt a moment of concern as she thought about all of the times their daughter had scampered intently after first this and that; always keeping the two of them on their toes. Jordan cast Amelia a look that said oh no and then smiled sheepishly at the medicine woman.

"This is not in concern of Amelia." The woman said as Jordan could obviously tell that she was struggling with some news; whether she should be the one to say or not.

"Please Aniahi, tell us." Jordan prompted as she laid her hand pleasantly on that of the medicine woman's. The woman nodded her agreement and then spoke very slowly so that Jordan and Lane might understand what she was trying to say. In the language of her people there was only one way to acknowledge this particular circumstance. She hoped that the two of them might understand.

"Previtinia ominia sentia o hondeazon." Aniahi confided in her own language as Jordan looked to Lane in confusion. Lane was wide eyed shaking his head.

"Ominia O hendosia sentia." Lane said as he was fervently shaking his head. Jordan was starting to become concerned. Lane's eyes were glazing over in tears. Fear clutched at Jordan. What was she saying? What was Lane saying? Hadn't she said that it didn't concern their daughter? Fear let up a little; but then claimed another peace of her as she thought of Lane; he had been to see her a week ago, right? Was he sick? Oh God she was at the edge of loosing her mind, and she of all people knew just exactly what that felt like.

"Ominia sentia o nehendosia." The medicine woman was talking again. That was it. Jordan was about to scream. She grabbed Lane's arms and yanked hard pulling him around to face her.

"What is she saying . . . what are you . . . what are you both saying?" Jordan nearly screeched.

Lane led Jordan to a pile of flour bags and prompted her to sit. "I don't want to sit down, Lane. I want to know what the two of you are saying. Are you sick?" Jordan asked in a strangled whimper, as she waited for her world to be ripped apart by the truth. He was part human and part angel, right? Maybe that wasn't good. Maybe his body couldn't afford the anomalies of both entities existing in one host. Fear gripped her throat threatening to cut off her air.

"Jordan, listen to me." Lane said as he grabbed her arms and hauled her to her feet making her face him. "She is saying that you are pregnant. I told her that was not possible that you are unable to have children." Lane explained as he allowed his shoulders to slump under the weight of what that meant. He had inadvertently done to Jordan what his own father had done to his mother. What could be worse? He had allowed his own selfish desires to have Jordan in his life to color his judgment. He had sentenced her to death.

"What did she say?" Jordan asked as she tried to keep the smile that was bursting forth in her heart from showing on her face.

"It doesn't matter." Lane said as he shook his head. "I'm so sorry Jordan. I should have never . . ."

"Don't!" Jordan commanded. "What did she say Lane?" Jordan insisted.

"What does it matter Jordan?" Lane said as he started to walk away. Jordan grabbed his arms spinning him back around to face her.

"It matters to me. Now please tell me. What did she say?" Jordan was almost pleading now.

"She said that nothing is impossible with God." Lane said as he looked further into her eyes; trying to make sense of it all. He guessed that in the forest when he had healed her that it had healed her body completely. Even passed wounds would be erased under the power of the Almighty God's healing hand. Lane tried to understand why God would bring them together just to allow them to be pulled apart in such a horrible way. And it would be horrible. Even now he could see the way his mother had died. It was gruesome; she had languished as all of the blood had left her body, evaporating into nothing. In the end she lay on the table gray and unmoving without her child or the great love of her life, his father.

Jordan reached up and touched his beautifully sculpted face admiring his half human half angelic features.

"That's right. Aren't you the one that has told me this whole time that we can do all things through Christ who strengthens us?" She asked as she slowly started to pull his face down to meet hers. "Show some faith." She said as she grazed his lips with her own. "God would not have brought us through all that He has just to let me die giving birth. Besides things aren't the same as when you were born." She allowed an errant tear to make its way down her cheek. "Modern medicine has a thing called c-sections. Women have them all the time. Women that aren't married to men with your particular . . ." Jordan waved at him as she thought of a delicate way to say what she wanted to make him understand. ". . . your particular set of circumstances." She said deciding that that was the best way to put it. "Sometimes women's bodies are just unable to afford the births of their children . . . Lane . . . it's just a fact of life. And those women aren't carrying children that are at least in part angel." Jordan searched his eyes praying that he was hearing her. This was a time to be celebrated; not dread. She was completely broken when she had learned that her father's cruelty had cost her the ability to have children, and now God had even granted her that kindness. It was as though the past had never existed. As if she had only started to live the moment that Lane had cast the demon out of her through God's allowing him the use of his power.

Lane studied her for a moment longer as he wrapped his arms around her and pulled her into a long embrace. He kissed her then, but it was only a hint of what was to come . . . this was all he could have ever wanted . . . to live in the most beautiful place on the planet, with the most breathtaking woman, bringing their rambunctious daughter up in the shadow of that beauty. while the miracle of their love gave birth to another generation.

"What are you thinking?" Jordan asked as they walked their loquacious, daughter back to their tent.

"I was just thinking that I am blessed. I would never think it possible to have all of this Jordan. God is good!" Lane admitted as he allowed their daughter's unending chattiness to bring a smile to his face. "Look at her Jordan." Lane prompted as his eyes took in the site that his tiny daughter made. She was hanging on to both of their hands allowing them to swing her back and forth as she regurgitated all of the knowledge she had gained form the medicine woman.

"I know . . ." Jordan said as she too admired their chatty daughter. Jordan's eyes misted with tears at the wonderment of the tiny being that God had allowed them to share their lives with. ". . . beautiful, and smart, all I could ever want my daughter to be." Jordan admitted as she again allowed Lane's luminous blue eyes to catch her off guard and take her breath.

"Just like her mother." Lane complimented; as he leaned toward Jordan allowing a small kiss.

"Hey . . ." The tiny voice of their daughter complained. "I'm swinging here." She said as she shined first Lane and then Jordan a toothless grin. Jordan was unsuccessful in holding at bay her laughter this time. She stumbled only for a moment and then righting herself she allowed a serious face to take the place of her smirk. "Yes ma'am." Jordan said as she cleared her throat refusing to look at Lane. She knew that he too would be lost in his own attempts at gaining control.

CHAPTER 38

It had been six months since the medicine woman's declaration that Jordan was pregnant. Jordan stood next to Lane trying not to burst with pride as she watched their daughter walk up the long path made by the villagers. Amelia seemed to be floating to the makeshift stage as she cast a glorious tooth-filled smile at all the willing recipients. The elder waited patiently as she made her way. Jordan missed her toothless grin, but even cuter, was the two large adult teeth that hung only slightly longer than the others; but just noticeable enough to give her that rabbit tooth look that marked a little girl as growing up. Jordan managed not to giggle out loud as she buried her head in Lane's arm. He cast Jordan a stern look; as he too stifled a giggle.

The men and women of the Cadotion tribe lined either side of a makeshift isle as there gazes floated easily to the stage that was made of tree bark and ground lily petals. In the middle of the stage stood a large male figure with an ornate silver and purple cloth draped lazily over his body. A chain of rose petals and dandelion stems with their yellow flowers standing out in stark comparison to that of the rose's dark red beauty trimmed the edges of the garment. The tribal leader, Zentoni, was the oldest member of the tribe and would serve his term as such until he was unable to hold the office due to old age, he stepped down, or the next tribe leader was declared. Each tribe leader was named such as they became not only the right age for the leadership role but cognitive and mature enough to accept the responsibilities. No tribe leader would be named if the present leader was able to continue in the position and the other tribe members respected the present tribe leader. A lack of respect for a tribe leader would lead to permanent and immediate impeachment. The Cadotion people were a simple people; so respect was easily given to those that followed the statutes of the tribe . . . mostly respect the rights of others, love your neighbor, always be willing to help and never cause harm to another tribe member . . . any member of the tribe caught in the act of harming another tribe member would be banished for no less than three months. During the three month period no contact could be made at all with the tribe. It was the one thing that all Cadotion people feared. The love that marked the Cadotion people's lives was easy to see . . . they were a social group and would never want to be banished from the other members of the tribe.

Jordan allowed the sweet smell of crushed flower petals to engulf her senses as she watched her tiny daughter march down the isle . . . her small body was wrapped in the usual green and brown hues that marked that of the medicine woman; green was for life and brown for earth. The medicine woman was charged with the health and welfare of all tribe members and as such had to adhere to long training sessions given by the present medicine woman. A woman was always chosen for the station because of women's natural ability to give care to others. A fact that made Jordan proud; after all of the years of believing that men cared nothing for women, only seeking to govern over, or take away their freedoms . . . the special place for a woman in the mist of these beautiful people was an honor and a privilege to be a apart of . . . but also a much needed reality check. One that allowed Jordan to see the truth; women were not being cast down into some darkened pit by men, they were living their lives in the shadow of the enemies hate and destruction, a destruction that was not aimed toward women alone but at every creature that made up God's creation. Satan hated mankind and he would stop at nothing to see them destroyed and sharing the bottomless pit with him and his demons.

Jordan could finally live in the light of God's love and His passion for all mankind without being distracted by Satan's lies; and that love was never more apparent than when she was lost in the eyes of her husband, caressing the bulge in her stomach that their unborn son made, or watching their beautiful daughter full of life as the future that she now embraced shined so brightly that it seemed to blind all that was in its wake.

Amelia took one giant step that threatened to topple her over, she was three now; but so much was the same. She was a little taller Jordan noticed, and of course she had her shiny new big girl teeth, but she was still the same rambunctious light of Lane and Jordan's life. The elder reached down and took Amelia's tiny hand in his huge one and the site made Jordan aware of just how tiny she was, and how she was growing up too fast. Jordan mindlessly caressed her rounded stomach as she pursed her lips trying to ward off the tears.

Lane caressed her back and shoulders, and then allowing his hand to snake around her side he rubbed the child she carried beneath her heart. The mindless action had no doubt caused him to worry. Jordan mentally chided herself, as she intertwined her fingers through his. She looked into his eyes, and almost lost her train of thought as the intensity of his worry shown there. She mouthed that she was okay.

The trip had been set, Jordan was now eight months and the two of them would be heading back to the states in order to set up for the c-section not long after the ceremony for Amelia was complete. Amelia would be staying with Aniahi to continue her training as medicine woman. Jordan would miss their daughter very much but it was necessary for Amelia to not miss out on any sessions due to her age. Jordan turned her attention back to their daughter as she tried desperately not to borrow trouble from tomorrow as the tribe members were accustom to saying.

Amelia was standing next to the elder now; waiting for him to hand her the first of many awards that she would receive for her accomplishments as tribal medicine woman apprentice. Jordan allowed a small sigh as the pride she felt for her tiny daughter overwhelmed her. Time seemed to be marching on at a velocity that Jordan was sure would bring her to her knees. It seemed just yesterday that she and Lane had stood in front of Anderson before God promising forever. Then the scene changed and this beautiful being was being handed to Jordan and Lane to cherish for always; now they were here watching Amelia make one of many steps toward her knew life and away from the two of them. She had tried so hard to not think of Amelia's success in this way. Of course she wanted her daughter to be successful. Didn't any parent? So what was this feeling that she was constantly being faced with; this loss . . . she couldn't shake the idea that the more her daughter stepped toward the things that would define her as a woman, her future self, the more she left behind the things of her childhood; a part of Jordan prayed that she and Lane would not be counted among those things lost. Jordan smiled as she knew that this was just part of it; being a mother that is . . . just another right of passage, on life's sometimes treacherous sometimes wonderful highway.

Amelia was taking her award now and looking out at Jordan, obviously she had picked up on Jordan's anxiety. Jordan stood tall as she put her fears to rest and allowed the pride she felt for her daughter to have the upper hand in the emotional battle that had been ensuing inside of her mind.

God would hold her even in that season of life. Jordan knew that to be truth, because He had already brought her through so much. He had given her so much more than she deserved. Jordan was still smiling at her daughter when she felt a small nudge in her abdomen; just another reminder of God's goodness, she thought.

* * *

Boarding the plane was bitter sweet; Jordan could still smell the soft lavender scent of the flower petals she had bathed her daughter in clinging to her hands and face. It was no wonder she had buried her face in her daughter's hair, not wanting to let go for so long. Lane had finally whispered that she would have to let Amelia go. He was right. Wasn't it best to make the departure easier on the child? It mattered not that the adult was having a hard time with the separation, sure she wanted Amelia to know that she would be missed, but it was not her intent to scare the child to death.

Jordan sat at the window seat as the airplane started to taxi up the runway and she imagined her daughter's beautiful smile as she rubbed her face and assured her that things would be okay.

"You haf to go mommy . . ." Amelia's tiny voice sang out in its usual bells and chimes tone "Aniahi says you are bring me baby." Amelia struggled with the words in her little girl way. Each word overly pronounced or cut off in places. Jordan stifled a grin as she thanked God for Aniahi's wisdom in dealing with delicate issues such as this.

"I will baby. Daddy and I will be back soon though. And we will bring you a baby brother or sister. But you have to pray that God will make him or her healthy." Jordan smiled as she hugged her daughter to herself again.

"He will be mommy." Amelia claimed as she touched Jordan's face again and then nuzzled her nose to that of her mommy's in their usual show of affection.

"He . . . ?" Jordan asked as puzzlement filled her features. ". . . You hope for a brother?" Jordan asked as she tapped Amelia on her tiny nose expecting a generic answer.

"It is mommy." Amelia confided as she nodded her head vigorously in a show of confidants. Then she continued. "I know that it is a boy because of the way the baby is laying in your tummy mommy." Amelia admitted and then she tossed a knowing grin at Aniahi. Aniahi stepped forward taking Jordan's hand in her own as she apologized for the indiscretion.

"I only just taught Amelia of such things." Aniahi's face glowed red with the embarrassment that she was feeling. "I am sorry. I did not think that she would use the information on you. I just believed it to be a good time to teach her of such things . . ." Aniahi admitted as she allowed her hands to glide toward Jordan's protruding abdomen, she continued with her explanation. ". . . due to your circumstance . . . I believed it would interest Amelia . . . and so be a good time to teach such things." Aniahi said as she again apologized for any inconvenience the knowledge of their child's sex may have on the surprise. Some couples did not want to be told of the sex of their child.

Again Jordan allowed her mind to drift lazily back to the present as she took in the warmth of Lane's body sitting next to her. She smiled as her eyes glazed over with sleep. She nuzzled down in the chair and laid her head on Lane's shoulder. Soon she was lost to sleep as she felt the plane lift in a slight jerky motion into the sky. The flight felt as though it was taking forever. Jordan had awoken and dozed back off three times, each time the looks of concern escaping Lane's bright blue eyes were not lost on her. The pilot had assured the passengers that all was well during a bout of turbulence and then fell silent until the next uncomfortable batch of sky bumps had claimed the serenity of her sleep. Jordan smiled lazily as she pushed against his hard shoulder determined to soften it for use as a pillow.

Jordan examined her thoughts remembering back to another trip that she had taken to meet her brother, during a very dark time in her life; odd she thought how different she had become. She could feel the stress as it unfolded its unyielding pathways through her nerves . . . she could remember a time that she would bask in the sensation becoming increasingly angry at herself for falling asleep and missing the opportunity to ride the wave of adrenaline that the rush of fear dumped into her veins. Now she couldn't find the same solace in the fear that heights caused as she had in the past. She focused worriedly on Lane and the unborn child beneath her heart as she prayed for the flight to come to an end. She shifted her weight as she tried without success to find a comfortable position for her large midsection to rest.

Lane jerked to an upright position as the pilot's voice broke through the silence asking that the passengers on the plane stay calm. Lane was unable to make out the reason for the pilot's soothing attempts, until he peered through the small bi-fold-door separating the patient compartments . . . just three isles past the door where he peeked through was a man holding a woman around the waste and threatening to kill her if everyone did not do as they were told.

The woman's eyes bulged in fear as hot tears made torrent trails down her terror-filled face. In the man's free hand was a large silver object that Lane could only identify as a weapon, but was not sure of its origin.

Jordan's eyes fluttered open lazily as she smiled sleepily from Lane to the window next to her. Lane tried without success to calm his jittery limbs from moving in bouts and jerks giving his nerves away. If Jordan was allowed to see what was transpiring in the next compartment Lane was sure that she would fall over the edge, tripping headlong back into the old Jordan. This was no time for Jordan to try to run to anyone's rescue, and Lane had no doubt that upon seeing the woman in distress that she would place herself directly in harms way.

Lane eyed Jordan as he tried to keep the fear that was oozing through his veins from registering in his eyes. He had to find a way to help the woman, and keep Jordan out of . . . "The know" . . . . But how . . . ? Lane leaned in as he placed a tender kiss on Jordan's forehead and then adjusting her cover he grinned sheepishly at his wife.

"I have to go to the men's room." He pretended . . . "Will you be okay?" He added for good measure.

"Of course . . ." Jordan said as she scrutinized Lane a long moment before allowing her mind to drift back into the oblivion it had been in only moments before. As sleep claimed her yet again she could not help but wonder if angels could have heart attacks.

As Lane stepped through the door and into the next passenger compartment he closed the bi-fold-door behind him hoping that it would be enough to keep Jordan out of harms way. Nothing would stop her from getting involved if she could see what he was now coming face to face with.

The woman's feet dangled helplessly in the air as the massive man claimed her upper body easily crushing her to him and covering her mouth with one hand. He had to be two feet taller than Lane. The idea sent another bout of terror skidding through his veins as he thought of the massive hulk-like man claiming Jordan's slight form. He could easily dismember Jordan and the baby . . . the thought seared through Lane's mind like hot coals leaving a blazing trail of rage in its wake. Lane crushed his body against the door of the bathroom as he contemplated his move. How would he disarm the man without getting the woman killed, and alerting Jordan to the problem?

Lane closed his eyes as he allowed his senses to become still and he focused on God once more. In a blinding reality he could see the inside of the plane again as if his eyes were wide open for the first time, as if he had not seen the situation at all before. The man that was holding the woman was indeed one of the descendants . . . he too was from the same fallen angels as Lane. But how much of the blood was still lingering in his tissues? Lane knew from his own experience that the fallen blood of the angels could make demands that he had no desire to satisfy. He too could have walked in the footsteps of those gone on before him had it not been for God's intervention in the matter. Nature verses nurture was a big deal. Fallen angel's children had a tendency of becoming evil members of society, taking what they wanted without remorse . . . hence the senseless deaths of the human women, through the conception and births of their children. children that were left to negotiate the twists and turns of life without the love of a father. More than the man's origins were being revealed to Lane as he stood completely still taking in the plane's cabin in his mind's eye. He knew that God would reveal the answer to him, if only he would be still and wait on him.

Just as suddenly as the thought blazed its way through his mind Lane was able to pull the object in the man's hand into focus. The object was long and had jagged edging and was crushed tightly against the woman's neck. Lane could even see the woman's carotid artery as it pulsated heavily against her neck announcing in its own way the fear that she was absolutely being consumed with. In that moment Lane knew what he had to do. Just above his head his mind drifted to something that he had not picked up on before, a small glass casing had fell open revealing a lever that read in case of emergency. Lane noted that the lever had an illustration depicting oxygen mask falling. Also to Lane's immediate left was a luggage compartment that hung open slightly revealing a bag inside that Lane recognized as a pool-stick carrier.

Lane inched slightly forward as he caught the eye of a frail lady in the back seat, her deep-brown eyes pooled with unshed tears. Lane placed his index finger over his lips to indicate that the woman should remain silent and then winked at her as he grasped the pool-stick carrier bag and pulled it silently to himself. Then he reached up quietly and pulled the red-lever that would free the oxygen masks. The masks fell with lightening speed startling the man as he stumbled back loosing his grip on the woman and inadvertently shoving the woman to the isle on her face where she crawled whimpering to a young couple that helped her to safety. The couple tucked the woman between them as the young woman started to sooth the woman's sweat dripping hair back from her face and whispering calming words into her ears. The woman shivered as strangled cries escaped her throat. She hunkered ever closer to the younger woman's soothing administrations.

Lane had already opened the bag to view the contents and was pleased to find not only a pool-stick but also a cue ball. He had not seen a cue ball in a pool-stick bag before but he did not have time to analyze it now. He calmly took the cue ball into his fisted hand and with calculated precision he thrust the ball in the man's direction; striking the bewildered giant in the temple.

The force at which Lane had thrown the cue ball was not meant to kill, but rather to stop the giant of a man long enough for Lane to collect the two halves of the cue stick from the velvety case that they were nestled in. Lane almost hated to use the equipment, surely it would be destroyed in the battle that was soon to start, but there was no choice. He would have to do what ever it took to keep the passengers in the compartment safe. The pool stick was but a slight price to pay for that end.

With lethal intent coloring his pale-sunken eyes the giant started toward Lane unaffected by the blow. Angry huffs punctuated his breathing as his massive arms bulged with the adrenaline pumping through them. Upon the man's second step in Lane's direction; Lane was already twirling the two halves of the pool-stick like batons. Lane pushed forward toward his opponent as he regarded the passengers with a side glance. There would be no way to avoid having the altercation in their mist. Lane would never have chosen a battlefield with so many innocent bystanders, but the decision was not in his hands. It was now or never. Lane knew from the callus way that the huge man had held the whimpering woman, as though she were a toy in the hands of a spoiled, defiant, toddler that he would plow through the passengers showing no mercy.

Jordan's eyes fluttered open. Something had woken her form her restless slumber. At first she was unable to figure out the source of distraction, and then like a blinding light, on a midnight highway she knew . . . she could no longer sense Lane's presence; the warmth of his massive body pressed against her side, showering her senses with security, a comfort that only he could give. With some effort she forced her bloated body forward and eased into the aisle. She considered for a moment the possibility that Lane could be in the men's room. It was with that likely revelation that she decided to go relieve her own bladder, which was completely filled, a common occurrence since she had become pregnant, she noted.

Moving forward the angry man pushed through the aisle as he pumped his fist and scowled in Lane's direction. Lane for the first time felt the slightest bit of doubt concerning who would be in the victor's corner at the end of the battle. What affect would wooden sticks be if a marble-ball had only managed to rile the man to a state of frenzied malice? Lane prayed a silent prayer for the strength and cunning he would surely need, this was no ordinary man. Lane knew without a doubt that he was a descendent of the fallen angels. He was a Nephilim, the offspring of the fallen angels; though Lane was certain of the man's origins he had never before witnessed one of this man's extreme girth and height.

Lane gave a silent thanks to the Creator as at last he saw the passengers begin to climb over the seats, apparently not one of them wanted to be in striking distance of the impending struggle. Lane allowed a slight backward glance in the elderly woman's direction. He nodded his head only slightly indicating that she should make good her escape into the coach portion of the airplane. The woman made a hasty retreat.

Jordan had just stepped out of the ladies room feeling refreshed to have shed what felt like tons of water out of her overfilled bladder, as a slight elderly woman brushed past.

"Honey you should come this way. That's no place for a girl in your condition" The woman said as she raised a gnarled finger indicating the direction she had just come from. Jordan patted her swollen abdomen lost for a moment in the marvel of actually being the 'girl that was not in any condition' to go into the other passenger compartment. The idea seemed so foreign and beautiful that Jordan allowed her emotions to be swept away for only a moment. Reality bounding down like an avalanche covered the surreal moment with doom. What could be happening in the other passenger compartment that someone in her condition wouldn't be safe? Jordan had to force the question; she didn't want to know, not really. For once she was blissfully unaware and it felt good. But she would have to ask there would be no way around it.

"What? I'm sorry . . . what seems to be the trouble, ma'am?" Jordan asked sweetly as she took the woman's hand in her own and patted it lightly.

"They're going to fight honey." The woman's pale blue eyes glazed over with tears as her ashen face twisted in fear.

"Who . . . who's fighting?" Jordan prompted with a soothing voice, trying to be careful not to scare the woman any further.

"Well . . . I don't know exactly . . . just that there are two large gentlemen fighting in the next compartment." The elderly woman said with a shaky voice, and then she was pulling Jordan along. "Come on honey lets get you some place safe." The woman's gentle eyes pleaded as she tried desperately to propel Jordan forward. Jordan gently pulled her hand free of the woman's slight grasp as she ushered her into the next compartment. The blood was already draining from her face, because she knew with innate certainty that Lane was one of the 'large men' that the small hunched old woman spoke of.

"You go on I'll be right behind you. I have to go back to the restroom." Jordan lied as she patted her swollen middle praying the woman would believe the lie and also praying for forgiveness for having lied to the woman at all. Jordan knew that the woman would never leave her alone any other way, there was a fight that Jordan understood in the woman's eyes. Jordan stepped into the ladies room again as she allowed a small sheepish grin in the woman's direction. She closed the door slightly waiting for the woman to leave. Finally when the woman was gone Jordan emerged from the restroom and started in the direction of the other passenger compartment.

Lane was happy to see that the woman had taken a moment to close the bi-fold door separating the two passenger compartments. There was no time for him to do it the impending battle was on the verge of starting, and he had no intention of allowing Jordan to be anywhere near the fight. No matter what he had to keep Jordan and their unborn child out of harms way. Turning his attention back to the fight, Lane was now face to face with the massive man, and if he seemed big form a distance. He was down right mammoth from two feet away. The man had both arms raised above his head, and was hammering his fists down in an attempt to pommel Lane to the ground. Lane jabbed the end of the pool stick that had the protruding silver tip bulging from its surface into the enormous man's midsection. Then with lethal precision he thundered the other end side long into the giant's chin; pushing the man back a few feet.

The man staggered only a moment and then was moving forward, as he lumbered in Lane's direction. Lane twirled the ends of the pool-stick in an attempt to thwart the man's focus.

Continuing to twirl both halves of the pool-stick Lane pressed slightly forward. Searching for the proximity of his next attack, Lane scrutinized the enormous man. Lane's knees buckled slightly as his mind registered the small sound from behind.

Jordan opened the door and peered just inside. Her blood filled with ice as her eyes took in the two massive men filling the aisle. Her mind could scarcely accommodate the thoughts flooding through it. Lane stood twirling two sticks looking every bit the fearless warrior but what was keeping her lungs from filling was the sheer mass of his opponent. The man had to be eight feet tall. His angry mass of black hair fell to just below his shoulders, his eyes were dark pools sunk back in his reddened face, and his massive arms protruded a tight-fitting white tank-top commonly known as the 'wife beater'. Anger mixed with fear and mounted becoming a raging volcano of desperation. Jordan started forward as she felt the tiny nudge from inside her bulging abdomen.

Lane was desperate to end this. His worse fears had come to fruition. Jordan was exactly where he had been praying that she would not be.

"Jordan please go." He was almost begging. The giant's eyes darted in Jordan's direction.

"Oh . . . not at all Jordan, by all means stay. You can play with me after I kill your husband." The man's deep bass voice rose filling the compartment with vibrations.

"I wouldn't miss this for the world." Jordan purred coolly. "I think I'll stick around. Besides I'd like to see my husband dismember you." She claimed as she rubbed her stomach tenderly and then slid into the nearest seat as if she were merely choosing a desirable seat at a theatre. "As you were . . ." She prompted while she examined her fingernails in an overt attempt at appearing bored.

Lane cast Jordan a confused glance as he turned his attention back to his adversary. He definitely would be having a long conversation with his wife, provided he survived this experience. As Lane turned his attention back the man was giving Jordan an appreciative once over. The giant then pulled his fist back into a battle-ready stance.

"Maybe I'll keep her for myself. She's got brass . . . got to get rid of the kid though." The man spat mockingly. "No use for kids."

He growled as he shook his head. Lane growled angrily as he thrust the stick in his right hand forward slamming it with brute force into the man's mouth. Blood splattered, painting Lane's shirt, a few rogue droplets sprayed a couple of passengers just a few seats up from where the two of them were fighting. The couple's puzzled glares were all that was offered for the viscous disturbance of their usually quiet lives. The giant's face contorted into a sadistic mass as an ugly grin lined his blood-soaked lip, he swiped the back of his oversized hand across his mouth as again he offered an appreciative smile.

Lane swung his left arm again aiming for the man's smug-grotesque face. With thundering force the man hurled his right arm up countering Lane's effort. Then with ease seeming uncommon to his massive size he struck out with his other arm slamming hard, his knuckles met with the flesh of Lane's face, just above his right eye. Lane staggered a few paces as he crumbled to one knee. The man pushed forward grabbing a fistful of Lane's hair, and hauling him mercilessly to his feet. An errant groan escaped Lane's lips, betraying him, and allowing Jordan insight as to how much the blow had overcome his senses and how close he had come to giving into the darkness that had shrouded his vision.

Jordan held at bay the gasp that struggled to free itself from the core of her being. She could not allow the giant of a man to feed off of her fear. For she recognized the demon that was calling the shots . . . of course she did. How could she not? She too had falsely believed it to be an old friend, the only constant in a darkened existence. She too had fallen prey to its murderous intentions, almost loosing not only what was left of her own humanity, but Lane as well. Now here again behind the dark-dead eyes of the massive enemy crouching ready to claim all that was dear to her; was the same dark presence . . . Hate.

Jordan sat waiting as hope drained from her soul, threatening to thrust her anguished heart into oblivion. She could not allow her fear to betray her in the canvas of her face. She knew that any show of fear would only serve as kindling to the raging fire that no doubt burned behind the dead eyes of the large man. Jordan silently prayed to the creator of all for a way out, an answer to the conundrum that unfolded in front of her. She obviously could not just engage in the fight. She either would have to sit idly by on an airplane that now soared thousands of feet above the ground and watch as the giant dispatched her husband, or she would have to figure out a way to help from the side lines. Looking around Jordan begged the Almighty for a clue. In her present condition hand to hand combat was out, and she did not have her six inch blade . . . what could she do? It was as that question breathed across her tortured soul that her eyes landed on an egg-shell colored object at her feet. Rolling aimlessly across the floor of the airplane, after Lane had thrown it at the enemy, the cue ball had finally settled at Jordan's feet.

Jordan took in the sight of the two men making sure that the giant was not watching her. Satisfied that she was under his radar, Jordan scooted the ball between her feet and bent her knees upward. She bent slightly to the side as she retrieved the ball and again checked the man's attention, which was mercilessly aimed at Lane. With another massive blow the man brought Lane crashing to his knees again. Raising his fists high above his head, as Lane's body swayed in a slight circle, the man was readying himself for the death blow. The giant's face contorted into a mask of euphoric bliss, obviously the sweetness of the kill already filled his veins.

Jordan seized the only opportunity afforded her. With precision and power born of answered prayers, she stepped into the aisle and thrust the ball in the enemy's direction. The cue ball and the giant's head collided with deadly force.

Lane drew on what was left of his waning strength as he thrust the pool-stick forward lodging the silver-screw-tipped end between two of the giant's ribs. An angry burst of air exploded from the man's mouth and nose. At the same moment his head was being forced backward by the force of the cue-ball Jordan had flung. As the man's body crumbled into a pile of flesh and bone at Lane's feet, Lane turned a bewildered look in Jordan's direction. Jordan crumbled to the seat, as a weak smile filled her face.

"Thank you." Lane mouthed

"Thank God." Jordan corrected.

CHAPTER 39

Jordan sat on the edge of the river laughing as Lane tossed water in Amelia's face. Amelia was four now, and just as chatty as ever. She loved her daddy, Jordan mused. Spending every moment that she was not with the medicine woman, with Lane . . . Jordan loved that. She would never have had anything to do with her father. She had only bad memories of the man. She could still remember the way he had tormented her and her mother; but it had lost its sting; as the awful memories of her past, dwindled a little more everyday in the brilliant light of her knew life.

Gurgled laughter persisted from the blanket next to her. Jordan looked down into the gaze of her baby son; as she sat admiring his father's blue eyes against the back drop of her dark curls. So much a representation of the two of them . . . Tristan Lane Gates the second, they had named him; was now a year old. He was just learning to walk a little and was just as rambunctious as his sister had been.

Fear of the unknown concerning his birth had nearly clouded the happiness that should be ever present during the preparation of any child's impending presence blessing a family, with the warmth and love that only one so tiny and so filled with trusting wonder of a new place could give. Soon after arriving at the hospital to prepare for Tristan's birth, their fears had been silenced. Jordan was given another ultrasound to prepare the medical staff for any birth anomalies that may occur. The gynecologist had been told that Lane's genetic pool was chocked full of enormous birth weights. The doctor had assured them that high birth weight was not an uncommon occurrence in the medical field and that the situation was well at hand. The doctor pleasantly, making conversation asked Lane how much did he weigh at birth. Not believing that his answer would be accepted as anything more than a joke on Lane's part; Lane had stopped at the hospital where he was born and got a copy of his birth certificate. Lane handed the document to the doctor and waited. The doctor took the envelope that held the birth certificate and pulled the document free. Lane stepped forward placing a protective hand on the doctor's shoulders as she swayed under the realization.

"Fifteen pounds and five ounces?" The doctor breathed. "I've never heard of such a recorded birth weight." The doctor placed a gentle hand on Jordan's protruding belly as she again turned to Lane. "Your mother?" Again the slight inflection of question caressed the words. Lane shook his head slightly as his eyes filled with tears.

"No matter." The doctor assured as she straightened her back to the daunting task of saving the lives of both Jordan and her unborn child. "We will take necessary precautions."

The doctor ordered a 3D ultrasound and soon realized that while Tristan was a good size baby he was not in his father's weight class. Jordan was placed in a room and was made comfortable. She was a week a way from her due date and because Tristan was an impressive eleven pounds and six ounces, the doctor wanted to call the shots at all times. Two days before Tristen was to be born the doctor opted to induce Jordan's labor. Two hours later Tristan was born, and though there was some complications, their beautiful baby boy made his grand entrance into their lives . . . he was the image of both Jordan and Lane. As though the two of them had been melted down and sculpted into one being.

Lane turned an admiring eye to the picture that his wife and son made. "Why don't the two of you join the two of us?" Lane said as he cast Jordan a rueful smile.

"Can the two of us . . . trust the two of you?" Jordan grinned as she gave Lane and their daughter a knowing look.

"Oh yes mommy. We'll be good." Amelia said in her little girl voice as she crossed her fingers behind her small back.

Jordan gave the two of them her best I doubt it grin, and then turned her attention to her son. "What do you think? Should we trust them?" She cooed as she shook her head from side to side nuzzling her nose to Tristan's tiny one. A tiny coo-like-gurgle sounded in his throat as he grabbed both sides of her face pulling her closer to him, so that he could give her liquid kisses; as Jordan called them.

"Okay . . . you're the boss. Here we go." Jordan teased as she adjusted his weight and started for the river. "But, if they turn on us . . ." She arched her brow in mock seriousness. ". . . It's on you, little man." She said as she tossed him in the air and gloried in the brilliant laughter that she had coaxed from him and his sister.

"Do me next mommy." Amelia pleaded as she stretched out her arms toward Jordan.

"Looks like you won." Lane conceded. "You have stolen my only ally." Lane feigned a pout as he tossed his hands in the air. "Oh well if you can't beat them; join them." He winked at Jordan as he took baby Tristan from her arms so that she could toss Amelia.

"Boy you are getting big." Jordan laughed as she pulled Amelia into her arms; first nuzzling noses with her beautiful daughter and then tossing her into the air.

"I'm not a boy mommy. Tristan is a boy remember and daddy too. We're girls." Amelia corrected as she looked at her mother through tiny concerned eyes. Jordan stifled a laugh and then squeezed her tiny daughter. This was it wasn't it? This moment and all of the moments that had culminated to make this moment and all the moments to come; these were the moments that defined exactly what Jordan would have chosen for her life, for the life of her children . . . here in this place with Lane. She loved this, the easy way that she and Lane had with their children. The way they seemed to be two parts of the same whole bending and meshing together until there was no way to know where one of them began and the other ended.

They played like that a while longer that afternoon, enjoying the sunlight on their skin; and the easy banter that should be present with family, no matter how the family was defined. It was the love and the closeness, the respect that tied them together; not bloodlines. Jordan believed that now more than ever, as she watched her daughter grow everyday into a beautiful young woman. And as she knew even now that her daughter would some day grow into the medicine woman of the tribe, with all of its ups and downs. She also knew that she and

Lane would stay and that they as well as Aniahi would guide Amelia in all of her future endeavors, for as long as they were needed.

Jordan knew too as she took in the site of her son in Lane's loving arms, they would always be this way, and that yes someday they would spend an eternity in a place where there would be no pain, where perfection graced every bend, and the luminous essence of Lane's Savior, of her Savior would wash over all that lived in that place, and there would be no more tears. All that had stolen anyone's happiness would no longer hold vigilance waiting to destroy its victim's lives, with its rottenness-hate-filled lies . . . because it would no longer have power in that domain. Jordan smiled as the thought took root and allowed a contented sigh.

"I love you." She admitted.

Lane looked satisfied with her declaration as he pulled her into his arms.

"And I love you." He claimed. "I will forever." His tone was slight as he looked out into the surrounding trees that hedged the beach, and then back at Jordan. "Forever . . ." He said his voice but a whisper as he allowed the word to drift between them as a constant reminder of the eternity that was promised.

Jordan lay her head on his shoulder and then allowing her head to fall slightly back she gave into the urge to become lost in his liquid blue eyes. Forever . . . she thought. That may not be long enough to be this content.

CPSIA information can be obtained at www.ICGtesting.com
Printed in the USA
LVOW050256260213

321666LV00001B/5/P